THE BILLIONAIRE

USA TODAY BESTSELLING AUTHOR
MARNI MANN

Visit my website at: www.MarniSMann.com
Cover Designer: Hang Le, By Hang Le, www.byhangle.com
Editor: Jovana Shirley, Unforeseen Editing, www.unforeseenediting.com
Proofreaders: Judy Zweifel of Judy's Proofreading, Kaitie Reister, and Chanpreet Singh

ISBN-13: 979-8410280037

To B.

For being my constant.

My inspiration.

And the reason I know anything about love.

PROLOGUE

JENNER

"Damn it, Jenner, you're drooling."

I heard Walter's comment, but my attention was on the brunette who was making her way across the restaurant. She had one hell of a body, wearing a tiny, low-cut red dress. Full Cs on display. The bottom of her dress hitting the center of her thighs.

And, goddamn it, it was climbing.

With each step, the hem rose half an inch. By the time she passed our table, I was hoping she wouldn't bother pulling it down, giving me the view I was after.

I bet her pussy was fucking perfect.

Her stare, locking with mine, was the kind that mentally stripped off my suit. Her slight grin only confirmed that, those plump lips promising a blow job I'd never forget.

"Do you need a napkin?" Walter added.

The brunette continued to hold my gaze until she passed us, turning the corner into the entrance of the restaurant.

Now that she was gone, I shifted my attention back to Walter. "Holy hell." I shook my head, lifting the dark cloth from my lap to wipe the corners of my mouth. "Did you see her?"

"She certainly had eyes for you."

Walter Spade was my largest client. A hotel mogul I'd been doing business with since I'd passed the bar. For tonight's meeting, I'd chosen the highest-rated steak house in LA, the scotch he was sipping over five hundred dollars a glass.

I smiled. "Do you blame her?"

He chuckled. "Tell me, are there any skirts in LA you haven't looked under?"

I pushed my back into the chair, rubbing my hands together. "Hers."

"Should I wager a bet that you'll have her naked before we're served dessert?"

This certainly wouldn't be the first time a woman's glance had enticed me enough to meet her in the hallway outside the ladies' room and carry her inside, fucking her against one of the walls of the stall.

But Walter wasn't just some client I could leave for thirty minutes.

Walter was *the* client.

The one who had helped me become a billionaire.

I got our waitress's attention and pointed at our tumblers, signaling we needed a refill, before I replied, "The only thing we're betting on tonight is the success of your upcoming hotel." I shifted in my seat, crossing my legs under the table. "I know you mentioned you have several locations in mind. Have you made any decisions?"

Spade Hotels was the biggest independent chain in the world with twenty-six five-star hotels in his portfolio. This meeting was to discuss his plans for the twenty-seventh, which he wanted to open within the next twenty-four months.

Each build-out was becoming more difficult, unraveling

hundreds of unchartered complications. The city would tie me up in permit issues, and the seller would bury me in thick, daunting negotiations. There was often litigation over the height of the hotel, the zoning, if the land housed animals or endangered vegetation. Months of research went into these projects, and that was before construction even began, which was another stage I legally oversaw.

"I do have a few ideas," he started. "One that's been marinating for over a year."

Walter approached new ventures unlike the way I pursued women. He was strategic, not impulsive. He wanted to analyze each endeavor, plan the exploration, process the possibilities.

I wanted to taste and please and come, and then I wanted to wake up in my own bed.

Alone.

"Let's talk about it," I told him.

"Before we do, I want to hear your thoughts." He turned his glass in a circle, the amber-colored liquid sloshing against the sides. "You've traveled the world, Jenner. You're in a plane more often than you're on the ground. You're at the age where people start having more disposable income and they like to travel in style. They might still fly coach, but they want thousand-thread-count sheets covering them at night. Where do the young and wealthy, like yourself, visit nowadays?"

I had two brothers who I used to do most of my traveling with. Since my youngest brother, Ford, had his daughter, Everly, his getaway time was more limited. My oldest brother, Dominick, was tied down with Kendall—his client turned girlfriend. The extent of my trips now happened solo, but when I was able to drag the guys away, there were a few spots we visited most often.

One in particular that had everything I was looking for in a destination.

"When a guy is in his twenties, he wants action," I told him. "The pulse and vibrance of big, entertaining cities like Vegas, Miami, Manhattan, where they have the convenience of twenty-four/seven amenities. When men hit their thirties, their careers are more strenuous, and their mindset shifts. Rather than a slice of pizza from a pushcart and warm canned beer, we want a Michelin-rated restaurant and a fireplace across from our bed."

"Wait until you hit your fifties." He laughed, taking a large drink. "That fireplace will need to come with a remote with no less than a hundred channels on the TV, and if they don't offer a two-hour massage at the spa, forget it." He leaned his arms on the table, cradling the twenty-five-year-old scotch with both hands. "Tell me where this magical place is."

I could see the scenery without closing my eyes. The vibrant colors of the fall foliage, the crispness of fresh, clean air, the snow-covered peaks. "Utah."

ONE

JENNER

UCLA was ahead by twelve points with a half still left to go. I needed them to beat Baylor University by at least fifteen to cover the spread, or I would lose the ten grand I'd wagered on this game.

March Madness—my favorite time of the year.

The boys and I always spent at least a week of the tournament in Vegas, where we planted our asses in the sportsbook, only leaving to eat dinner and go to the club, each day the same until it was time to fly home.

What would make day two even better was if UCLA pulled out a win.

And I knew the guys agreed—we'd all taken the same bet, wagering different amounts—some of us more vocal than others each time Baylor scored.

Ford was the loudest, slurring, "*Fuuuck*," after the most recent dunk. He got up from his seat, pointing at the wall of TVs. "This game is making me fucking crazy." He looked at me and then at Dominick. His head moved in slow motion, his knees almost buckling. His first mistake had been drinking on an empty stomach this morning. "I'm hitting the head. Need anything?"

Unlike my younger brother, I was pacing myself after waking up with an unbearable headache from last night's shenanigans.

"You all right there, buddy?" I asked. "Do you need someone to hold your hand on the way to the restroom?"

He flipped me off. "Asshole." When his arm dropped, he had to grip the back of the chair, so he wouldn't collapse. "Jesus, I've turned into a lightweight. What the hell happened to my tolerance?"

I laughed. "Everly happened." I set my empty beer in the bucket and grabbed a fresh one. "Don't worry; by the end of the week, we'll have you right back to where you need to be."

"But it's going to be painful as hell to get there," Dominick added. "Tomorrow will be even uglier than today."

"Fuck me," Ford groaned, carefully taking a step back but almost tripping. "Need anything? Last offer."

"I'm good," I answered.

"Dude, we have a waitress," Dominick reminded him. "She'll get us anything we need, but I'm thinking we should ask her to get you some food."

"Good idea," I agreed.

"Hot fucking mess," Dominick joked the moment Ford stumbled to the restroom.

"I really hope you're not talking about Miami," a girl replied to Dominick. From the corner of my eye, I watched as she took Ford's seat. "I can't afford for them to be a hot fucking mess."

A breeze of her perfume found its way to my face.

With hints of cinnamon and pumpkin, she smelled like fall.

"Oh good, they're up by fifteen," she added. "You're definitely not talking about Miami, then."

She turned toward me, and I almost spilled my beer.

Fucking hell.

There was gorgeous—celebrities, models, social media stars.

And then there was her.

She had long black hair that seemed to never end. A petite, trim, well-taken-care-of body. Pouty, thick lips with a breathtaking smile and these screaming blue eyes that wouldn't let you look away.

A kind of beauty that made my mouth part, but nothing came out of it.

"So, who's the mess?" she asked me. "Or more importantly, who'd you take?" She grinned as she waited for my response, the glossiness of her lips taunting me. When I still said nothing, she continued, "I've got five hundred on Miami. I took the moneyline, parlayed the bet with the over." She pretended to fan herself. "I'm trying not to sweat it out, but it would be a serious travesty if I lost."

She knew gambling and basketball.

Goddamn it, that was sexy.

All I wanted was to keep her talking, so I could continue gazing at her mouth—the way it almost pulsed as she inhaled, how her tongue licked the corner of her lip, how they widened to take in the straw, sucking the plastic as she took a drink.

My dick was so fucking hard.

"I think you've got yourself a safe bet," I told her, suddenly finding my voice.

Her eyes dropped down my chest before she glanced at the wall of TV screens, her profile just as beautiful. A small, sloped nose, a stunning jawline, a collarbone that jutted out, begging me to lick across it.

I needed her attention on me again, so I asked, "Why Miami?"

"I live there." She tapped her heart. "I could never bet

against them."

"Fair enough."

"And I go there, so I'm slightly proud."

A college student.

Twenty-two—*maybe*.

If my guess was correct, I was eleven years older than her.

At eleven, I had already been telling my teachers I wanted to get into law. Even prior to middle school, I had known I was going to follow in my parents' footsteps and take over their firm the moment they retired. A role I would share with Ford and Dominick.

But this one—this fucking beauty—wasn't even out of the womb.

"Who did you take?" She lifted her palm in the air—the perfect size to wrap around my cock. "Don't tell me. I want to guess." Her lids narrowed, scanning my face. "UCLA?"

I took a quick drink. "How did you know that?"

"I'm a good guesser." She glanced down at her lap, a look of worry etched into those fascinating eyes. "Did I take someone's seat?"

"Why? Do you want to get up?"

Her head leaned back, exposing her throat as she laughed. "I suppose no. It is pretty comfy here."

Ford could sit on the goddamn floor at this point—I didn't care. There was no way I was having this girl move unless it was to my lap.

Before she glanced back toward the screens, I said, "You came all the way from Miami, huh?"

"It's March Madness." She moved her hair to one side, the black curls hanging past her shoulder, covering her tit. "Vegas sounded like a good place to watch it."

"My boys and I do this every year." I nodded toward Dominick, who was on the other side of her, and then pointed at the friends behind us—Brett, Jack, and Max, entertainment agents who hired our firm for a majority of their deals. "It's our tradition."

She turned, taking in their faces. "So, these guys belong to you?"

I laughed. "I'm not sure if I should answer that."

"What about the one who almost ran into me on the way to the restroom? Does he belong to you too?" She tucked a leg beneath her ass—a part of her I was dying to fucking see. "If so, you need to get that boy some bread and coffee, stat."

"He's my younger brother. We cut him some slack because he's a single dad." I held out my hand, wanting to feel the softness of her skin. "I'm Jenner."

To my surprise, her grip was stronger than I'd expected, her skin even silkier than I'd anticipated.

"Jo." Her stare dipped again, this time to my mouth, lingering there for several seconds before it rose. "It's nice to meet you, Jenner." She sucked in her bottom lip, chewing it.

"And you ... Jo."

Her hand stayed in mine much longer than it needed to. "Did you hear about Miami's shooting guard?"

"What happened?"

"Ankle injury. He kept it quiet, not wanting to start any rumors before the tournament. If he had sat out this game"—she shook her head—"oh man, that would have been brutal."

"You wouldn't be winning right now."

She bit the end of her straw, holding it in her mouth as she said, "Oh, we would still be winning. Don't you remember the Florida State game?" She paused, waiting for my brain to catch up. "Our shooting guard was out with the flu, and we still won seventy-one to sixty-five."

Most of the women I was with couldn't have this conversation. They didn't care about sports, they weren't loyal to any particular team, and they certainly couldn't recall any game statistics.

But, damn it, this was hot.

"How could I forget that game?" I said. "The guard for Florida State had one of his best games, and they still couldn't beat you guys."

"Their guard is soft."

I took a long drink of my beer, watching her the whole time. "Yeah? How so?"

"He sat out half the season with a broken toe." She rolled her eyes. "Our guards could climb Everest on crutches. Nothing would stop them."

"Except the flu."

"Oh my God," she groaned. "He was in the hospital with a hundred and five temperature and ended up with a nasty case of pancreatitis on top of having kidney stones. Stop being so tough on him. That boy's hardly a pussy."

She had a fight in her.

I liked that.

"Are you as knowledgeable with football?"

Her teeth tugged on her lip as she smiled. "Quiz me."

I wanted to do a hell of a lot more than ask her some irrelevant questions.

I wanted to carry her up to my room and fuck every sports fact out of her brain.

"How about—"

The vibration of my phone cut me off.

I held up my finger, pausing our conversation, and quickly pulled my cell out of my pocket, seeing a text from Dominick on the screen.

Dominick: I'm betting 5K you fuck her in the next ten minutes. You want the over or under?

I looked around Jo to glance at Dominick, laughing before I typed my reply.

Me: Over.
Dominick: I thought you were better than that. I'm disappointed in you, brother.
Me: I just want to spend a little more time looking at her.
Dominick: You'll be doing plenty of that when she's naked on your bed.
Me: You've never heard of savoring?
Dominick: LOL. We both know that's not your style.

It had never been my style; he was right.

But, fuck me, this girl was worth it.

She wasn't parading around the sportsbook in a bikini top and leather shorts, like the waitresses in this section. Jo didn't have to. Fully clothed in her cutoffs and oversize sweatshirt that exposed her shoulder and hot-pink bra strap, she was still a hell of a lot sexier than them. But there was so much more to her than just a delicious body. She had confidence that was more alluring than I'd ever seen along with wit, charm, charisma.

"No need to quiz you," I said, waiting for her eyes to return to me. "Besides, I have a feeling you can hold your own with football." I just noticed the tiny freckles under her eyes, and they were fucking adorable. "But I am curious how you knew I went with UCLA."

She tucked her other leg under her ass. "Jenner, you have LA written all over you."

Quick and smart.

Damn it, I couldn't get enough of this girl.

"The East Coaster knows the LA vibe. Interesting."

She smiled. "Do I have Miami written all over me?"

Flip-flops had covered her feet prior to her tucking her legs beneath her, the new position showing more of her lean, muscular thighs. The black hair and blue eyes were exotic, but they hinted at nothing.

"Aside from your tan, no."

"I'm just a giant mystery to you ..." She finished her drink and set it on the table. "Tell me, Jenner, what do you do for a living?"

"You don't want to guess?"

She laughed, adjusting her top, the shift now showing more of her bra. "Is that what you want?"

I exhaled, taking in the whole view. "There's something I want far more than you guessing my job." I downed the rest of my beer, not bothering to grab a new one. "I'm a lawyer."

A flash of red moved across her cheeks before she said, "Professional haircut"—her eyes were on my head and then lowered—"trimmed beard, a neck that could easily hold a tie." She circled the air with her finger, as though she were adding up each detail. "I can visualize it."

And what I could visualize was taking off that sweatshirt with my goddamn teeth, instantly sucking one of her nipples into my mouth, gnawing on the end. I'd position her on her back, leaning her up on her elbows so she could spread her legs around me.

"You're picturing the tie around my neck ... or somewhere else?"

Even her laugh was smooth. "Jenner, you certainly know how to make a girl blush." She gripped her hair, like she needed to hold on to something. "But if you want an honest answer, your neck isn't the only place I can envision a tie. I see many knots in a variety of places—some more interesting than others."

My dick fucking throbbed in my jeans.

"Your wrists?" I paused, analyzing her expression. "Or maybe you wouldn't want to give up your sense of touch?"

Her stare dipped to my chest, lowering to my waist, a heat moving through me as she slowly lifted. "It would be a shame to lose my ability to touch, especially if there was something in front of me—or even on top of me—that was worth feeling."

"Jo ..." I shook my head, folding my hands behind my neck. "You're taking my brain to some naughty fucking places right now."

"Oh yeah?" She cocked her head to the side. "Where's my brain?"

While I stared, I tried to decipher her thoughts.

"It's okay, Jenner. You can say it. You won't scare me away." She reached inside my bucket and took out a cold beer, twisting off the top and drinking down several gulps. "Maybe we should bet something—like this is what'll happen if you're right or this is what'll happen if you're wrong."

"As long as a win earns me your lips, I'm down."

"Which lips?"

Fuck me.

This girl had a fire that was roaring as loud as mine.

Each breath, each glance, each swipe of her tongue made it grow.

I used my head to nod toward her face. "I'd start with those." I took the beer from her hand, bringing it up to my mouth to take a sip. "If they tasted as good as I expect them to, then I'd go lower. Much lower ... until I found the others."

Her eyes answered me before she said, "I'll take that bet."

I set the beer down, my dick rubbing against my zipper. "Why wait?"

"What are you saying?"

"I'm saying ... if I kissed you right now, would you stop me?"

TWO

JOANNA

Jenner was nothing but trouble.

I'd learned that the moment I'd taken a seat in the sportsbook, fate somehow placing me next to this delicious man. Every word, every expression, every visual dip he made down my body only tempted me more.

It didn't help that he was positively gorgeous.

Even through his clothes, his broad shoulders and the outline of muscles in his arms told me he had a body I wouldn't be able to stop touching. Perfect lips surrounded his straight white teeth, followed by a path of thick, dark stubble. He had a small, pointed nose and emerald eyes that were wickedly sinful and extremely dominant.

Dominant like his personality—something I'd never experienced before in a man, but I was quickly learning it was a trait I couldn't stay away from.

No matter how many times I attempted to get up, the heat in my body forced me to stay seated. A heat that stirred a storm of sensations, a humming of tingles.

A burning need that trumped every warning sign in my

head.

Each sign signaling more trouble.

"If I kissed you right now, would you stop me?"

His words were simmering in my chest, his eyes so incredibly dangerous that it was making my blush grow deeper.

The spot between my legs was pulsing.

Throbbing.

Oh God, what is happening?

"No, I wouldn't stop you," I whispered, unable to speak any louder.

My reply hadn't been prepared; it hadn't been thought out.

The spontaneity a mistake the moment I realized he was moving closer.

His palm cupped my cheek, his fingers moving into my hair, and he was pulling me toward him.

He didn't slam his mouth into mine, like I'd expected.

He closed the gap, leaving an inch between us instead.

As though he was teasing himself.

As though he was preparing for how I was going to taste.

"I've been staring at this one." His thumb pulled at my bottom lip. "Thinking how badly I want to bite it."

I forgot that we were in a casino.

That we were surrounded by his family and friends.

That there was a massive wall of TVs and games and bets happening around us.

I could only focus on him.

This feeling in my body.

This urge that was controlling me in a way I hadn't ever experienced.

I sucked in a deep breath. "Then, what's stopping you?"

"The second I taste you, I'm going to want more. I'm a greedy motherfucker, Jo. I won't be able to stop with a kiss ..."

These were promises, not lies.

His eyes confirmed that.

Would one taste be enough?

I knew that answer.

In fact, every part of me could feel that answer.

"So, what are you going to do, Jenner?"

I held in my breath.

Waiting.

Longing.

"Follow me to my room."

He wasn't asking.

Did I want him to?

My skin was scorching, each swipe of his thumb igniting a new flame.

"Now?"

"Yes." He stood, towering over me, making me feel so tiny in this chair. "Right now."

He held out his hand for me to grab.

The second our fingers linked, a bolt of energy passed through me. I almost jumped from how strong it was.

There was only one place my feet were going to lead me.

There was no sense of even trying to talk myself out of this, to try to delay going to his room.

Having sex with this man was inevitable.

Because, in this moment, I belonged to Jenner.

With our fingers still gripped, I rose from my seat and followed him through the casino, his hand moving to my lower back as we approached the bank of elevators.

"Jesus," he growled in my ear. "Your fucking ass ..." His fingers lowered, teasing the top of it. "I knew it would be perfect, but goddamn it, not this perfect."

There were so many things I could say, so many ways I could derail this, but our connection was too strong.

I felt that in my bones.

I gave him silence, and he gave me breath, exhales hitting my neck, like foreplay.

But the moment we were inside the elevator with the door closed, one of the top floor buttons selected, he was moving me toward the back wall. A huff of air came out of my mouth when the metal bar pressed against my spine.

His hands surrounded my face. "So fucking gorgeous."

His eyes were piercing mine.

He had the ability to make me feel like he was taking all of me in even though our stares were locked.

I couldn't breathe.

Especially when he slowly closed the space between us. "Jo ..." His eyes turned even more feral. "I can't wait a second longer."

His lips fell against mine.

Claiming me.

Owning me.

I tasted the beer and the desire on his tongue, a hunger every time it entered my mouth.

A satisfaction the second it pulled back.

A wanting the moment it was gone.

With his hands on my waist, holding me against him, there wasn't even air between us.

When the door opened, he lifted me into his arms, carrying me down the hallway. Once we were inside his suite, he began tearing off my clothes before he even put me on my feet. The sweatshirt I'd thrown on in a hurry was tossed to the floor, my bra not far behind, and the jean shorts slipped down my legs, followed by my thong.

Now that I was standing, I did the same to him, pulling, tugging until there was only skin left.

God, I was right. His body was as perfect as I'd thought. Ripples of muscle across his chest, down his shoulders, causing both biceps and triceps to bulge. A sexy, thin line of hair ran down the center of his abs, each one etched into his stomach, deep enough that my fingers could get lost.

The hair continued to his cock.

My eyes bulged as I stared at his long, thick shaft, the crown widening and then narrowing toward the tip.

Unlike the boys from my past, Jenner was a man.

And that could be seen from every inch of his body.

He took a few steps back, and that was when I realized we were in the living room of his suite, standing completely naked, his eyes devouring me.

"Goddamn it." He shook his head, his lips pulling into the most provocative grin. "I'm the luckiest motherfucker in the world." His gaze crawled up and down me. "You're breathtaking."

His hands circled around my back and began to bend me, leaning me away from him so he could kiss down my throat. His mouth lowered to the tops of my breasts and then the center of my stomach.

"Your taste ..." He gave me a sample of his tongue work, swiping it across my belly button. "It's fucking lethal."

As tempting as it was, I didn't ask for more detail.

Because I knew.

And because I felt the same way about him.

Once his lips rose to mine, I put my finger on his lips and said, "Your turn. Where do you want my mouth?" I traced his upper and lower lips. "Here?" That same finger ran down his chest. "Here?" I continued until my hand hovered above his dick. "Or here?" I sucked in a mouthful of air and cupped his tip, my pussy throbbing as I imagined what it was going to feel like when he was inside of me.

Penetrating me.

Fucking me so hard that all I could do was scream.

"*Mmm,* Jo."

That sound, my God, it was erotic.

"I want all three." His hands tightened, holding my face steady. "And I don't want you to rush."

THREE

JENNER

When it came to sex, there was only one role that had been designed for me.

The lead.

I needed the control, the domination, to follow the build and get lost in the release.

It was the only time I could escape the thoughts of work, when I was truly out of my head, when my responsibilities melted away and I was focused on something else.

Right now, my complete attention was on Jo.

And that fucking mouth of hers.

She wanted to know where I wanted it, and at first, I told her I wanted it everywhere. But that direction needed some clarification because my cock was throbbing much harder than my lips.

"Get on your knees."

A blush moved across her cheeks, reaching as high as her eyes. "You want my mouth on your dick? This doesn't surprise me."

"I need to feel how well you suck."

As she got into position, she took ahold of my shaft, pumping it with her fist. "From your body to this, there's nothing small about you, Jenner."

I chuckled.

The moment she'd taken off my clothes, her stare had told me she appreciated how much I worked out. I was certainly a fan of the way she took care of herself—a body built for running with toned limbs and the most flawless ass, perky tits that weren't any bigger than my palms.

As she claimed more of my cock, I held the back of her hair and said, "It's yours, Jo." I wrapped the long locks around my wrist. "And you don't have to be gentle." I hissed the moment she surrounded my tip, exhaling, "*Fuuuck*," as she licked across my crown.

She swirled over the top edge, and as she lowered, adding more pressure, her mouth became a goddamn vacuum.

"Oh fuck."

She was taking me in deeper, adding more friction to the tip, licking me like I was a fucking dripping cone.

With my fingers buried in her hair, I tried to guide her.

But she didn't budge.

This girl wanted to do things on her own.

And if I wanted her mouth, I just had to accept that.

"Hell yes," I moaned, handing the control right over to her, wondering what the fuck had gotten into me. But that thought dissolved as she dipped to my balls, licking each one into her mouth. "Goddamn it, that feels good."

When her mouth returned to my cock, her hand twisting over my base, rising to the center to meet her lips, my head fell back.

She wasn't blowing me like it was her job. She was blowing me like she was trying to get the fucking job.

"Just like that," I roared.

I urged her deeper, to feed her more of my dick.

She didn't move.

But the moment I let up, she dived down, giving me the suction I was after.

Bob after fucking bob.

Testing my limits.

Tightening her mouth, keeping her tongue wet like she wanted me to come.

And that was going to happen if I didn't make her stop.

Her lips made a popping sound when I pulled out my cock.

I immediately reached for her hips and hauled her up against me. My condoms were in my suitcase in the bedroom, so that was where I carried her, placing her on the bed, where she waited while I took one out of the box, tearing off the corner of the foil with my teeth. I rolled it over me as I walked back to her and lifted her in my arms, wrapping her legs around my waist, and I held her against the nearest wall.

I rubbed the outside of her pussy, making sure she was as wet as I needed her to be.

And, goddamn it, she was.

"How fragile are you?" I devoured her mouth before she could reply, needing to taste her before I continued. "I can try to play nice ..." I glanced down her chest, the hardness of her nipples begging to be bitten. "But, fuck, Jo, I don't know if I can."

"Then, don't."

I smiled. "You're sure about that?"

"No ... but yes."

She moaned as my tip entered her, and I instantly felt the tightness of her pussy. The wetness that soaked across the rubber. The narrowness as I slid farther in.

"Fuck!" Her pussy was holding me hostage, to the point

where I didn't know if I could go in any deeper. "You have the most perfect cunt."

Her response wasn't words. It was a sound that vibrated through my goddamn chest.

"Oh God," she breathed.

Her nails dug into my shoulders, like she was holding on to the reins and I was bucking beneath her.

And that was what happened the moment I was fully inside her.

I stilled for a few seconds, giving her time to get used to my size, and when she lifted her hips, sinking back down over me, it was time to start the pounding.

Our skin slapped together, my balls banging against her, the top of me rubbing against her clit.

Her nails dug in harder. "Jenner!"

She had found muscle, stabbing straight into the center while she tilted her head against the wall, so I went in for her neck, pulling her flesh into my mouth before biting it.

"Oh fuck," she cried. "I'm coming."

I could feel it.

The way she was closing in around me.

How she ground her hips to get me in even deeper, each of my strokes allowing me to feel the quiver from inside her.

But it wasn't enough.

I wanted more.

I needed more.

I waited until her orgasm passed, and then I carried her to the bed and placed her on the mattress. While I stood on the floor in front of her, her legs spread around my waist.

"Fuck me," I roared.

And that was what she started doing, moving her hips, meeting me as I thrust into her.

I didn't expect the participation, especially after she just came. But she wouldn't stop; she wouldn't still.

Pleasure was this girl's drug.

When it became too much, the explosion threatening to erupt in my balls, I flipped her onto her stomach and crawled up behind her.

"You're so fucking tight," I growled after entering her. I knelt on the edge of the bed and gripped her hips, finding a ruthless rhythm. "And so fucking wet."

I slid into her with no effort—she was that turned on—and I felt her contract with each plunge. From here, I had the perfect view of her body, the sleekness of her arched back, the sides of her tits, the roundness of her incredible ass.

An ass I was dying to be inside of.

I grasped her tit, her nipple teasing my fingers as I pinched it.

She must have liked the sensation because she bucked against me. I did it again, this time harder, pulling, rolling across the tip.

"Oh God!" she shouted. "Yes!"

I moved to the other side, doing the same, and then I lowered to her clit—a spot I knew would give her an even stronger reaction.

The second I touched her there, she slammed against me, her sounds vibrating through the whole room, sounds I couldn't get enough of.

"Jenner!" she gasped. "Don't stop!"

Using the pads of two fingers, I shifted back and forth against her clit.

It only took a few passes before I felt her coming.

Shuddering.

"*Ahhh*!" She paused. "*Ahhh*!" she yelled even louder.

A tightness came through, constricting each plunge, and then a wetness dripped over me as I continued to fuck her.

And I did.

Without hesitation.

Without mercy.

Without stopping or giving her time to recover from the sensitivity because I wanted to bring her right back to that place.

But not here, not like this.

Once I knew her orgasm had passed, I flipped her around and settled her on my lap. I aimed her pussy over my tip and growled, "Fucking ride me."

It took her a moment to catch her breath before she really started to pick up speed. She rose to my crown and sank down, circling her hips at the base. While she kept up that pattern, she held my shoulders, her lips hovering near mine. The closeness allowed me to taste her exhales, each one ending in a moan.

"That's it, Jo. Fuck."

Now that my hands were free, they could wander, feeling every inch of her body, tracing spots I hadn't been able to reach before. I started with her ass, clutching the thickness, the curves of her hips, urging her to take me. To fuck me. To let me own that pussy.

Her tits bounced in my face, and I surrounded a nipple, sucking it, flicking the end with my tongue.

"Oh God," she cried. Her hands dived into my hair, pulling me closer. "Your fucking cock."

I bit her, holding that little bud between my teeth before I ordered, "Take it."

If she wanted the control, then she needed to demand it. She needed to ride me with all the strength she had left.

Because in this moment, my fucking dick was hers, and that wasn't something I ever gave up.

"Own it," I told her. "Show me how much you fucking want it."

She did.

She ground over my shaft, twisting her body at the bottom of each dip, caging me inside her cunt.

"*Fuuuck.*" I released her nipple. "If you keep that up, it's not going to be yours for much longer."

"Maybe that's what I want." She breathed against my cheek. "Maybe I want to feel you come because there's nothing sexier than watching a man lose himself."

Damn it, that was hot.

A woman who wanted to please me as much as I wanted to please her.

"Then, fuck me," I told her. "Fuck me like I've never been fucked."

It was as if a switch went off.

Her speed wasn't what changed, nor was it the power she used.

This was deeper.

More intimate.

A tightness that came from within.

She reached behind her back to cup my balls while she bounced over me, keeping my shaft lodged inside her, turning her body in different directions to gain friction from every angle. And as she tickled my sack, my balls started to tighten.

The sensation building.

"Damn it." My fingers rubbed her clit, my other hand squeezing her tit. "Fuck me!"

She did—harder.

Her pussy became wetter.

She was practically clutching my cock, milking the cum from me.

She wanted me to blow.

And she was going to get it.

I gripped her waist, holding on.

Taking it.

Allowing her to work my orgasm through my body with each dip of her cunt.

"Jo," I groaned as I was about to hit the peak, the intensity at its strongest, the feeling consuming me. "You're making me fucking come."

"Me too! Oh God!"

Pump after pump, she sucked me dry, filling the condom.

And while she rode the hell out of me, my eyes stayed on hers.

Watching her.

Viewing every second that she possessed my cock.

The moment I fell apart, she did too, rocking her hips, shaking over me, our moans matching.

"Oh God, yes!"

When she finally stilled, when there was nothing left to drain out of me, she kept me inside her and flattened her hands against my chest.

Her breath came out in pants. "I wonder if my girls are looking for me." She laughed. "I told them I was just going to check the score."

Her satiated stare made me smile. "Do you think another twenty minutes will matter?"

She cocked her head to the side. "Twenty minutes?"

I flipped her onto her back, my mouth diving into her neck. "Maybe thirty." I moaned, knowing I was about to change the condom and do this all over again.

FOUR

JOANNA

"Where have you been?" Monica asked as I reclined over the lounger next to hers.

After I'd left Jenner's room, I'd hurried up to mine, seeing a text from Monica that said the girls had gone to the pool, and I'd quickly changed into my bikini and rushed downstairs.

I pushed my sunglasses even higher on my face and rolled my head toward my best friend. "I've been … busy."

"Take your glasses off."

"Why?"

She sat up on her elbows. "Take. Them. Off."

I lowered the metal frames to the end of my nose, feeling the heat from her gaze as she diagnosed me. Her stare narrowed, dipping to my neck and back up to my forehead.

She gently slapped my arm. "You just got laid, didn't you?"

I couldn't stop my smile from spreading. "No."

"Liar."

I laughed. I couldn't help it. She knew me better than anyone in this world.

That was what happened when you had met your best

friend your freshman year in college, assigned as dormmates, and had been inseparable ever since. I couldn't life without her, and that was why, within a few seconds, she knew I would give her every juicy detail.

At least, most of the details.

Some I wanted to keep to myself.

"Okay, okay ... I got laid." I used my hand to fan my face. "Girl, it was hot. Like smoking, scorching, *oh my God, I'll never recover from this* kind of hot."

She slipped off her own glasses, like she needed a better look at me. "You just went to check the score of the game, and you met a dude that quickly? How does that even happen? Who is he? I'm beyond floored right now."

I shrugged. "I took a seat in the sportsbook, and before I knew it, I was going up to his room."

"Jo ..." She gripped the spot she had just slapped. "He could have murdered you. Or trafficked you. Or tortured you, Dexter-style."

"I love you."

"I'm not kidding."

I sat up in the lounger, folding my legs, wrapping my arms around my stomach. "I know you're not, but trust me, I assessed the situation, and I was completely safe."

"Promise me you won't do that again?" She grabbed her pink drink and downed half the glass. "You know, unless I'm with you and I can give him my seal of *he won't murder my best friend* approval."

I grinned. "Promise."

She set the cup down. "Now that we've got that settled, tell me everything." She glanced toward the pool, where Lex and Courtney were standing in the shallow end, talking to two guys. "Unless you want to wait for them? You know you'll have to repeat all of this the second they get out."

"It's fine." I lifted her drink, holding it against my cheek, still feeling flushed from Jenner. "Monica, all it took was a flirty conversation. I think we were talking about neckties—I don't even know—and I was suddenly a puddle at his feet. That's how magical that man is."

"Tying you up? Okay, that's way hot." The waitress walked by, and Monica ordered two more of the drinks I was still holding against my face. "So, did he?"

I sighed. "No, but I was mentally tied to him in every possible way. He knew my body, like he'd been studying it for years. And he made me feel things"—I shook my head—"things I'd never felt down there or anywhere before."

"I'm literally shook right now." Her eyes widened. "You're not the girl who sleeps with a dude on the first date—or even the third, never mind a man you knew for twelve seconds."

"It was more like fifteen minutes."

"That's not the point we're going to debate right now." She rolled her eyes. "I really need to get over the fact that my best friend was having mind-blowing sex while I was fighting with Lex and Court over what bathing suit I should wear because we all ironically chose the same color and that's just a pool day no-no."

I touched her greasy, suntan-oiled arm. "You know when you stare into the eyes of a man, and in a single second, a jolt comes through your body that tells you he owns every ounce of you? And no matter how hard you try to fight it, he's going to win you?"

"No." She shook her head for extra effect. "I've never experienced that in my life. Hotness, yes. Sexiness, yes. Drunk sex, unfortunately, yes. But a man owning any part of me? That's where you lost me."

I laughed. "Remember this moment. When it happens, this

conversation is going to make much more sense, and then you'll tell me how right I am."

She grabbed the two drinks off the waitress's tray and handed me one, taking back her previous cocktail, which I'd just downed. "So, what now? Will you ever see him again? Where does he even live?"

Her questions had weight, and I felt the heaviness of each one. "LA."

"I was afraid of that."

"I gave him my number. Who knows? Maybe he'll reach out. Or maybe I just had the best sex of my life and—" My voice cut off when my cell vibrated from the table between us. I'd forgotten that I'd even set it there.

I glanced at the screen.

Unknown: It's Jenner ... I can still taste you.

I looked up just as Monica said, "It's him, isn't it?"

I nodded. "I think I just died." I held the phone toward her, showing her the message.

"Damn ... I think I just died too."

"How the hell do I respond to that?"

She grinned. "You know exactly what to say to that man." She nodded toward my phone. "You have some serious magic too. Now, go work it, girl."

"All right, wish me luck."

Me: I can still feel you inside me.
Jenner: I want to taste you again.
Me: Yeah? How badly?

Monica cleared her throat. "Jesus, you're glowing." I gazed

up at her as she added, "I mean, legit fucking glowing. Like you used a highlighter instead of bronzer."

I touched my cheek with the back of my hand. "I don't have any makeup on."

"You have him on you—that's as good as concealer." She took a sip of her drink. "What's he saying?"

"That he wants to taste me again."

"And?"

My glasses were still at the end of my nose, and I pushed them higher on my face. "And I asked him how badly."

"*Ooh*, that's good."

Jenner: Badly enough that I can't wait until tomorrow.
Jenner: My room. 7 tonight.

Monica had made us dinner reservations for eight thirty, which gave me time for a quickie.

If Jenner even knew what a quickie was.

Me: You have me until 8.
Jenner: I'll take every second I can get.

"So?" Monica said the second I set down my phone.

I picked up my drink and rested it against my chest, needing to cool down again. "I'm going to his room before dinner. Don't worry; I won't be late."

"You're getting the D; you can be as late as you want. We'll get you a to-go dinner if we need to since I know how hangry you get."

I looked toward the girls in the pool, watching them flirt with complete strangers who were eyeing my friends like candy. "What am I doing?" My stare connected with Monica's. "Really, what in the fucking hell am I doing?"

"You're having fun." She leaned back in her chair, hands linked under her head, arms spread wide. "And you're getting some ass." She laughed. "Which is something you've needed for a while."

"Thanks ... dick."

"Listen, I'm just speaking the truth, and we both know it." She paused to watch two guys walk by, both handsome, but neither had anything on Jenner. "How long is he here for?"

I couldn't remember at what point he'd told me, but I recalled him answering that question, so I said, "He's here for the rest of the week."

Which was the same as us.

"One check in the *hell yes* box." She clinked her glass against mine. "What else do you know about him?"

I sucked in a deep breath. "He's a lawyer, he lives in LA, he's here with friends and a brother or two."

Her face was like the heart-eyes emoji. "A lawyer? I just died—again."

"And he probably has a good ten years on me, maybe more."

She sat up and faced me, crossing her legs. "Age is hot. It makes him experienced; it makes him established and successful and independent—things we can't say about any of the fools we go to college with."

"That's definitely true."

She leaned forward, squeezing my knee. "You need to promise that you won't get shit-faced and end up married and wake up the next morning, not remembering a damn thing. I've seen far too many movies like that." She looked up at the sky, like she was entering dreamland. "I already know how I'm going to design my maid-of-honor gown and every ruffle and piece of satin that's going to go on it, and I won't settle for an

Elvis drive-through at three in the morning, somewhere off the Strip."

"Let's not forget, you'll also be designing my wedding gown." I winked, smiling, until I thought of the other scenario. "You don't have to worry; my parents would murder me if I married someone without their approval, and then my father would disassemble him limb by limb." I didn't even want to put that thought into my head. "Jenner and I live on opposite sides of the country, and we're in totally different worlds. This week is all about fun, like you said ... nothing more."

FIVE

JENNER

"Where's dinner?" I asked Jo as she slipped the dress over her body.

One I'd stripped off.

One that had been on the floor of my suite for the last hour.

"Some steak house on the Strip," she answered. "My best friend, Monica, picked it. She handles that kind of stuff. I just do the eating."

The dress was as tight as skin, showing every curve, and she had those for days, starting with her hips, lowering to her ass, bulging at the corners of her cleavage. And in this outfit, her tits looked even larger since the dress was so low-cut.

"Fuck," I moaned, leaning into a table as I watched her adjust the fitting. "You'd better run."

She grinned, and it was so beautiful. "What happens if I don't?"

"That dress is going to be shredded from your body."

She laughed as she slipped into her sky-high heels. "No shredding. This is one of my favorites. It would hurt my heart if there were only pieces left."

I couldn't stop devouring her with my eyes. "I'd buy you another one."

It would be worth it.

Because the last hour hadn't satisfied the need I had for this girl.

It didn't matter how much I'd tasted, that my mouth had been on every inch of her.

I wanted more.

What the fuck is happening to me?

One taste had always been enough.

But now, I found myself walking toward her, hugging her against me the second she was within reach, my dick already hard again.

Her hands surrounded my face as she looked up at me. "You can have me later." Her thumbs brushed over my beard as she took in my eyes. "But not now. I have to meet the girls."

I squeezed her ass. "I don't like that answer, but I'll accept it."

She leaned up on her toes, giving me that gorgeous pout and the chance to breathe her in. Jo's flavor was different. The fall scent followed her deep into the night. But it was more than just that. She had an appetite that was similar to mine, a desire, a charisma I just couldn't get enough of.

"I'll text you," she whispered against my lips. She pulled away and adjusted her dress, glancing down her body. "I look like I've been through war."

"If you didn't, then I didn't fuck you hard enough."

Her head fell back as she laughed—something she'd done before and something that drove me fucking wild. "You definitely fucked me hard enough. I don't even know if I'll be able to walk tomorrow." She headed for the door and waved before opening it.

"I'll see you later, Jo."

As she left, I took in the view of her ass. Even though I'd just been holding it, even though I'd kissed across her cheeks when she was spread over my bed, I still couldn't stop staring.

That body.

That freshly fucked pussy.

That satiated smile she gave me as the door closed.

Goddamn it.

Who the fuck is this girl?

I turned and headed into the bedroom, putting on the outfit I'd laid out for the evening—a pair of jeans and a button-down, a sports coat on top. I made a quick stop to the bathroom to brush my teeth and spray on some cologne. As my hands were under the faucet, water pouring onto my fingers, I decided not to clean my face. Doing so would wash away Jo's scent, something I could still smell on my beard.

I wanted to taste her for a little bit longer even if that meant wearing her to dinner and the club.

She was just too good to get rid of.

Goddamn it, I've lost my fucking mind.

I went back into the bedroom, ensuring I had my wallet and phone and room key, and I headed down the hall to Dominick's suite.

"About time, motherfucker," Dominick said as he opened his door. "I was wondering if you were going to show up."

I pounded his fist and replied, "I've been busy."

"I hope that means you've been with Jo?"

When I'd returned to the sportsbook several hours ago, I'd shared a few small details with the guys. They hadn't given me a choice—the questions had started the moment I sat my ass down.

"You know it," I told him.

He gripped my shoulder. "Fuck, man. Getting it in on your second day in Vegas. Now, you're making me proud."

Brett handed me a scotch when I walked into the living room. "To pussy," he said and clinked his glass against mine.

I took a drink and looked at Ford, who was reclined in one of the chairs. "Feeling any better?"

He nodded. "The nap helped, but I'm not hitting the booze until dinner." He held up a bottle of water. "Meet my new friend."

I laughed. "At least you're not in bed, ordering room service, which is what I was expecting from you."

"And never live it down?" He shook his head. "No, thank you. The fall might be ugly, but it's the rallying that counts."

"Ain't that the goddamn truth?" Max said. He took a seat next to Ford. "One thing we know how to do—and do well—is give an endless amount of shit."

Max was right about that.

Too drunk to go to dinner and clubbing was an instant invitation to getting called out whenever the opportunity arose. With these guys, our best friends, the teasing would be fucking relentless.

"You good?" Brett asked, his arm going across my shoulders as I walked toward the balcony, where Jack and Dominick were talking.

Since Dominick had started doing business with The Agency—a company of entertainment agents, including Brett, Max, Jack, and Scarlett, their other partner who sat out for guys' trips because she said it was too much testosterone—they had become fixtures in our lives.

"Real good," I told him. "But I'm ready to get shit-faced and have a hell of a meal."

His grip tightened. "That makes two of us."

Dominick's room was like mine with a balcony running across the back that gave him a full view of the Bellagio fountains and the unique, lit-up high-rise hotels on the Strip. Just as

Brett and I stepped outside, the sky was turning dark, giving this city an entirely different feel. Aside from the fun we had here, the scenery was my favorite part about Vegas. The mountains framed the perimeter, the belly an explosion of lights and energy and color.

Normally, I would take in this view and think of all the work that was waiting for me on my laptop.

But work wasn't what ate my mind tonight.

It was Jo.

"Two times in one day," Brett said, our hands resting over the wooden banister that edged the top of the glass wall outside. "That's more than a one-night stand, my friend."

Another reminder.

I could still see her body, still feel the softness of her skin, still hear her screams as she shuddered over my cock.

Women didn't take up real estate in my brain.

They left as quickly as they came. I didn't have time for them to stick around. My life moved far too fast for that—traveling, work, traveling for work, a vicious cycle that repeated weekly. Since graduating from law school, I didn't ask for phone numbers. I didn't memorize addresses. Women were like a bold, heavy cabernet while eating a five-hundred-dollar Kobe steak. They enhanced the experience, but they weren't the star of the show.

The star was work.

It always had been; it always would be.

Except this little beauty with long black hair and glittering blue eyes was etched in a space I couldn't erase.

And I didn't know what the fuck to do about it.

I turned toward Brett. "She might become a multi-night stand while I'm in Vegas, but this is where it'll end."

"You sure about that?" Brett asked.

As I was about to answer, Jack walked back inside, and

Dominick came over and said, "If you're talking about Jo, he's already fucking pussy-whipped."

I looked at my brother. "Do you have something you want to say to me?"

Dominick smiled. "Do you really want to hear it?"

I laughed.

I knew where this was going.

Since Dominick was dating Kendall now and Brett was engaged to James Ryne—the most popular actress in Hollywood—they thought they knew it all. They had every goddamn answer. Like they were fucking psychologists in any situation that involved women.

I couldn't wait to hear this.

"Sure, bring it," I told him.

"You like her, and you don't know what the fuck to do about it."

Now, I really laughed. In fact, I laughed so hard that my head fell back.

The action instantly brought back a memory from earlier in my room.

Fuck.

"Listen, you two, I know you both think you're the latest and greatest Dr. Phil, but you have no idea what the hell you're talking about. She lives in Miami, and she's in college. I have no business even entertaining a thought like that, never mind pursuing her."

"So, she's a bit of a cub," Dominick said. "That's a moot point. She's legal—that's all that matters."

"And you know half my relationship has been long-distance while James is on location, filming." Brett nodded toward Max. "He and Eve haven't always lived in the same city either." He then pointed at Jack. "And you know he and Samantha have had their time apart."

I glanced between Brett and Dominick, not believing my fucking ears. "Hold up. I got my dick sucked a few times today, and suddenly, you're marrying me off and visualizing my white picket fence?" I shook my head. "I don't know what the fuck has gotten into you two, but, Jesus, you're laying it on thick." I glared at Dominick. "Especially you, the guy who lived an identical life as mine."

"But do I now?" Dominick asked. "I learned that lesson and almost pushed away the best thing that's ever happened to me."

I emptied the scotch in my hand, my patience running out. "Are you done?"

He put his hand in the air. "I'm just saying, be open to possibilities. You shut them out before they even turn into chances. Whether it be with Jo or the next girl, I want you to stop and consider what could be."

I set my glass down, wishing one of them had brought the bottle outside.

Am I considering anything they're saying?

Fuck no.

This is a waste of a conversation.

"I've heard you. Now, I think it's time for dinner," I said.

I wished that dismissal caused the thoughts to leave as well.

But they were there, front and center.

I had almost a week left in Vegas. Jo did as well.

If these temptations continued ...

No, I wasn't putting my brain there.

"You seem to be forgetting all the hell you and Ford put me through when I kept rejecting the idea of dating Kendall," Dominick said.

The start of his relationship had been a rocky ride. And Ford and I had been there for it all, holding his damn hand.

"I get it," I told him. "But this is premature."

"I thought that, too, at the beginning," he admitted. "Except the second I laid eyes on my girl, deep down, I knew she was going to be mine. That feeling came over me, and I fought it for as long as I could, but I couldn't get her out of my goddamn mind."

Fuck me.

The only thing I wanted in this moment was to wrap my hands around her ass and haul her body up against mine, attacking her mouth with my fucking tongue.

I pushed away from the balcony and said, "I'm leaving. It's time to get drunk. Are you two coming?"

I didn't wait for an answer. I continued inside, joining Max, Jack, and Ford.

But I could hear Brett and Dominick laughing behind me, followed by, "That motherfucker doesn't even know what just hit him."

SIX

JOANNA

"Shake it," Monica sang as I ground my ass against hers, the music flowing through me.

Going to clubs and dancing was a big part of our nightlife in Miami, so it only made sense that we would do the same while we were in Vegas. The best thing about doing it here was that this city was full of strangers. The chances of us running into someone we knew was beyond slim. We could dance however we wanted, dress however we liked. We could just let loose and not care and let the music take over.

At least, that was what I thought.

Until I looked up from the speaker we were dancing on and saw Jenner and his crew in the VIP area.

Oh God.

I was positive he hadn't seen me because none of the guys were looking in our direction.

I wasn't surprised he was here. This was one of the most well-known clubs on the Strip. Whenever I read about celebrities visiting Vegas, it was always mentioned that they made a stop here. I was sure they were seated in the same section as

Jenner—an area my girls and I couldn't enter, as we didn't have the right passes. We hadn't tried to get those passes because we only came here to dance.

"Monica ..." I tugged her arm, getting her attention. "Look." I pointed toward Jenner and watched her face as I said, "That's him."

She glanced back at me, almost spilling her drink. "Like *him*, him?"

I nodded. "Yes, that's Jenner."

"*Daaamn*, girl." Her eyes widened as she took him in. "He's like a much sexier, younger version of Ben Affleck. The J.Lo version, not the Jennifer Garner version."

"Right?" I hadn't made the connection, but she was dead accurate. "Man, he's delicious."

"Are those his brothers on either side of him?" She was practically meowing. "If they are, you need to hook me up. Like, I can't even ..."

"Yep, that's Ford and Dominick, although I'm honestly not sure which is which. The guys across from them are their friends."

They were all certainly good-looking.

But they weren't Jenner.

His face was so sharp, edges that made him so manly and sexy, his scruff such a natural addition that I couldn't imagine him without it.

And then there was his body.

Sigh.

"I don't know if it's all the liquor we've downed tonight or what, but, holy hell, you look like you're in heat, woman."

I giggled as I faced her. "He's irresistible. I seriously can't help it."

And he was dangerous, but I didn't add that description.

I kept that one to myself.

She touched my face, like she was taking my temperature. "He's that good, huh?"

"You have no idea."

She lifted my cup, forcing me to take a sip. "Did he know we were going to be here?"

I swallowed before I responded, "I never said a word about where we were going for dinner or after."

"Then, it's fate, baby."

"What's fate?" Courtney said from behind us, wrapping her arms around both our shoulders, as Lex moved to my other side.

"Jenner's here," I told her.

"*Whaaa*?"

"I know," I agreed. "But it's not like it matters. We're just having fun, and he's here with his boys, probably looking to pick up another girl—"

"It matters," Lex said, cutting me off. "And he's not picking up anyone. There isn't a single girl at their table."

She had a point.

From what I could see, it was just the guys and several bottles of booze.

Still, whatever this was, it couldn't extend beyond Vegas.

We were different ages, living in much different worlds, and there were a million other reasons why we wouldn't work.

"So?" Monica said.

I turned toward her. "So, what?"

She pushed my butt. "So ... go talk to him."

"You're nuts."

"She's right. You need to go talk to him right now," Lex said.

"And then score us access to the VIP area, so we can see if there are hotter boys up there than down here," Courtney added.

I glanced at all three of them, not believing my ears. "You're kidding, right?"

Monica laughed. "I think you know I'm positively not kidding."

Courtney turned me around, so I faced Jenner, and said, "Go tease that boy," in my ear.

"And hurry," Monica added. "I need to get a better look at those brothers and see if they're as juicy up close."

I chuckled, but it was more out of nerves.

I wasn't just teasing that boy. I was playing with fire.

I attempted to turn around, and the three of them said in unison, "Go!"

"All right, all right."

The speakers that we were dancing on ran across this whole side of the club, leading past the VIP area, where Jenner was sitting. The problem was, my girls and I weren't the only ones on them. They were packed full of people. If I was going to get Jenner's attention, aside from texting him, this was the only way.

But I needed to be careful, or I would fall at least ten feet to the ground.

To keep my balance, I flattened my hands on the wall and apologized to everyone dancing in front of me as I weaved my way toward him. The closer I got, I saw that he was in deep conversation with one of the guys, his back still facing me.

When I was only a few feet away, I tiptoed the rest of the distance, making sure not to trip in these heels, and shouted, "Jenner!" When he didn't respond, assuming he hadn't heard me, I tried again, "Hey, Jenner!"

He turned, a smile warming his face when our eyes connected. He stood and leaned over the banister that separated the two sections, putting us closer together. "What are you doing here?"

I held the spot next to his fingers, clinging for dear life as two girls twerked behind me. "I came with my friends." A grin moved to my face—I couldn't help it. "How about you?"

"This is the best club in Vegas. We always find our way here." His stare dipped down my body, a look of satisfaction filling his eyes. "Fuck, you look gorgeous"—he slowly made his way to my face—"but I still like having that dress on my floor." A heat burst across my cheeks as he added, "Why aren't you in the VIP area?"

The grittiness of his voice and the hunger in his gaze made me wet.

It had only taken seconds, and that was something that had never happened before.

"We have no way to get in," I told him.

He pointed toward the front of the club. "The VIP entrance is near the door. Meet me there. I'll get you in."

"My friends too?"

He nodded. "Of course."

I blew him a kiss, surely the result of all the vodka Monica had fed me tonight, and I retraced my steps, returning to the girls.

"He's getting us in?" Lex asked once I reached them.

"Yep, come on." I grabbed her hand, making sure Court and Monica were behind us, and I got us down from the speakers, hurrying through the dance floor toward the front of the club.

Jenner was standing at the access area with one of the bouncers, talking to him like they were best friends.

I wasn't surprised.

Someone like him had connections everywhere, including the hottest club in Vegas.

"These are the girls?" the bouncer asked Jenner.

He smiled. "Yes, all four of them."

"I need to see IDs," the bouncer said to us. "Then, I'm

going to place a bracelet on your wrist. Don't take it off until you leave."

My friends and I had our licenses ready, and once they were checked, the bouncer wrapped the paper bracelets around our wrists, and we went up the stairs. But not before Jenner slipped something into the bouncer's hand, a quick flash of his grip showing me it was a hundred-dollar bill.

This club was so hard to get into. I assumed there was another hundred tucked behind it.

The moment I cleared the last stair, Jenner's arm snaked around my waist, pulling me toward him.

"I haven't been able to stop thinking about you." His hand lowered, squeezing my butt. "And this."

"Trust me, I feel the same." I quickly glanced at my girls, and Monica winked at me. "Thank you for getting us in."

He gave me a kiss, and I could taste the whiskey on his lips, the desire in his movements, the lust that was dripping between us. "My pleasure."

Those two simple words were the sexiest when they came from him.

Even though I'd been hesitant when the girls pushed for this, I was happy I'd listened.

The feel of his arms around me was something I could definitely get used to.

Because even when he was gone, his touch continued to consume me, and I hadn't stopped thinking about him since I'd left his suite.

I placed my hands on his stomach, the hardness of his abs teasing me.

Taunting me.

Something was rushing through my body, and I couldn't control it.

It wasn't just the thought of getting him naked or his tongue or the naughty things he would do to me.

It was something more.

Oh God, Jo, what are you doing?

"There's no way I'd have let you stay out there ..."

His eyes told me he wanted to say more. That he was being protective. That he was stopping the vultures from scooping me up.

That he wanted me all to himself.

But he left it at that, voicing nothing more.

With our eyes locked, our bodies pressed together, I already felt like I belonged to him.

And when he leaned down, giving me his lips again, that feeling was only confirmed.

A tingle burst down my body, one that started in my throat and ended between my legs.

Even after he pulled his mouth away, it took a few seconds for my eyes to open. To realize we were still by the entrance. That my friends had found their way to the bar. That we were in an extremely busy, loud, dark section of the club.

Because it felt like it was only us.

"Are you going to introduce me to your friends?"

I'd been so mesmerized that I'd completely forgotten.

How rude of me.

"I'm sorry." I shook my head, pulling myself back into reality. "I see them at the bar. Come on."

I linked our hands, an action that felt so natural that I didn't realize the meaning behind it until we arrived at Monica's side and his fingers slipped out of my hold, gripping my lower back instead.

"Ladies," I said, clearing my throat, "meet Jenner."

Monica's face said it all—shock with a heavy dose of approval. I assumed she was surprised by how good-looking he was or the fact that I'd immediately fallen into his arms or that we couldn't keep our eyes off each other.

The bartender set a round of drinks in front of her, and she handed me one and then reached for Jenner's hand to shake. "It's so fab to meet you. What can I get you to drink?"

"Likewise," he replied. "And I appreciate the offer, but we have several bottles at our table. There's no need for you girls to pay for anything tonight."

I took a long, heavy gulp, and while he shook hands with Lex and Court, I stared at Monica, easily making my way into her thoughts. She was impressed and as smitten as me, and that was clear as day.

I had to stop myself from laughing.

When Jenner pulled his hand back, his arm returned to my backside, and he said, "Why don't you all come sit with us? I'll introduce you to my friends and brothers."

The nervous energy was, for some reason, still there, and it increased at the thought of meeting his friends and family. Even though I'd seen them in the sportsbook, this felt different.

It felt more intimate.

Especially as we walked over with his hand on me, all of their eyes on mine as we approached the table.

"This is Jo," Jenner said to the group.

As he voiced each of their names, I recited it in my head and shook their hand, trying to memorize who they were. And when I released Jack's fingers, the last of the group, I said, "It's nice to meet you all." I gave them a wave and continued, "These are my girls. This is Monica, Lex, and Courtney." I pointed at each one.

"Ladies, come sit," Ford said, and he got up from his seat, calling the waitress over to get more chairs.

Dominick and Brett rose as well.

My friends were reluctant to take their places, but when the boys insisted, they caved.

Jenner sat in the only empty chair, the one he'd given up to meet us at the entrance, and he pulled me onto his lap. The second my butt landed, I felt his hardness, and he wasted no time pushing it into me.

If I'd thought I was wet before, nothing compared to this.

And when his lips pressed against the back of my neck, my body began to scream.

"Jo, where are you from?" I heard.

It took a moment for me to work my way out of this Jenner fog, but when I did, I realized Dominick was the one who had asked. While waiting for the waitress to return with chairs, he stood behind us.

"Miami," I told him, and I pointed at the girls. "We all live there."

"Do you come here for every March Madness?" he asked.

"Some of the girls aren't even twenty-two yet," I shyly admitted. "So, no, this is the first year we've been, now that we're really able to enjoy Vegas."

"You're just babies," he replied.

I laughed.

But he was right.

As I hung out with Jenner and his friends, dressed in sports coats with cuff links at the ends of their sleeves, having immediate access to the VIP area and not even blinking at the cost of bottle service, I certainly felt the difference between them and college guys.

But as Jenner's lips moved down my shoulder, those thoughts dissolved.

And once again, I could think of nothing but him.

"You're making it impossible for me to pay attention to this conversation with your brother," I whispered.

His mouth moved to the back of my ear, where I felt a quick flick of his tongue. "And I haven't even touched you yet."

That was a warning.

Because seconds later, his fingers found me, pressing against the center of my stomach, his thumb rubbing circles, like he was threatening to go lower.

"You're killing me," I groaned only loud enough for him to hear.

"I'm not trying to ..."

But he was.

He knew exactly what he was doing.

"Don't you want me to make a good impression?"

As he exhaled, goose bumps lifted across my skin. "Jo, you already have."

SEVEN

JENNER

There was no way I could sit at this table with my brothers and friends and Jo's crew and ignore my cock.

A hard-on that was fucking raging to be inside of her.

Every bit of small talk was making my patience thinner. Every question directed at her was only making me want her more.

I couldn't wait a second longer to have her alone.

I downed the rest of my drink and growled in her ear, "We're going to dance."

She said nothing, not even putting up a fight as I stood from the chair and lifted her into the air, taking a few steps before I set her on her feet.

Dominick glanced at me before I turned, and I mouthed, *We'll be back*, before I led her through the VIP area.

We descended the steps, and I brought her to the back of the dance floor.

This was where I wanted her, where we could escape those familiar eyes. Where she only had to focus on me.

Where I could feel the beat blast through her body.

Where I could watch her shake her ass, appreciating the way she moved, how her hips fucked the air, how they found a rhythm as though she were bouncing on my dick.

"I'm surprised you wanted to dance," she said as I backed her all the way into the corner, the darkest, most private area I could find.

I needed to feel her ass first, so I flipped her around, pressing those perfect cheeks against my cock. I held her waist, my mouth going to her ear. "I want this."

She circled her arms around my neck, shimmying her body lower, feeling the music. "You have it, Jenner."

"Fuck me," I moaned, teasing the bottom of her tit. "You're fucking delicious."

I couldn't hold in my thoughts, especially as her back arched, urging my hands up. I moved to the flatness of her stomach, the dips of her hips before I cupped her tits, grazing her nipples, rubbing my fingers over them. There were cutouts in her dress that ran along her sides, even more slits across her back, the dress hanging low on her chest. The only way she could look sexier was if she was naked. And the best part of these small openings was that they gave me access to her skin.

Skin that I wanted to touch freely without any barrier between us.

Flesh that I wanted to caress.

This position gave me the perfect angle to do both.

"God, you feel so fucking good."

I dipped into the hole on her back and slid below the fabric to her stomach.

She leaned into me, encouraging me to go further, to feel more of her.

I quickly glanced around us to make sure there wasn't anyone nearby, that no one was paying attention.

We were in the clear.

I had Jo all to myself.

And I planned to take full advantage of that.

She was shifting her ass across my cock, rubbing the length back and forth. With each grind, she pressed harder, her movements intentional.

Goading me.

When I turned her cheek to bite it, I saw the grin pulling on those gorgeous lips.

"Someone's ready to play," I hissed.

"Jenner ..." She leaned forward, and even though she was dancing, she was taunting me with doggy style—one of my favorite positions. "I want you." She moaned just as the bass lowered, drowning out her sound.

But it hit my body.

It vibrated through my goddamn chest.

I pulled her back up, holding her neck against my chest, growling, "I want to bend you over that speaker"—I paused, pointing her toward the section of the dance floor that I was referencing—"and fuck you until you fucking scream."

She brushed her hand over my cock, holding it, jerking it through my jeans. "How badly do you want to come?"

I sucked her earlobe into my mouth, gnawing the end. "I can't stop thinking about your pussy." I kissed down to her collarbone. "I can't stop thinking about how wet it's going to be." I licked the top of her shoulder before working my way back up. "How tight you're going to clutch me when you're coming."

I slapped her ass, earning myself a yelp that I swallowed as I moved across her throat.

"How badly?" I asked, returning to her question. "As badly as I need to hear you come." I lowered my hand under her dress until my finger hit her clit, pleasantly surprised to find she wasn't wearing any panties. "I need to feel it."

"Here?" She quivered. "Oh God."

I brushed across her clit, rubbing it in a circle, spreading the wetness that was dripping down her.

"I feel like everyone is watching."

As we faced the dance floor, the darkness encompassing us, the lights didn't even hit any of the space near us—the main reason I'd picked this spot.

"They're not," I assured. I dived into her neck as I lowered to her pussy, probing that tight fucking hole. "But maybe you want them to." I used my free hand to pinch her nipple. She wasn't wearing a bra, her tits free and bouncing as I ground my cock into her ass. "Maybe you want them to see how good I'm about to make you feel." I moaned in her neck. "How wet you're making my fingers." I dipped fully inside her, sliding in so easy—she was so fucking worked up. "How hard you're about to come."

I couldn't hear her breathing, but I could feel it.

Each gasp.

Each exhale.

I pinched her nipple, and she bucked, her back arching, her chest heaving for more.

"Or how much you turn me on," she breathed against me. "That's what I want them to see."

"*Mmm*," I groaned. "You dirty girl."

And right now, that dirty girl was mine, and she needed to be rewarded.

My thumb went to the very top of her pussy, a second finger pushed inside her, and a pattern started of lapping her clit and thrusting into her cunt. She was clenching around me, showing me how tight she was, making me jealous of my fingers.

They got to feel the perfectness of her pussy, the narrowness.

She was sucking me in and not letting me go, the same way she did to my cock.

Fuck.

I wanted nothing more than to taste what was soaking my fingers, to be on my knees with my face buried between her legs. That wasn't going to happen here. I'd have to wait until we got back to the hotel. But that didn't stop me from moving my hand faster, giving her the pressure she needed.

"Jenner ..." Her nails stabbed the back of my neck. "Oh my God."

I could feel the build happening inside her.

Her breathing changed.

Her hips swung, moving with me, bending her body with each plunge.

"Yes!" She shook. "Fucking yes!"

Her head leaned against me, and I pumped her with the same speed and power as the music blasting through the speakers.

Owning that fucking pussy.

And it didn't take long before it was fully mine, her body shuddering so hard that I had to hold her stomach so she wouldn't fall.

"*Ahhh*!" she moaned. "*Fuuuck*!"

She felt so good. I could do this over and over again, never stopping, just listening to that sweet, sexy moan on repeat. The desire to please her was a need I'd never felt before.

And, goddamn it, I couldn't get enough.

The moment she calmed, I pulled my hand out and turned her around. As she watched, I swiped my tongue across my finger, licking the drops off my skin.

Savoring her.

Swallowing her.

"Fuck, Jo." I made sure all the wetness was gone before I

held the back of her head, moving her face closer to mine. "You taste so fucking good."

She kissed me, sucking my tongue, gripping me with all her strength, her movements almost animalistic.

"You want more?" I said against her lips.

"I do." Her hands slipped down and clasped mine. "Follow me."

I said nothing as she led me through the dance floor and back into the VIP area. Instead of returning to the table, she brought me into the hallway where the restrooms were located and into the men's room, walking us into a stall that she locked the moment we were both inside.

She instantly lowered my zipper, navigating my cock through the hole of my boxer briefs. Once my dick was out, she got on her knees, licking those pouty fucking lips.

"Jo ..." I stared down at her as she surrounded the base of my shaft with her fist. "*Fuuuck.*" I spread my arms out, palms pressing against both walls of the stall. "What the fuck are you doing to me?"

"I'm taking what's mine."

Mine.

I needed to know.

I needed to fucking clarify.

"And that is?"

She looked at me through her long, thick lashes. "Your cum."

Watching that word come out of her mouth was the hottest thing in the world.

She wanted to make my balls throb. She wanted my nut in her mouth.

She wanted to own my pleasure.

She surrounded my tip, swirling her tongue across it, and

my head fell back from the sensation. "It's all yours," I exhaled. "Take it."

Her hand focused on the bottom, twisting, turning, rising to meet her mouth in the center. She added so much of her spit that her tongue was like a fucking sled.

"I want it," she begged as she surfaced. "I want you to come." She bobbed harder, picking up speed. "Give it to me, Jenner."

I held the back of her head, burying my fingers in her hair, watching her choke as she took more of me in. But she never stopped, never paused. She relaxed her throat and sank down, pumping her hand before she rose to the tip and did it again. She knew the amount of tightness I needed, how hard to suction in her cheeks when she was on my crown. How to flatten her tongue when she circled down the middle.

This girl knew how to give some fucking head.

"*Yesss!*" I took in her face, the way her cheeks expanded around me. "That's it." I squeezed her hair. "Suck it. Fucking suck it, Jo."

My balls were tightening.

My fucking legs turning numb.

"Come for me, Jenner."

Each order became hotter.

More of a turn-on.

Demanding in a way where I wanted to give her whatever she needed.

And this one triggered the build in my body.

She still had a free hand, and knowing I was watching, she slipped it between her legs, moaning the second it touched her pussy.

The vibration moved across my cock.

"Fuck ..." I rocked my hips forward. "Let me see you finger yourself."

She only had to lift her dress a few inches before I saw her cunt.

And she had two fingers buried deep inside it.

The same place my hand had been.

The place I couldn't stop dreaming about.

"Make yourself come," I ordered. "I want us getting off at the same time."

She had both arms moving, drawing out the most intense feelings from both of us, our sounds matching as they hit the air.

I couldn't hold off for much longer.

Not with the way she was fisting me, not with the way she was chugging me down.

It felt too good.

And every time I glanced at her, she was finger-fucking that gorgeous pussy.

Each of her breaths hit my cock; each of her moans dragged me farther in.

"Jo," I barked, the orgasm beginning to take hold. "You'd better fucking come."

My eyes wanted to close, but I wouldn't let them.

I needed to see this.

I needed to watch the shudders move across her body.

"Tell me," she cried. "Oh fuck, Jenner, tell me."

I reared my hips back, the explosion of tingles moving through my balls and into my shaft, and the first burst shot out of me.

She didn't need the warning.

She could feel my movements.

She could taste me in her mouth.

But if she needed words, I would give them to her. "I'm fucking coming."

There was a change in her mouth and the way she was

circling my shaft. They both came with a harder suction, like she wasn't just taking my cum, but also trying to suck it out of me.

And with that came a whole new wave.

A whole new build.

And with each dip, she milked me more with her tongue, the shift in her throat telling me she was swallowing me down.

I clenched her hair in my fist and roared, "Oh fuck."

I'd never felt anything like it, nothing this engrossing, this amazing.

Pleasure spread across her eyes as I shot another load, and I knew that was when she was coming, her body shaking, her balance almost wavering. But she didn't let up. She gave me exactly what I needed, draining me, emptying me, pulling every fucking moan out of my body.

She didn't pause until I eased my cock out of her mouth.

But once that happened, I realized her hand was still on her cunt, continuing to finger-fuck herself. And now that her mouth wasn't full, I could really hear her sounds.

"Jenner, oh God, yes," she cried, squeezing my shin.

One last quiver came through her body before she finally stilled.

I helped her onto her feet. Grabbing her fingers before her hand dropped, I brought them up to my mouth, licking them. "That taste ..." I shook my head, making sure her skin was dry. "Goddamn it, Jo. I can't get enough of you." I held her face, staring into her eyes. "Who the fuck are you?"

Her body stiffened for just a second, and then she wrapped her arms around my neck. "Someone who wants to swallow you again."

EIGHT

JOANNA

When I'd gotten off the plane in Vegas, my friends and I in a ride-share on the way to the hotel, I didn't expect this week to be anything more than just fun—partying, hangovers, tanning by the pool.

But it had turned into so much more.

And now that we were on our last day here, flying out tomorrow morning, I was devastated that this trip was coming to an end.

Mostly for one reason.

A reason I didn't want to admit.

Jenner.

Monica had seen this coming, like it was a celebrity alert broadcasted across the world. She wanted this for me—she wanted us to work.

But there were so many factors that went into play. Long-distance was only one. Relationships were hard enough. Living on opposite sides of the country, constantly missing each other, felt impossible.

Besides, Jenner hadn't even hinted that he wanted anything

to happen beyond this trip. We had exchanged phone numbers, and that was the extent of our commitment, but we were still hanging out almost nonstop. I'd spent every night in his bed, and now, both of our crews were at the pool together, celebrating our final day.

The guys had rented a cabana, and waitresses kept it filled with appetizers and liquor and mixtures. Even though we were all partying as a group, Jenner's attention was never far from me.

Neither were his hands.

As we stood in the shallow end, they were circling my lower back, tracing the bottom of my bikini.

"What time is your flight tomorrow?" I asked him—a question I'd avoided until now because it felt so final.

But I needed to prepare myself.

"The plane should be here around one."

I wasn't surprised he was flying private. I would have been surprised if he wasn't.

"If you were on the way," he said, "we'd give you and your friends a lift home."

I loved how he treated private flying like it was an Uber.

"What time do you take off?"

I pressed my back against his chest, holding in my breath, feeling the coarseness of his dark hairs and the hardness of his pecs. "Our flight is at nine." I sighed. "I'm not a fan of anything early, but the girls wanted to be back at a decent time to get in some last-minute homework."

I almost cringed when I said that—another reminder of how young I was compared to him.

I stared at the girls, who were trying to keep up with his guys, guzzling vodka under this wicked heat. "I think it's going to be a rough morning." I laughed.

"I don't think you're wrong."

He turned me around, placing my back against the side of the pool, surrounding me in his arms. His cold, wet lips found mine. I could taste the liquor on his tongue, the neediness in his grip. The fire that was building between our bodies.

"*Mmm*," I moaned the second he pulled his mouth away.

It didn't matter how many times I had this man inside me—even if it was three times a day, like we'd been averaging; it wouldn't be enough. I'd gone to bed last night after cowgirl. I'd woken up to doggy style this morning.

Yet now, just a few hours later, I was fantasizing about what position he would put me in this afternoon.

He held my chin as he asked, "Do you girls have plans for dinner?"

Monica had tossed around a few ideas but hadn't made a reservation.

"Nope," I replied.

He pulled my lip into his mouth, biting the end before he released it. "We're going for sushi, and we have a private room. I can easily add four more to the table." His hands dipped to my ass, circling my cheeks. "And we also have tickets to see The Weeknd tonight. If you want to come"—he nuzzled his face in my neck—"I can score those for you too."

"You're kidding."

A man with endless connections.

I found that so incredibly sexy.

"This isn't the only hotel I've opened on the Strip." He pulled his face back, his lips now close to mine. "My job earns me perks all over the world."

"You're a lucky guy."

He sighed. "I work hard for it. Trust me."

"I don't doubt it one bit." I smiled. "Fair warning: Monica is going to die when she hears this. She's obsessed with The Weeknd." I turned around, facing her back, watching her in deep conversation with Max. "Hey, Mon," I said, waiting for her to give me her attention. "Want to go for sushi tonight with the guys?"

She nodded. "Sounds yummy to me."

"And how about going to The Weeknd concert after?"

Her eyes widened. "Shut up. You're not serious. I tried to get us tickets, and they were just so ridiculously priced. I couldn't swing it."

I'd wanted so badly to buy them as her graduation gift, but Monica wouldn't even let me think about it.

Now that she was getting to go anyway, I couldn't be more excited.

"I have club-level seats," Jenner said to her. "With backstage passes." He nodded toward Max and added, "Max represents him."

She shook her head. "I can't even." Waves lapped onto my chest as she hurried over to us. "I might propose to you right now," she said to Jenner, giggling. "Is this real? Or am I dreaming? Because I don't think I've emphasized enough that The Weeknd is my favorite artist of all time."

"It's happening," I told her. "You just have to say yes."

"*Yesss!*" she screamed over the music in the pool, and people nearby looked in our direction. "Hell yes!"

"What's going on?" Lex asked, moving closer, Courtney joining her.

"We're all going to The Weeknd concert tonight," I replied.

"*Whaaa?*" Courtney said. "We are?"

"Oh, we are, girlfriend. We are," Monica told her.

I placed my arm across Jenner's shoulders, his eyes already on me. "You've made my friends really, really happy."

"And you?" His stare was boring through me.

I chewed on my bottom lip. "I think you know the answer to that."

Monica joined the other two girls, squeeing so loud that I couldn't stop laughing at them. But my demeanor immediately changed when Jenner's mouth pressed against my neck, rising to my ear.

His hands continued their sexy assault across my body as he growled, "You're going to have an amazing time tonight."

He was making a promise.

One I didn't doubt.

And one that proved to be true because hours later, when I was standing at the edge of the VIP box, staring into The Weeknd's face, I couldn't drop the smile from my lips.

I couldn't stop dancing.

I couldn't shake the tingling bursting through my body.

The Weeknd was belting out one of his most popular songs that Monica played on repeat in our apartment. My best friend was living her best life, and so were Court and Lex. The guys were moving around the box, eating the catered food, pouring drinks. And Jenner was behind me. Our bodies had been pressed together all night, swaying in sync like we had at the club.

"You weren't lying," I whispered to him after several songs. I pressed my face against his shoulder, inhaling his cologne, memorizing it. A scent that was spicy and crisp and unforgettable. "This is amazing."

We were close enough that I could see the sweat on The Weeknd's forehead, where the energy in the arena was pulsing through me, where I could feel the beat as though I were standing on a speaker.

But the concert wasn't what made this night so special.

That was Jenner.

And this was an evening I would certainly remember forever.

"I'm glad I could do this for you."

I gave him a quick kiss before Monica grabbed my hand and lifted it into the air, twirling me in a circle. Jenner released his grip on me, and Monica hugged me against her.

"I can't remember the last time I had this much fun," she said, dancing with me, finding our own rhythm. "But I have to tell you something. Whether you want to hear it or not, I just need to get it out."

She was speaking directly in my ear, and I pulled back to look at her, trying to read her expression, judging where she was going to take this conversation.

"He's the best." She paused. "And the best thing that's ever happened to you."

There was a tightness in my chest, a throbbing reminder that after tomorrow morning, everything would be different.

"Monica ..." I shook my head, not knowing what to say.

But I agreed with her.

I just didn't want to admit it out loud.

I didn't want to put that kind of weight on the future.

"Don't fuck this up," she warned.

I swallowed, staring at my best friend, my heart clutching.

"Promise me?"

I nodded, giving her the best answer I could, and then I wrapped my arm around her and ground my hips against hers, getting her mind back on the music.

But that wasn't where mine was.

Mine was on Jenner.

"Good morning," Jenner whispered against my forehead.

I stirred awake as I felt his words move across my skin, my eyes not even having to blink with the sun barely peeking through the long, heavy curtains.

I didn't know what time we'd eventually crawled into his bed last night, but it wasn't all that long ago. Once the concert had ended, Jenner's limo had taken us back to the hotel, and we'd all spent several hours in the bar before Jenner and I came up here.

"Morning," I grumbled, nuzzling into his neck, trying to find my bearings. Talking this early wasn't one of my favorite things, but our time together was so limited. I leaned up, checking the clock on his nightstand. "Ugh, I have to leave soon."

I rested my face against his chest, running my fingers through the small patches of hair, my lids closing as I tried to burn this memory into my head.

How he felt.

The warmth of his skin.

The feel of his body on mine.

Because the moment I left, I didn't know if I would ever get this back.

Or if I would ever feel this way again.

But if I kept this as a memory, I could return to it whenever I needed, whenever I missed him.

Even though I already did.

"I'm not looking forward to saying good-bye," I admitted, regretting it the second I finished speaking. I tilted my face up to look at him. "I just mean, I've had so much fun with you."

His fingers ran across my cheek and into my hair. "You're the best thing I never expected to find ..."

I didn't know what that meant.

But I liked the sound of it.

His hand lowered to my bare back, where he traced circles over my skin. The sound of his heart pattered against my ear, a drum that made me close my eyes and take in this moment again.

And every one we'd had together so far.

From the second we'd met in the sportsbook to the way he'd brought me up to his suite, the evenings we'd spent in this bed, and last night's finale.

It had all gone by too fast.

How could I tell him I wanted to relive it all over again, that I wanted things to last beyond Vegas, when what we had was just fun, nothing more? Two people who had hooked up on vacation, and it had been the best sex of my entire life.

I needed to accept that.

To convince myself.

To repeat it in my head until I believed it.

"I should probably get going," I whispered, pushing myself up, wanting to do just the opposite. "I still have to pack and round up the girls. I'm sure they're still sleeping off their hangover."

When Jenner and I had left the group, they had been doing shots in the bar. Something told me today was going to be a challenge in many ways.

He released me, and I got out of bed, finding my dress where I'd left it on the chair. I quickly slipped it on and hurried into the bathroom, taming down my hair and rinsing the smudged makeup from my face. I even took some of Jenner's toothpaste and finger-brushed it over my teeth. When I came out, he was leaning against one of the chairs in a pair of gray sweats, a bottle of water in his hand, my clutch in the other.

He held the bag in my direction and said, "Come here."

The second I was within reach, he pulled me against him, holding my face to his chest, like we were back in bed. My eyes closed, and my arms circled around him, gripping him with all my strength.

He kissed the top of my head. "Get home safe."

I looked up, our eyes meeting, the room now starting to fill with morning light. "Thank you for the most incredible week."

He pressed his lips to mine.

He never parted them.

He never gave me his tongue.

He just breathed me in, our mouths locked, his hands possessively rolling across my back, my shoulders, moving to my face, where he held my cheeks steady. His palms stayed there, keeping me in place, his thumbs pushing the sides of my lips, like he was trying to get me closer.

But that was impossible.

Not even air was separating us.

When he eventually pulled away, his stare continued to devour me, sending a jolt straight through my body.

"Go," he demanded. "Before I make you miss your flight."

I would never forget those words.

I tucked my clutch under my arm, my heart pounding in a way that reminded me of running, the last quarter of a mile when you just wanted to get home.

My throat was tightening.

Emotion was lifting, and I wasn't sure why.

Or why I couldn't stop it.

It had only been a week.

Such a minuscule amount of time.

How was it possible to feel this way, this ache that wouldn't leave, this pain that wouldn't lighten?

Before a tear fell, I took a step back and then another, turning to walk to the door. When I reached the knob, I faced him, the need to see him one last time so overwhelmingly strong.

He hadn't moved.

Neither did his expression.

The only change was his eyes, the intensity of his gaze, like any second, he was going to pounce.

"Good-bye, Jenner." My voice wasn't any louder than a whisper.

Before he said anything, before he made a move that would stop me from leaving, I hurried down the hall, letting his door slam, and rushed inside the elevator.

The minute I hit the button for the top floor, the first tear fell. I wiped it away, knowing plenty more would follow. When the elevator arrived on my floor, I stepped out and rushed to our room, my chin quivering, my nose starting to run.

I heard silence the moment I opened our door.

I went into the master bedroom, the room I'd shared with Monica before staying with Jenner. I found her facedown on the bed, wearing the dress from last night. There were even heels still on her feet.

I flipped on the lights and sat on the edge of the bed, shaking her awake. "Mon, you have to get up. We need to go to the airport."

"*Ughhh,*" she groaned, covering the side of her face. "I feel like death."

"I know, but we have to get going." I left her to grab my suitcase, lifting it onto the bed and opening it. "If we miss our flight, we'll have to fly standby, and it'll be a nightmare."

"I can't move."

"But you must."

I ran to the second bedroom, where Lex and Court were passed out in similar positions. "Ladies, get up!" I flipped on their lights as well, and they stayed still. "Move your butts, or we're not going to make our flight."

They moaned a reply I couldn't understand.

"Fine, suit yourself. You'll just have to spend the whole day at the airport, hungover and in hell, while you wait for an available flight."

"*Stooop*," Lex cried.

"I hate that she's right," Court grunted.

"You have less than thirty minutes, so haul ass."

I went back into my room and opened the drawers of the dresser, taking out my clothes and dumping them into my suitcase.

"Jo," Monica said as she sat up, squeezing her temples.

I avoided her eyes, making several more trips between the dresser and my suitcase.

"Jo," she said again, louder, wincing from her headache. "Look at me."

I didn't want to, but I paused and faced her.

"Babe, do you want to talk about it?"

I shouldn't be surprised. She knew me better than anyone.

I shook my head, slumping on top of the bed. "No. Yes. No." I wrapped my arms around my stomach. "Fuck."

"Come here." She opened her arms, and I fell into her, the scent of booze filling my nose as she hugged me.

I hadn't realized how badly I needed this.

"I know you're not all right."

The tears were back, flowing harder than before. "Not even close."

"You care about him much more than you realized."

"Yep. That." My chest was so constricted; I didn't know how I could get air in. "I told myself I had to be okay with this. It was a vacation fling, nothing more. I couldn't have feelings beyond today." I wiped my nose. "But I do, Mon." I held the back of her dress, squeezing the material. "I just need the hurt to stop."

She pulled away. "I wish I weren't so hungover. I feel like

I'd have all the words, but right now, I'm just trying not to throw up."

"Don't worry; this isn't the last time we're going to talk about him."

She went to laugh and held her head with both hands. "Maybe we should miss our flight on purpose. What time is he leaving?"

"No." I shook my head as I thought about her offer. "We said our good-bye, and it has to end sometime." I took a breath. "Why not now, right?"

"Babe ..."

But there was nothing she could say.

Nothing either of us could do.

We were headed back to Miami, Jenner was going to LA, and that was just the reality of our situation.

But I knew one thing for sure.

Feelings that developed in Vegas ... didn't stay in Sin City.

NINE

JENNER

"Jenner, it's Ralph," my client said as I held the phone to my ear, not two minutes into my Monday.

The leather on my seat was still cold, my coffee untouched.

"Ralph. Good morning." I cleared my throat, reaching for the mug my assistant had just delivered. I was tempted to start the ticker on my computer to track the length of this call, billing Ralph for the time. The software was so precise that seconds were rounded up to minutes. But Vegas was still running thick in my veins, and I just didn't have the energy yet. "What can I do for you?"

"I'm interested in building a warehouse, totaling upward to a million square feet. Whatever I don't use, I'll subdivide for rental income until I can utilize the whole space."

I took a sip of the hot, dark drink. "An excellent way to generate revenue. Based on the price per square foot you can get for a rental in both Malibu and Marina del Rey, you'll more than cover your nut."

Ralph, a longtime client, was a boat dealer, specializing in yachts, cabin cruisers, and center consoles. Since I was so familiar with his business, I knew the warehouse would store the overflow of his inventory and allow him to expand his service department—something he wanted to do more of.

"Except I won't be building in either of those spots, Jenner. I have news. I'm expanding."

"Fantastic to hear. Whereabouts?"

"Miami Beach."

I shook my head, silently laughing.

Out of all fucking places.

"Great spot," I told him, picking up a pen and tapping it against my desk. "A paradise for boating, and now, you'll have real estate on both coasts."

"I need you to weigh in on the land and build-out, handle the zoning. There's going to be some red tape involved with this one."

"That's my specialty."

"And that's why I keep you on retainer."

I turned my chair, facing the windows, squinting at the sun as it burned the sleep from my eyes. "Send me the paperwork. I'll take a look at everything and let you know what I find."

"My secretary will email you in the next hour." He paused. "How quickly do you think you can meet me here?"

"Here?" My brows rose as I stared down at my coffee like it was spiked. "You're in Miami now?"

"Standing on the lot as we speak. I'd like to make an offer in the next few days before someone else scoops it up, which means we have to move fast. You know how hot Miami real estate is at the moment."

I exhaled, clicking my mouse, waking my computer. I pulled up my calendar, quickly reviewing the next few days. Each was packed with meetings along with a trip to Seattle on

Friday. I was sure I could take several of those calls from the plane and have my assistant rearrange the rest.

"It's going to take some heavy lifting to pull this off. Give me an hour, and I'll get back to you."

"I appreciate it, Jenner. In the meantime, I'll make sure the paperwork gets sent."

"Sounds good," I said and hung up, immediately calling in my assistant.

As she stood in my doorway, I explained the situation with Ralph, letting her know I'd need at least two days in Florida, possibly three. As she left to work on my schedule, I leaned back in my chair and closed my eyes.

The coffee wasn't giving me the energy I needed to get through this day, never mind this morning. I hadn't even been home for twenty-four hours, and that sexy, beautiful girl was still so present in my mind.

A mind that should have been cleared of her the moment I stepped on the plane.

Just because she had owned my thoughts and occupied my hands while I was in Vegas didn't mean that had to continue.

I was home.

I was back to my lifestyle.

Thousands of miles separated us, and so did far too many years. Years that were important, that were full of development, that put us in different stages of our lives.

It didn't matter that there was a chance I could be flying to her city this week. Seeing her would only delay the inevitable. It would only tease me.

And the best thing for me—the best thing for both of us—was to push our time in Vegas far out of my fucking head.

"Jenner," my assistant said, returning to my doorway. "I worked a miracle. I don't know how, honestly, but I did. I have you on the company's plane tomorrow morning and then flying straight to Seattle on Friday."

She closed my door, and I stared at the black screen of my phone.

That gave me three nights in Miami.

Goddamn it.

I wasn't going to call her.

I sure as hell wasn't going to see her.

Yet I found myself searching for her name in my Contacts and holding the phone to my face, listening to each ring.

There were only two before she picked up and said, "Hello?"

"Jo ..."

She took a deep breath. "God, that voice. The last time I heard you say my name like that, you were moaning it."

I chuckled.

That fucking mouth.

One of the many things I liked about her, whether words were coming out of it or it was swallowing my cock.

"Do you want me to moan it again?"

There was silence on the other end and what sounded like movement and then, "You're into phone sex, Jenner? How naughty of you."

I pushed my chair away from my desk, leaning back as far as I could go. "Not that I'm opposed to it, but I think it would be much hotter if I was moaning it against your lips."

I could hear her smiling when she voiced, "Tell me how you're going to make that happen."

"I'm coming to Miami tomorrow for business. I'll be there for three nights."

She exhaled, the sound almost sinful. "Does that mean I get you all to myself for those nights?"

I stared out the window, the LA skyline almost glittering

under the morning light. "I'm sure I can make that happen ... and possibly even a few days."

"I like that answer even better."

I held my coffee against my lips. "So, you're telling me you're available."

"For you, I'll make it happen, although I might have to squeeze in a class or two and a tiny bit of homework."

I growled, "I don't think I can let you do that."

"No?"

My lids shut as I thought about her body and the things I wanted to do to her. It had only been since yesterday that my hands were on her, that my lips had grazed her skin.

It felt longer.

Like months.

"I don't think I'm going to let you leave my bed once you step foot in my room."

"*Mmm*," she moaned. "How do you plan to spend that time?"

Her voice was as good as her silky, wet tongue licking down the center of my shaft.

"I'm going to start with rope, making sure you can't move."

"Tell me more ..."

"Or handcuffs," I clarified. "Whichever I end up bringing with me, but I want you chained to the bed, your legs spread wide open." I adjusted my dick as it hardened in my suit pants. "I want you available for my mouth, my hands, my cock—whichever one I want to use."

"Jenner ..."

"Are you wet?"

"Oh God, yes."

I couldn't control the need erupting inside me, the urge, the craving coming out through my voice. "How fucking wet?" When she went to answer, I cut her off and said, "I want you to put your hand down your pants and dip into your pussy and tell me just how wet you really are."

There was movement, like she was balancing the phone with her shoulder to free up her hands. Her breathing increased and hitched. "It's on my inner thighs."

"Fuck," I hissed.

"And it's dripping along my pussy. My finger is sliding down my slit."

I rubbed my hand over my hard-on. "Goddamn it, yes."

"That's what you do to me, Jenner. You make me soaked."

"That tight, little, wet cunt so fucking ready ..."

"For you."

My dick was throbbing, wanting to be freed from my pants, to sink inside Jo's pussy.

"Touch yourself for me," I ordered.

"You'd better be doing the same."

Just as that thought started to resonate, to really take shape in my head, and I went to reach for my zipper, my door opened, and Ford peeked his head through.

"Fuck me," I groaned as I stared at him. "My brother just walked in ..."

She laughed. "Now, that's shitty timing. Tell Dominick or Ford I said hello. As for you, I'll be seeing your sexy ass tomorrow. I can't wait."

"That makes two of us," I said and hung up.

Ford closed the door and took a seat in one of the chairs in front of my desk and said, "Jo?"

I nodded. "She says hello."

He smiled. "Interesting."

I rolled my chair forward, pushing my legs under the desk to hide my raging erection. "What is?"

"That the guy who wasn't going to start anything beyond Vegas is talking to her the morning after he returns."

"Did you come in here to give me shit? Or did you stop in for a more important reason?"

He pulled at his tie, shaking his head before running both hands through his hair. "The latter. I'm fucking overwhelmed, man. I've got this four-year-old who can't survive without me, and, fuck, I don't want to fail her, but I feel like I am."

"Are you really doubting your parenting right now?" I lifted my coffee, wrapping my hands around it. "You're the best father I know."

I took a quick glance at the photo on my desk of Everly and me. It was about six months ago when I'd taken her to Disneyland. She was still so little, but we'd had the best time, her face lighting up whenever she saw a character, her little jaw dropping when the fireworks went off.

"You don't know what it's like, being responsible for someone and being their everything."

"You're right; I don't, but what I do know is that you do a hell of a job at it. I know how good you are to her. I know how much she loves and admires her daddy."

He leaned forward, crossing his hands between his legs, his head hanging low.

"You're doing the best you can, Ford. You should be proud of that. I know I'm proud of you."

He finally lifted his head. "How can I be when something like this happens?" He reached into the inside pocket of his jacket and pulled out a piece of paper, placing it unfolded on my desk.

I took the sheet into my hands, seeing that it was a drawing Everly had done. Not that I could distinguish her art from anyone else her age, but pink was her favorite color, and almost the entire drawing was done in magenta. The picture was of a table, two stick figures sitting in chairs around it.

But there was a third placement—a section that was scratched out in black crayon.

A spot where her mother was supposed to be sitting.

You didn't have to be a psychologist to understand what was happening here.

"She's angry," I said, looking up at him.

"And resentful."

I knew how much this was hurting him. I needed to say something that would make my brother feel better.

"Listen, she doesn't understand. She's too young; her mind can't process this yet. But when she sees that empty spot at the breakfast table, dinner table, wherever, she has feelings, and I don't blame her. I have feelings about it too."

"That's my fault."

I folded my arms over my desk. "That you're not with her mother anymore? Don't you dare start blaming yourself for that shit." I took a drink of coffee, trying to calm myself down. "One day, Everly will see the whole picture and understand the layers, and it won't just be pink and black to her."

"And until then?"

"Take your daughter on vacation and let her play in the sand and boogie-board across the waves. Let her drink virgin strawberry daiquiris and eat McDonald's and not all that organic, unprocessed, unbleached bullshit you fill her with."

He gripped the armrests of the chair, but his posture was becoming slightly more relaxed. "You know, that isn't a bad idea."

"You just spent a week in Vegas. Now, it's her turn. Spoil her—even more than you already do." And because he needed to hear this, I added, "Let's not forget you were a fucking animal before Everly came into your life. You partied every night; you slept with every skirt in LA. But the moment she came into your world, you did a one-eighty. You went from being a selfish motherfucker to Everly's father, and not every dad can say that."

He sighed, rubbing his hands over the wooden armrests. "I appreciate that." He huffed out more air. "You know, I still wake up sometimes, shocked as hell that I'm a father and she's mine."

"I'm pretty sure every parent says that."

"You're probably right." He was quiet for a few seconds and then said, "What about you? Are you good?"

"I'm headed to Miami tomorrow for three days."

There was finally a change in his expression, and that was because he was laughing. "Jesus, I knew it."

"It's for work, asshole. But, yes, I'll be seeing her."

"And when the Miami opportunity presented itself, you jumped all over it—no need to confirm. I already know."

He wasn't exactly right.

But he was right enough.

"So?" I inquired.

"So ... this is shaping up to be a long-distance thing. The one thing you said you didn't want. And when I caught you almost rubbing one off, your expression told me everything I'd suspected."

"Which is?"

"You're fucking wild about her." He put his hand up as I attempted to respond. "Whether you want to admit it or not, she's the one."

"She's twenty-two years old, Ford."

He rolled his eyes, like his fucking daughter. "Not again with the age reminder. We know how old she is. It doesn't make a difference."

"You're wrong." I shook my head. "I like what she does to my cock. End of story."

"Yeah, yeah." He got up and walked to the door. "I don't

know how you became a fucking billionaire, doing law, because you have the worst poker face I've ever seen in my life."

I pointed to the door. "Get out."

He chuckled as he opened it. "God, it feels good to be right."

TEN

JOANNA

"Giiirl," Monica sang from the doorway of my room. "My God, you're even turning me on; you're so hot. Twirl. I need to see the whole view."

I laughed at my best friend as I stood in front of the full-length mirror, slowly turning in a circle, giving her every angle of my outfit.

Her outfit.

The one I'd stolen from her when I was searching for something to wear.

"What do you think?" I asked. "Is it enough?"

She fanned her face with her hand, gawking at me. "Enough?" She huffed. "If this doesn't make Jenner fall to his knees, then there's something seriously wrong with him." She came closer, adjusting the shoulders of my sweater, tightening some of the curls that had fallen loose. "He's going to die." She shook her head. "I mean ... *diiie*."

I smiled. "I hope so."

I faced the mirror, checking out the costume one last time. The short, pleated skirt ended at the top of my thighs, and the matching low-cut sweater vest and plaid tie showed off my belly button. Monica had been the naughty schoolgirl for Halloween, and when I saw this hanging in her closet, the idea sounded perfect, especially since Jenner had said he wouldn't let me sneak away for class or to do homework.

"I promise you," she said, "there's no hope involved when it comes to men and sex." She grabbed a tube of lip gloss off my dresser and dabbed some over my mouth. "He's going to open the door to his hotel room and lose his mind. His dick'll be so hard that he probably won't even be able to talk."

"Oh my God."

"What? It's true." She pulled out her phone from her back pocket and checked the time. "Are you still meeting him in twenty?"

I nodded. "I only get three nights with him, Mon." I swallowed. "It doesn't feel like enough time."

"Hey, it's better than nothing at all, and that's all you can ask for right now." She grabbed the long coat I had to wear over the costume and helped me slip my arms through before resting the strap of my overnight bag over my shoulder. "Go have fun, do everything I wouldn't do, and text me the juicy details if you ever come up for air."

"I feel like *Pretty Woman*." I glanced down at the long jacket. "It's over eighty degrees outside. How obvious is it that I'm hiding something underneath?"

She lifted my chin. "Stop stressing over everything and go have earth-shattering sex—that's all I want you to think about, nothing else, do you hear me?" She walked me out of my room.

At our front door, I turned to her and said, "Love you. So much."

"Love you more." She spanked my butt. "Now, go."

I laughed as I headed down to the parking garage on the first floor of our building and climbed into the driver's seat of my car. Jenner's hotel was only a short drive, and I tried to stay as invisible as possible while I carried my bag through the lobby and into the elevator.

I held my breath as I knocked on his door.

It hadn't been long at all since we'd seen each other, yet it felt like months. Because now, I was back to my life—school, homework, the grind of my senior year—but I didn't feel like the same person, and I looked at everything differently. Before Vegas, I'd never experienced this type of connection with someone. I'd never wanted anyone like I wanted Jenner.

The thought was terrifying, and it felt impossible.

Maybe that was why I wasn't prepared for the feelings that smacked me in the chest the second he opened the door.

"Hi," I said so softly as I stared at his devastatingly handsome face.

Eyes that were boring through me.

Exhales that I could almost feel hitting my skin.

Lips that I remembered so fondly on my body.

Oh God.

He was dressed in a navy suit, his silver tie loosened, the glistening of cuff links on his wrists. I'd never seen him so formal, but I didn't think he could ever look as sexy as he did now.

The outfit screamed lawyer. Success. Maturity.

This was no college boy standing in front of me.

This was all man.

My teeth sank into my lip as I added, "That suit looks amazing on you."

A subtle, extremely hot grin tugged at his mouth. "My meeting ran late. I didn't have time to change."

"No complaints here."

He reached for me. "Get in here."

I was suddenly in his arms, our bodies pressed together, my

bag falling from my shoulder as I wrapped my arms around him, his mouth ravishing mine.

He tasted just the way I remembered.

The way I'd been dreaming about.

Of lust.

Desire.

Sensuality.

And the harder he kissed me, the more I felt.

He left my bag where it had landed and led me into his room, bringing me straight to the bed. He took a seat on the edge while I stood between his legs. His stare danced down my body, taking in the sight of me, the same way I had done to him in the doorway.

"It's too warm out for that coat." His gaze turned so hungry. I was instantly wet. "Jo, what's waiting for me under there?"

"A present," I whispered.

I pulled at the tie that kept the jacket secure, the sides falling open, revealing the costume.

"Fuck ... me." He pulled my jacket off and gripped my waist, holding me so tightly. His eyes dipped all the way to my four-inch heels, like he'd never seen me before, like his mouth hadn't kissed every inch of my skin. "This is all for me?"

I felt like a plate of wagyu and Jenner was a ravenous carnivore.

"Every bit of it."

He finally gazed up. "God, I'm one lucky motherfucker." Our eyes met again. "You look fucking gorgeous." He licked across his lips, as though he were getting ready to eat, gently tracing the area between my shirt and skirt. "Man, *mmm* ..." He shook his head. "My dick is fucking throbbing."

"What are you going to do to me, Jenner?" I widened my stance, revealing more of the garter belt. "I've been a bad, bad student."

"Oh yeah? What kind of trouble have you gotten into?"

I shrugged so innocently. "I was caught doing something with my mouth." I pulled on my bottom lip even though it was covered in gloss—gloss that had left a little sparkle on his lips from all our kissing. "Something that involved swallowing."

"Jesus ... yes."

I got on my knees, the skirt lifting so high that it showed my ass as I unclasped his belt and unbuttoned his pants and lowered his zipper, freeing that delicious, long, wide cock. "Something like this ..."

The tip had a small bead of pre-cum, glistening from the overhead light. When I'd done this in the club, the restroom stall had been slightly dark, and I'd had quite the buzz, so I couldn't take my time or appreciate the view.

But now, I was sober.

I could see every inch of him—the veins that ran through his shaft, the bulge of his crown, the small slit with my gift at the end, the little translucent dot of cum. I stuck my tongue out, using just the tip to lick it up and swallow.

"Fuck," he hissed, his eyes glued to me. "You are fucking naughty." His hand went into my hair, gripping my long locks, trying to guide my mouth lower.

But I stayed at the top, teasing around it. "Is that what you want?" I looked up at him naively. "My mouth on your cock?"

The look in his eyes was animalistic. "Fuck ... yes."

I should make him wait, test his patience, turn this into a torturous game that would result in him tying me up just to get my mouth.

But the truth was, I wanted to suck him off as badly as he wanted it.

So, I didn't wait.

I parted my lips, and in one dip, I took in as much as I could until my throat threatened to gag.

"Goddamn it," he roared, a sound so incredibly sexy.

I cuffed my hand around his base, leaning to the right and left as I bobbed, giving him pressure on both sides, at every angle, raising my fist to meet my lips. Even though I was sucking, my cheeks going concave, I still used my tongue, swiveling it around, allowing it to steer me up and down his dick.

And, my God, it was such a tasty one.

Wide to the point that I was almost having a hard time breathing, far too long to fit it all the way into my mouth, but a length that would easily hit that spot that was deep inside me, that would make me come after a few pumps.

A spot most men didn't even know about.

But Jenner knew my body like we'd been intimate for years.

As though he'd studied the places that gave me the most pleasure.

As though he'd mastered me.

I didn't let up. I didn't slow.

With his cock teasing my throat, my tongue turning in every direction, I continued my assault until he pulled out of my mouth and said, "Get on the bed."

His tone was hungry. Full of longing and dominance.

And that made every part of me tingle in anticipation.

I went to take my heels off, and he stopped me and said, "Leave everything on."

The second my knees hit the mattress, he gave me a spank. A tiny yelp came through my lips. A sting followed that made me even wetter. I crawled to the head of the bed, knowing the skirt was so short that he could see my bareness, and I turned around to face him.

"Spread your legs."

I bent my knees and gradually widened them, watching him stare at my pussy.

"Damn it, Jo." His lips were parted, feral. A want so thick

that I could taste it in the air. "You have the most stunning pussy." He continued to gaze for a few seconds more before he said, "Don't move."

He went over to the closet, disappearing inside. When he returned, he had something in his hand that was white, revealing just a flash of it as he moved his arm behind his back.

"Do you trust me?" He stood at my side, his knees close enough for me to touch.

He'd never asked me that before.

He'd also never given me a reason not to trust him.

"Yes."

"You're sure?" His eyes narrowed. "Because this is all about trust ..."

Trust.

Air was caught in my throat, making it so difficult to take a breath, my body almost shaking. "Yes."

He brought his hand around, showing the two pieces of coiled-up rope and the blindfold sitting on his palm.

Now, I understood the question.

He was taking away my ability to touch.

To see.

And if I didn't trust him, this wouldn't work, nor would it be enjoyable for either of us.

I'd only known him for a little over a week, but I didn't sense he would do something I couldn't handle. From what I could tell, Jenner was all about pleasure even if there was a small amount of pain involved.

"I trust you."

He waited in case I changed my mind.

When he felt like he'd given me enough time, he lifted my arm and wrapped the rope around my wrist, tying me to the headboard. It wasn't tight enough to burn me, but it was strong enough that I couldn't move. He did the same to my other hand and then knotted the blindfold behind my head.

My world went completely dark.

I felt him move somewhere between my legs.

I heard his breathing.

Since I had to rely on my other senses, they were heightened, on overdrive, taking in every hint.

"Do you know how fucking beautiful you are?"

His words vibrated through me, and I felt each syllable.

"Tell me," I whispered.

"You're breathtaking—every fucking bit of you. I can't stop staring at you. I can't believe that I get to lick every inch of you and fuck you and do whatever I want to you ..."

My back arched, his words as stimulating as foreplay, like a wave of air passing over me that made every part of me shiver. But as I flattened against the bed, there was movement from him, and my body immediately broke out in goose bumps when his hand landed on my thigh.

My breath hitched.

His fingers only gave me a light skim, but I still felt them everywhere, the fire igniting within me and spreading.

"*Ahhh,*" I moaned.

"It feels different, doesn't it?"

He knew.

Because I was sure he'd done this before, and that didn't surprise me.

"Yes," I admitted, gasping as he traced my other leg. "Completely different."

"Sensitive in a way you've never felt."

I sucked in a mouthful of air. "*Yesss.*"

His lips were on me now—the only way I knew was from the wetness of his tongue. They started at my knee, kissing higher, leaving crumbs of tingles. His mouth wasn't moving fast, but it was still hard to distinguish his whereabouts because his hands were everywhere—across both legs, flirting with the bottom of my skirt, taunting my inner thighs.

It all felt so good.

I wasn't breathing.

I was only moaning.

And I couldn't stop.

When I could finally suck in a breath, each exhale dragged through my lungs before I quickly filled them again. I couldn't hold on to air for too long. I needed the release. I needed to control something, my breathing the only thing I had power over.

His lips went higher.

I still couldn't tell his precise location. Sensations were starting to jumble, touches were turning to licks, kisses were now bites. My body was overwhelmed. I couldn't grip, I couldn't see, I couldn't prepare.

I just had to take it.

And listen.

And feel.

And when his mouth eventually landed on my pussy, there was a pounding in my ears, a tightness in my throat, a lifting of my back.

"*Mmm,* Jo. You taste so fucking good."

His tongue shot a bolt of energy through me, and I no longer felt my movements.

I'd even lost control of that.

I only felt him.

And it was a kind of pleasure I'd never had before.

Never one that was this intense. Never one that dragged a full scream from my chest as the mere flick of his tongue.

A flicker across the top of me. A long, thorough lick over the whole length. A quick bite, and then he sucked me into his mouth, brushing my clit with his tongue, instantly starting a build from somewhere in my body.

"Jenner!"

His fingers were teasing my pussy, circling, spreading my wetness before they plunged inside.

Not one.

I could feel two.

This was the most ruthless, melting combination.

The nibbling and licking.

The sucking.

The fingering.

I was gone.

Lost to what was happening in this incredible darkness that seemed to only bring me there faster.

"Oh fuck!"

I strained my wrists against the rope, trying to reach for him, for something, to hold on to anything, but I couldn't.

And it soon didn't matter.

"Tell me, Jo." He licked harder. "Fucking tell me how good this feels."

His tongue took no pause. It was after one thing, and my body was giving it to him.

"Oh God, I can't make it stop."

"Then, don't."

My knees fell inward, and he pushed them apart. My head fell to the right and then left, my back rising.

"I want to feel you come."

That was all it took—that one tiny order—and my orgasm was stretching across my navel, into my nipples, going as low as my feet.

"Jenner!" I cried. "*Yesss!*"

It held steady, never wavering, never letting up.

"God, that's one fucking gorgeous sight."

I shouted, "*Fuuuck,*" and my fingers clenched like a pillow was underneath them.

"You look so sexy when you come."

And it was still building, still throwing me toward that highest peak, where I felt nothing but this wild, pure satisfaction.

But something happened.

Something that made it even more mind-blowing.

He put a wet, primed finger in that forbidden back hole.

I couldn't tell how far he went in, but an entirely new feeling was moving through me at a speed as fast as my climax.

A feeling so foreign because no one had ever been back there before.

I didn't know what to expect, if it would add to what I was already experiencing.

But when I took my next breath, I moaned so loud that it felt like my body was making just as much noise as my mouth.

The combination was beyond words.

Beyond enjoyment.

And he was giving me quickness and more pressure, pulling what he needed from me—all of it adding to this storm.

My orgasm erupted.

"Oh my God!"

The rush, the shudders—now, I really couldn't breathe.

"That's it." He licked. "That's the cum I wanted to taste ... and now, you're finally giving it to me." He was whispering, talking directly to my clit, suddenly so gentle. When his tongue stilled, he kissed the top of my pussy like he was saying goodbye, and he pulled his hand away.

As I tried to recover, he took off my skirt, and before I could even protest, he ripped the sweater off me, hearing the fabric shred from my body.

"Jenner!"

"It was taking too long," he growled.

I was so sensitive. I yelled the moment his teeth surrounded my nipple, tugging on it through the thin lace of my bra.

"*Mmm*," he moaned. "More beauty."

There was the quiet opening of a drawer and the sound of foil, a snap of rubber.

He was back on the bed, and I couldn't hold in the scream when he positioned himself between my legs, poking at that spot still buzzing from his tongue.

"If I'm too rough, I need you to tell me."

"Rough?"

His lips were on my neck, lowering to my nipples, gnawing on one, and then the other, like he owned them. "I don't think you realize how badly I want to fuck you." His hardness probed my pussy, sliding in just the smallest amount before he pulled back out. "How I thought of nothing else during my flight here and during those long, excruciating hours I was in that meeting, thinking of all the things I was going to do to you."

And now, he was teasing himself.

Again.

Building up the want.

The need.

And building me up.

"I think I can tell." I inhaled and swallowed. "I can feel it." The back of my head pushed into the pillow. "You're so hard." There was movement, and I hollered, "*Ahhh*!"

He was biting my nipple again, this time so much harder, sucking the end after to soothe it.

"You can't, Jo." His voice was like a lion's roar. "You can't even begin to imagine." He was lapping one now, his tongue wide, giving me slow, torturous licks. "First, the wait, then watching you come. Now, staring at your cunt, knowing how fucking wet and tight it's going to be." He moaned, going in just a tiny bit deeper and immediately backing up. "You have no idea what hard feels like."

"But I'm here now ... and I'm all yours."

His face hit my neck, his whiskers scratching the softness of my skin. "Say that again." He kissed across my throat, dragging his beard. "Say those fucking words, so I can taste them."

"You"—I quivered as he lowered, my body blazing—"have me now."

In one quick thrust, he was fully inside me.

"Oh my God!"

This was entirely different than when his mouth was on my pussy.

But both completely overwhelmed me in opposite ways.

"Damn it, I was right. You're so fucking tight."

My body had been built for Jenner. There was no way I could take another inch. And each thrust, each pound of his hips, reinforced that.

But, oh God, it was the best feeling of my life.

"Yes!" I yelled. "Fuck me!"

Even though I was still recovering from his mouth, I could handle this. And I wanted more. I wanted to reach that place again that he'd brought me only minutes ago.

He pulled out and lifted my legs off the bed, circling them around what I assumed was his waist. He arched my hips in a way I could tell he was kneeling in front of me, drawing my ass up higher until I met his tip. That was when he gripped me hard, keeping me in place, and plowed into me.

My breath was gone.

My brain couldn't process what I was feeling.

I could only take what he was giving me, and that was fierce, carnal strokes.

Ones that made me beg for more. "Pl-ea-se ..." I cried, his pumps causing the air to stutter through me. "Do-n't st-op."

"You're so fucking wet."

That sent me right over the edge. Like fuel, each time he entered, a new flame licked through me.

"Jenner!" The build was coming on so strong. "Oh fuck, I'm going to come."

That seemed to be what he wanted.

To own my orgasms.

To deliver them back-to-back.

Because instead of slowing, instead of letting the moment gradually happen, he increased his speed. He doubled his power. He twisted his hips to give me more friction.

And he hit that spot.

The one that was so deep inside me that no one had found it before.

But Jenner's tip grazed across it each time he entered me.

And I couldn't stop shaking.

I couldn't control what was happening.

I just knew how good this felt and how lost I was.

I pulled against the rope, the burn not even registering. When I clung to his waist, I didn't even realize it would send him in farther.

But I took it.

And I screamed, "*Ahhh,*" as the trembles shook my stomach and shot toward my chest, all the way down to my thighs. The shudders were like echoes, each pass wrecking me all over again.

"Fuck yes," he barked. "I can feel it."

The peak was holding steady, not dying, not even weakening.

"Jenner ..." I was frozen in ecstasy. "My God!"

Just as it began to let up, my limbs turned numb, my breath leaving my lungs like it was never going to return.

And because he could always read my body, his movements

slowed, his powerful thrusts softened.

His hand slid down my torso until he reached my nipple, gently brushing it.

"*Mmm*," I moaned.

My pussy needed healing, and he was giving it to me, allowing me to find air again.

"I could watch you come all fucking day."

His cock gave me a sharp jab, my back automatically lifting off the bed, and I was shocked that it hadn't hurt. Rather, I wanted it. Needed it. An urge sprouting completely out of nowhere.

"Over and fucking over again."

I shook my head over the pillow. "I don't know if I can."

He laughed.

A noise I hadn't expected.

One that was almost sinister.

"Don't test me, Jo. We both know I can make you come whenever I want to."

There was pressure around my wrists, and then the rope loosened, my hand falling out of the hold.

He released the other one, and I went to reach for the blindfold and heard, "Leave it on."

My hands dropped to the bed; the second they landed, there was more movement.

A repositioning.

He was lifting me, and suddenly, I was kneeling on the mattress.

I felt around, hitting hair and muscle.

His chest.

I was straddling him.

"Ride me, Jo. Make me fucking come."

He was no longer inside me. But there was still wetness between my legs. So much that it was dripping out. I reached down, lightly tapping different spots until I found his cock, moaning when I had my fist around it. I led his head toward my pussy and tensed once I lowered over him, a friction and soreness I hadn't expected.

"It'll go away," he promised, as though he were inside my head. "Once you get used to me again and once I start doing this."

His actions earned an, "Oh!"

He was rubbing my clit back and forth, the surge returning like it had never left.

Like this was the first time he was making me come.

I dropped all the way to his base, using his chest to balance, and rose to his tip.

He was right; within a few dips, my body was accepting him again, need and desire replacing the soreness.

And there was even an ache to come again.

"Fuck ... yes." His fingers bit into my waist. "Own that fucking cock."

I couldn't imagine what I looked like while I rocked over him, but I could feel my breasts bouncing, my head falling back, my hair hitting the top of my ass. This new position placed him differently inside me, hitting a whole new spot, and it only took a few shifts of my hips, a couple twists, before I was right back to that place.

That feeling.

That build bubbling to the surface.

"Look at me."

I straightened my head, trying to find my whereabouts, the blackness making it so difficult.

And then, out of nowhere, the blindfold was gone.

He ripped it from my face.

The light blinded me.

I froze, trying to get used to the sunlight and brightness in the room.

But he grabbed my hips and ordered, "Fuck me. Don't you dare stop."

I squinted until I could handle more and found my rhythm, feeling myself close in around him, hearing my wetness. Now that I had my vision back, I could appreciate his face again. His delicious emerald eyes, his delectable lips, the beard that had felt so incredible as it scraped my inner thighs.

Oh God.

"Look at me when you come." He held my cheeks, locking our stare. "And fucking kiss me."

I was breathless.

Sweaty.

So spent from all the orgasms he'd given me, but I leaned forward and smashed our lips together, his tongue filling my mouth.

I circled it, sucked on the end, until he pulled away and roared, "Fucking ride me, Jo."

I could feel how close he was getting by his short, hard pumps, his hips jerking forward as he gripped me.

I wasn't far behind.

I arched my back, using all the speed and power I'd saved for this moment.

"Fuck!" I cried.

Everything was starting to feel so good again, so sensitive, especially when he began to meet me in the middle, plowing his cock into me right before I lifted off him.

"Jenner!"

I was seconds away from losing it.

So, I leaned my face back, giving him my eyes like he'd demanded.

"Hell yes." He held my neck. "Fucking come."

And I did.

The orgasm completely owned my body, making everything inside me shudder and burst. The only thing I could focus on was his tongue as it returned to my mouth and these crests that washed over me, not even letting me gasp for air.

"*Fuuuck!*" he shouted, thrusting faster, harder. "Jo ..."

I clutched him, waiting for him to break, and when he did, I wrapped my arms around him and took over the movements.

"Milk it." His hands circled my back. "Fucking milk it."

I gave him everything I had left, the bold, needy, quick sway of my hips, the turning that added the extra friction, a kiss that would drive him mad.

And it did.

He filled the condom, moaning, "Jo," after each shot, and I didn't still until his voice turned silent.

I kept him inside me, panting.

Relishing.

He pressed his nose to mine. "You're a fucking animal, you know that?" He clutched my hair, pulling on the locks until my lips were aligned with his. "It's like your pussy was molded just for me, and I'm the lucky bastard who gets to have it for the next three nights." He pulled my lip into his mouth, sucking on it before he added, "We're going to go take a shower and get this sweat off our bodies, and then we're going to one of my favorite restaurants."

I could barely decipher what he was saying.

I was full of sex.

Heat.

And him.

But I'd caught a few words and grunted, "Food. Yum."

He grazed his teeth over the same lip. "A steak house ... I know you have meat on the brain."

It took me a moment, but I laughed.

"Not just any meat, Jenner. Only yours."

ELEVEN

JENNER

There was gorgeous ... and then there was Jo.

A category all to herself.

With a spicy, confident personality, a wickedness when it came to sex, and a body that could turn me into a submissive.

I knew she'd put on a sexy dress for dinner, but every time I saw this girl, she surprised me.

Pleasantly so.

She didn't show off half her body, like most of the women I went out with. Aside from the little costume she'd worn today, her clothes were seductive but tasteful. There was a provocativeness in her eyes, something women couldn't fake or achieve —they had to be born with it.

Like her.

She could make me hard with her stare.

Her smile.

Her kindness and trustworthiness, traits that made her unique.

That made me crave her.

That made me wrap my arm around her when we got out of the SUV. The men we passed on the sidewalk stared at her. I knew they were fantasizing about her body, that they were praying she would glance in their direction, hoping to score a second of her attention. Women were no different, their eyes instantly finding Jo.

She was someone to gaze at.

But I kept my arm tightly around her ...

Like she was mine.

That was what I thought about as I took the seat across from hers at our table.

In the past, so many women had wanted a commitment. I wouldn't give them one. Most of the time, I wouldn't even consider it.

Jo was different. Jo was making me feel things.

Things I didn't want to surface because single was the life I'd chosen to live.

But, fuck, she had a face I could wake up to every morning. She was someone I could take for a midnight dessert on a random Tuesday. Someone I could carry onto my jet in the middle of the night, so she could wake up somewhere beautiful in the morning.

But to even consider that, I needed her on my coast, minutes away, giving me access to her whenever I wanted.

Miami wasn't that.

Goddamn it, there were just too many obstacles with this one.

This had to be just ... fun.

That was what I repeated to myself. That this would be over once I returned to LA.

But even as she opened her menu, her long eyelashes taunting me over the flickering candlelight, I was dreading that plane ride back.

She looked at the food selection for only a second and then back at me.

"Tell me, Jo ..." I put my hand on my water glass, needing to feel the coolness from the ice. "What are you going to do when you graduate? It's happening soon, only a few months away." Once my fingers were wet, I gripped the wine menu, taking a quick peek so I knew what to ask for once the waitress arrived.

She moved her napkin to her lap. "I'm a marketing major. I would like to go into the field, not necessarily at an agency, more like apply my skills to a business and do the marketing and social media and influencing for a company. Those are the things I'm good at."

"Have you decided what kind of business?"

She sighed. "That's the hard part. I'm still not sure. I did an internship last semester for a set of privately owned gyms in South Beach, and they offered me a job for when I graduate. I also did some work for a local art dealer who owns several galleries throughout South Florida, and she would love to employ me full-time, but I just don't know. Although I enjoyed both jobs, neither angle is exactly what I'm looking for." She shrugged. "I guess time will tell."

"I didn't have that luxury."

"No?"

I shook my head. "I went from prelaw to law school."

"Did you always know what you wanted to be?"

"I did, but I also knew what was expected of me, and with that came a lot of pressure."

She leaned her arms onto the table. "Explain."

"My parents founded one of the largest, most successful law firms in California. They opened it shortly after graduating law school, and they've single-handedly built their practice to what it is today, which is several locations across the state, hundreds of attorneys on staff, a focus on almost every practice of law, and relationships with the DA of each county." I chuckled, remembering pictures that had been taken in our nurseries, the scales of justice painted on the wall above our cribs. "We were bred to be lawyers while in the womb. There were expectations. Thick ones."

Her brows rose. "Isn't that the case for most family businesses?"

"I suppose."

"Were you at least able to choose what kind of law you wanted to practice?"

I leaned back in my seat, crossing my legs under the table. "I don't want to make it seem like I was tied to law with rope around my wrists." I smiled at her. "My brothers and I had a choice. No one forced us or gave us an ultimatum. We went willingly, and to be honest, I don't know what I'd do if I wasn't a lawyer. I certainly enjoy my job, and I've made it my own. I have a passion for real estate, so it only made sense to make that my focus."

"Why?" She folded her hands in front of her. "What is it about real estate that attracts you?"

"The freedom." I glanced up, the dark sky hanging over the patio we'd been seated in, the stars just bright enough to show off their glimmer. "I don't like to be grounded for too long. I love being in the sky. I like new scenery, a new pace. I want to wake up in the mountains and go to bed on the beach. That's how I've always been."

"A wanderlust. I can definitely appreciate that."

I eyed her face, her approval telling me we also had that in common.

"My clients have acquisitions all over the world. They need me on the ground, assessing the land, helping with the construction, endlessly negotiating every contract. It works perfectly for me. I don't spend that much time behind my desk; therefore, I don't have time to get restless."

"What's your endgame?" She twirled a long piece of hair between her fingers. "I mean, will you be going at a hundred miles per hour forever?"

I shrugged. "Until I get bored. Then, I'm sure I'll find something else to occupy me. Maybe that will be travel."

"You say that ... because you haven't fallen in love yet."

There was so much seriousness in her eyes.

In her lips.

I couldn't hide the laugh; it took over my face, my chest.

Dominick had lived the same life as me until he met Kendall.

He fell in love, and everything changed.

He'd become the person he'd sworn he'd never be.

Will that happen to me?

Even though I considered spending more time with Jo and I'd thought about her nonstop since meeting her in Vegas—more than any other woman—I couldn't see it.

I didn't care how enticing she was.

"How do you know I've never been in love?"

She chewed that lip, the bottom one that I loved to suck. "I can tell."

As she was about to elaborate, the waitress came to our table and asked what we wanted to drink.

"Does red work for you?" I asked Jo.

She nodded. "Sounds delicious."

I ordered one of their highest-priced cabernets and handed the waitress the wine menu.

As soon as we were alone again, Jo said, "Listen, I consider myself a pretty observant person, but you don't have to be into detail to see how independent you are. That tells me you were either in the wrong relationship that kept you tied down and prevented you from exploring, and that's why you can't stop now, or you haven't found a bird to be caged with." She tilted her head while she stared at me. "I suspect it's the latter."

Air came huffing out of my lungs. "Jesus ..." There was something so fucking sexy to be under her microscope. "You're not wrong."

"I know." She winked. "I was just trying to be nice with my first guess."

I chuckled.

She had an adorable sense of humor.

Kind but honest.

I liked that.

Nah, I fucking loved that.

"You know what's interesting, Jenner?" She took a drink of her water. "You're not looking for a relationship, you don't want to be tied down, yet you're here, with me, just a day after returning from Vegas." She moved all her hair to one side, the locks hanging well past her tit. "I must be one lucky girl. Not only did I get you for a week in Vegas while you were with your friends and brothers, but now, I also have you for three nights while you're in Florida."

I thought about every word she'd said.

I processed each one.

And as they resonated, I learned something.

Jo was right.

I didn't need three nights with my client. I extended the trip to give me more time with her. And as soon as I'd found out about Miami, I'd called her—the hesitation hadn't lasted for more than a few seconds.

"Jo ..."

"I hope you don't mind, but I brought Bordeaux glasses," the waitress said, her approach cutting me off, placing the long-stemmed glasses in front of us.

"Not at all," I voiced. "It's what I prefer."

She showed me the bottle, earning herself a nod, and then she began the process of opening the top and pouring a sample.

But the entire time, my eyes were on Jo.

And as soon as the waitress filled our glasses and left, I held mine toward the center of the table. "To more time together."

Jo smiled. "Interesting ... I'll cheers to that."

We both took a drink, and she placed her wine on the table, holding the stem between her fingers, twirling the thick rod so the dark liquid sloshed against the sides.

"I want to know what you like to do, Jo. Where you want to visit. The things you dream of when you close your eyes."

"*Hmm.* Good questions." She paused, her face a mix of thoughts. "I like to see things I've never witnessed before. Things that take me by surprise. That make me smile. That make me cry."

"You want to cry? I don't think I've ever heard a woman say that before."

She leaned in closer. "I want to be rendered so speechless that I only have tears to shed."

"Has that happened?"

"Yes."

I crossed my arms over my chest. "Tell me about it."

Her chest rose and fell several times before she started. "Monica—my best friend you met in Vegas—has a brother who's in the military, and he's been stationed overseas for the past two years. The calls aren't as frequent as her family would like. He can never FaceTime because his location is confidential. I happened to be at her parents' house when he returned for a visit." Emotion was moving into her eyes. "He told no one he was coming; he just walked through the door while we were all in the dining room, eating cake for Monica's birthday."

She looked down at the top of the glass, the wine now still.

"Seeing the way her parents wrapped their arms around him—that's a scene that makes you speechless. That fills you with tears because there are no words to describe that kind of love. I swear, I watched her parents take a breath like they hadn't breathed in two years." She halted again, appearing to fight whatever was threatening to come through her eyes. "Two days later, he left. He'd only had a couple days off, and he'd made the long trek home just to celebrate his sister's twenty-first birthday."

I exhaled, shaking my head. "All right, you won that round."

She took a long pull of her wine, holding it in her mouth before swallowing. "It's those kinds of moments I want to see. The ones that teach you, that show you another side of yourself." She broke our connection to glance around the restaurant, eventually returning to me. "As for travel, I was fortunate to grow up with parents who liked when I tagged along, and they took me on most of their vacations, but there are so many places I want to experience. Like boating down the Yangtze River in China and soaking in a salt pool in Egypt. I'm dying to see the waterfalls and cliffs of Milford Sound in New Zealand."

There were standard answers—Rome, Paris, London, Dublin, the regular European and UK tourist traps that I almost always heard whenever I asked this question. And then there were people like Jo and me who wanted to go off the radar and see the deeper parts of the world.

Not even my brothers were game for that.

But she was.

I held the glass of wine against my chest, staring at her before I took a sip. "What do you dream of?"

She took a deep breath, breaking our contact once again until she spoke. "I dream about making someone overwhelmingly happy. About becoming a mother. About having a successful career, where I can make a difference at the company, where I can make a name for myself. I don't want to just fit in. I want to be remembered."

Jo's maturity was something that constantly shocked me.

I never felt like I was speaking to a college student. She had more intellect than half the attorneys I worked with.

"You will be." I grinned. "I have no doubt about that. Once you pick the opportunity that feels best to you, you're going to flourish."

She said nothing as she gazed at me, her lids eventually narrowing. "It's not that easy."

"No?"

She shook her head as the waitress approached.

"Have you had a chance to look over the menu?" the waitress asked.

The thick binding was open in front of Jo, and she glanced up at me and said, "May I order for us?"

That was something no woman had ever done for me.

I was curious about what she would select and if it would meet my expectations.

But I still gave her the chance, handing my menu to the waitress, my stare fixed on Jo when I replied, "Impress me."

"We'll start with the ahi tuna, please," Jo instructed. "We'll then share the porterhouse, cooked medium, with a dry baked potato along with the au gratin potatoes, and an order of the marinated mushrooms." She paused. "Can we have hollandaise and béarnaise sauce on the side?"

"Delicious choices," the waitress responded. "Anything else?"

"Sage butter," Jo said, selecting my favorite from their extensive butter list. "And we'll also start with the bacon."

My mouth watered—the bacon was one of the items this restaurant was known for.

"I'll put the order right in," the waitress said and disappeared from our table.

Jo turned in her chair, folding her arms over her chest, her legs crossed in the aisle between our table and the one next to us. "I did good, didn't I?"

I shook my head, acting disappointed. "I was thinking of ordering the salmon."

Without pause, she snapped, "Bullshit."

I laughed. "I couldn't have done better, honestly."

I reached across the open space, my fingers landing on her thigh.

The move didn't startle her—she had seen me coming.

But it startled me in the way she felt.

The warmth of her skin, the way it welcomed me.

The placement that felt so right.

So fucking perfect.

"How else can I surprise you tonight, Jenner?"

You just did.

But something told me she already knew that.

TWELVE

JOANNA

"Do you go to the beach in California?" I asked Jenner as we sat in lounge chairs on the sand, the warm Florida sun shining down on us, the waves lapping not far from our feet.

South Beach wasn't the dreamiest beach in Florida, but it was still so beautiful, calm, and relaxing.

But the view had nothing on Jenner, not with his abs on full display, his pecs etched across the top of his chest.

My God.

That man was perfect.

No matter how hard I tried to look away, my eyes constantly went back to him. I was already staring when he rolled his neck toward me, blocking the sun even though he wore shades.

"No, never," he replied. "My parents have a place in Malibu. You'd think we'd go there and spend more time outside." He chuckled. "When we visit, we eat and then head right back to the city."

"What a shame."

He was quiet for a moment and said, "We should change that; you're right."

"Is it the lack of time or something else?"

He reached for his vodka soda, facing the water when he responded, "When you work with family, constantly making important decisions, your off time turns to shoptalk as well. Conversations about the weather turn to clients; talks about politics turn to employees." He shook his head. "I just want mindless chatter with my family, and we can't seem to make that happen. Before we even pour a drink, I'm already questioning how quickly I can get my ass back to LA. Jo ... my brain just needs a break."

"Wow." I sat up, rubbing some more suntan lotion over my legs. "That has to be heavy, so mentally daunting." I held my breath for a second. "I didn't grow up in a house like that."

"No?"

I squirted more lotion onto my hand and set the bottle on the table behind us. "Dad worked outside the home. Mom was an artist and had a studio off the garage. Their jobs were different animals, so their talks never seemed to go there."

"I wonder what that would be like—if my parents had different careers and the three of us boys had taken other paths." He put his arms behind his head. "What the hell would we talk about?"

I laughed. "The weather and politics."

"Man," he groaned, "that sounds even more boring than law." He smiled as he gazed at me. "Do you have any siblings?"

I reached into my bag, pulling out one of my floppy hats, and secured it over my head. "Nope, just me."

He rolled to his side, bending his arm, holding his face with his palm. "An only child, huh? What does that feel like?"

"In some ways, a lot like you and law—there's pressure."

"All the attention is on you."

I nodded. "Exactly." I held my fruity drink against my chest and watched the waves. "You know, my parents don't have other children to speak about who can soften the blow, like *Margie is in residency, Ralphie is working on Wall Street, but poor Jo is still trying to figure her life out.*" I frowned. "I don't have the luxury of figuring my life out. I need to give them talking points and reasons to be proud." I took a long sip.

"No matter what you do, Jo, you'll make your parents proud."

"Maybe ..." I gulped down another mouthful. "But what I can say is, being an only child has made me fiercely independent. I don't need anyone to entertain me. I'm not afraid of silence or being lost in my own head. I'm also not afraid of being alone."

Another major advantage was maturity, something that developed naturally, more so than my friends, because my parents never treated me like a kid.

I hoped Jenner felt that when he was around me—that despite being young, I was an old soul for my age.

He reached across the small space between us, his fingers landing on my bare stomach. "I don't know how you're not taken right now."

I didn't know how to take that comment.

I definitely didn't know how to respond.

And I wasn't sure I wanted to hear his reply if I asked him to elaborate.

What I did know was that setting expectations for Jenner and me would make me vulnerable for disappointment.

In what could be.

In myself.

I just had to accept whatever this was.

Even if I had fueled it.

I took in his eyes as his fingers lowered to my hip, circling the small area.

"Do you wish you had siblings?"

I appreciated the change of subject, my brain needing a rest.

"When I was younger, no. But now, I do. And I have one—her name is Monica." I grinned. "When you're an only child, it's fully acceptable to adopt a sister or brother, and she couldn't be more perfect. She picks up after herself. She shares. She even cooks."

He laughed.

I loved that sound.

It only encouraged me to keep going.

"No, really." I clarified, "We live together so well, and she's the most amazing best friend. I'm positive that no matter where we end up, it'll be together."

"Is leaving Miami on the table?"

I glanced toward the water again, a view I'd been admiring for the last four years. "I graduate in two months, and I have no job. The world is on the table, Jenner."

"I assumed you'd stay here."

I took the last sip and set the empty cup on the table. "If I take the job with the art dealer or the private gym, I'll be staying, but I'm keeping all my options open. Our lease doesn't end for another four months, so that gives me time to figure things out past graduation." I paused as the waitress approached and ordered another round for us. "Be honest," I said as she left, "is it strange to be hearing about this post-college-life stage? You've been established for so long. I imagine it's been a while since you've thought about any of this."

There were times when Jenner looked at me, and I could tell what he was thinking. I could read the thoughts in his eyes;

I felt his energy. And then there were times when I was lost, unable to decipher a single thought.

That was where I was now—lost.

"Admittedly, it's been a while since I've been in your shoes, but it's interesting to listen about your journey and compare it to mine."

My voice softened when I said, "Does it bother you?" I took a breath. "My age, I mean."

He stared at me silently. "I never really gave age that much thought before you."

"Because?"

I wasn't sure if I'd regret that question, but I still asked it.

First, there was a laugh, followed by, "I think you know why, Jo."

Because it was just sex before me.

Even if our future wasn't defined or our destination wasn't set, things with us had moved beyond sex.

That was where my brain went.

But my heart needed to confirm.

"Because I matter ..."

"I think I've proven that to you." He glanced toward the sand and back. "I'm here."

I exhaled, the tingles now in my lungs and throbbing in my chest. "I didn't expect to hear from you once I got home from Vegas." His fingers hadn't left my hip, and I intertwined ours together. "But having you here has been so fun."

He stared at me but said nothing.

The tingles turned to a heavy ache.

"I'm going to say something that isn't going to be easy."

I hadn't been able to read his eyes a few minutes ago, but I could now.

I could see his words as clear as the sky.

"If the circumstances were different ..." I voiced.

He nodded, the movement appearing to almost cause him pain.

And now, that pain lived in me.

My throat was so tight that air hardly moved through. "I get it."

That didn't mean I accepted it, that I didn't hate it, that I didn't want to scream at what could be.

But Jenner hadn't lied to me. He didn't try to play me. He didn't bullshit me.

He gave me truth.

And it hurt more than anything, but I understood.

How could we maintain something as magical as I wanted like this?

Different time zones, thousands of miles between us, my future so uncertain.

And those were just the things on the surface.

I had to be realistic about our situation.

But that certainly wasn't going to stop me from enjoying the rest of our time at the beach and the following two evenings he had planned. It didn't matter where we were or what we were doing. Jenner's hands were never far from my body, his attention never straying from me.

I felt like the center of his world.

I relished in it.

On the morning when he was scheduled to leave, I woke up, naked on his chest, my fingers running through his patch of dark hair. Instead of heading for breakfast, we decided to order room service, and once it was delivered, he brought it out onto the patio, overlooking South Beach and the beautiful, vast skyline that edged the water.

As we sat next to each other, nursing large cups of coffee, I finally dipped my fork into the cream cheese and raspberry jam that had squirted out the side of the stuffed French toast, and I brought it up to my mouth.

"*Mmm*," I groaned. "You have to try this."

I cut off a piece, the bite generous and dripping in maple syrup, and I held it out to him. As he surrounded the fork, I watched those beautiful, kissable lips and the bob of his Adam's apple as he chewed. His beard had thickened in the last few days, the hairs becoming even softer as they lengthened. I touched them as he swallowed, his face almost nuzzling against my hand.

He wiped his mouth with a napkin, my stare moving to his fingers, their length, the short nails at the end, remembering how they had felt on my body when I woke up to him rubbing my back.

"Delicious."

I nodded. "Isn't it?"

And so was the feeling inside me.

Damn it, I would miss him.

Such a big part of me was wishing we could do this every morning. The other part of me knew that was impossible.

That didn't stop me from dreaming.

Fantasizing.

Wanting to buy myself even more time with him.

I checked my phone, seeing that in only two hours, his private plane would be taking off.

I took a few more bites and placed the metal cover over my plate. "I know you were planning on taking the SUV to the airport, but I'd like to drive you."

He set his fork down, abandoning his eggs for coffee. "You're sure?"

"Yes."

Once his hands were free, he stared at me for several beats and tapped his lap and said, "Come here."

I got up from my seat and planted my butt on his thighs, wrapping my arms around his neck. A spot that was far too comfortable. A place that could so easily feel like home. I adjusted my body, snuggling my back against his chest, my feet balancing on the banister of the balcony, his chin resting on top of my head.

"Fuck ... I'm going to miss this."

My eyes squinted shut, the sensation in my heart becoming too much, his words sending me right over the edge.

I didn't respond. I just held his arms as they crossed over my navel, and I felt the slight sway of his body, like the ocean breeze moving past us.

"How often do you find yourself in Florida?"

I felt him breathe, the air warming my hair.

"At least once a quarter. I have several clients here."

"Are all the trips planned far in advance or surprises like this one?"

"Both." He paused. "I'd have to look, but I don't recall any more trips down here until the end of the year. That could always change though." His arms tightened. "What about California? Do you ever make your way out there?"

I filled my lungs several times, holding in the air after each inhale. "It's actually where I'm from."

"No shit?"

"Yeah ... I grew up in LA." I stilled, feeling the pounding in my heart. "I do go back—holidays, birthdays, special events, things like that. But now that graduation is coming up, I have too much to do, and I won't get a chance to return. Plus, my parents will be coming, so there's no reason to fly home to see them."

He turned my body to the side, so he could take in my face.

There were so many things I wanted to say, but I couldn't. They hurt too much. So, I hugged him against me, clinging to his back, remembering that I'd felt the same way when I left his hotel the morning I returned to Miami.

In a couple hours, I would be recalling this exact moment, wanting to rewind time.

Wanting to relive the whole weekend.

Wanting to recapture the happiness I felt when I was with him.

He pulled away and captured my face between his hands, drawing his mouth close to mine.

Kissing me.

It wasn't the kind of kiss we shared when we were naked and tumbling in bed.

This was different.

This was breath and softness.

Tenderness.

My eyes stayed closed as his lips left mine and slowly opened, the emotion sparking when his emerald gaze was so rich and vibrant.

"Our paths will cross again, Jo."

I smiled—for him, not for me. And without hesitation, I hugged him again, hiding my face on his shoulder, making sure he didn't see the tears that were threatening to fall.

I dug for my voice, keeping the sadness out of it, and whispered, "I can't wait for that moment."

THIRTEEN

JENNER

"Another round, please," Ford said to the bartender, pointing at the shot glass in front of him along with the ones in front of Dominick and me.

The bartender lifted a bottle of whiskey from behind the counter and refilled the small glasses.

Ford held his up in the air and said, "To getting shit-faced."

"I'm already there," I admitted. "Jesus. Enough. No more shots after this next one."

"You're tapping out?" Dominick dared.

I nodded, the movement so exaggerated that my head no longer felt attached. "Hell yes."

"The pussy says he's done," Dominick grunted at Ford. "You know what that means, don't you?"

"It means nothing," I said to them. "It means I have a meeting first thing tomorrow that I can't fucking miss. And it means you two are assholes if you try to goad me into drinking more."

Dominick held out his hand and said to the bartender, "Bottle. Please."

She placed the half-empty bottle of whiskey in his grip, and he refilled the glasses again, looking at me when he voiced, "Drink up, pussy."

"Fuck all three of you," I said even though there was only two.

Maybe I was including the bartender.

Hell, I didn't even fucking know at this point.

"Listen, dickhead"—my head dropped to see the time on my Rolex, my eyes squinting so the numbers didn't jump—"my driver is outside, waiting to take me home, and my ass is planning on being in that car in two minutes."

"And here I thought, you were about to redeem yourself," Ford said. "I have a sitter tonight. You're not ditching out early; you don't have the balls."

I threw back the whiskey Dominick had poured and slammed the glass on the bar top when I'd meant to just set it down. "My meeting is with Walter. I can't cancel. Out of *alll* people, I can't do that to him."

"Dude, stop crying," Dominick said. "You owe us. It's as simple as that."

Crying.

I could strangle the motherfucker.

But if I stayed any longer, the drinking wouldn't stop. Neither would the teasing, and my brothers were two people I hated to disappoint.

I got up from my barstool and pounded their fists. "I'll see you at the office."

My suit jacket was lying across a nearby chair, and I grabbed it, rushing to the door before either of them could stop me. Once I got outside, I found my SUV parked at the base of the lot and climbed into the backseat.

"Mr. Dalton," my driver said, "am I taking you home?"

"Please, Steven. Thank you."

As he began to drive, I took out my phone and tried to make sense of what I was seeing. I was too drunk to reply to emails, but that didn't stop me from reading some of the ones that had come in. Most were work-related. Clients needing contracts reviewed, questions about potential deals, issues that had arisen during acquisitions.

So many fucking billable hours.

I moved on to my social media, scanning through the pictures, my thumb swiping, making them move so fast that I just caught snippets of faces, bodies, scenery—nothing important. But one of them caught my attention, causing me to scroll back, stopping on the photo.

Fuck me.

Jo had posted the picture a few hours ago. It was of her at a Marlins game. Her hair was braided on the sides with a hat on top. She wore a team jersey that she'd tied to show off her stomach and cutoffs on the bottom.

I went to blow up the photo and accidentally liked it.

Goddamn it.

I moved on to the next picture of her in a long dress and a hat similar to the one she'd worn to the beach, and I realized I hadn't seen this photograph.

I'd followed her Instagram on the plane ride to Miami, but work had been keeping me so busy the last week that I guessed I hadn't spent much time checking out her account.

I had the time now.

There were photos of her with friends, but most were solo shots. There were ones of her in a bikini at the beach, posing in dresses with sunsets in the background, at clubs and restaurants. My favorites were the ones where she was cozy in her apartment, the faraway look in her eyes telling me she was fantasizing.

About me.

No wonder I hadn't checked her account before. It was dangerous as hell.

Just as fucking dangerous as it was to text her, yet I found myself pulling up the last message we'd exchanged, my thumbs hitting the keys.

Me: You're so fucking hot.
Jo: Sounds like someone's missed me. Are you a Marlins fan?
Me: Nah, I'm just a Jo fan.
Jo: Does that earn me rope? Or maybe handcuffs this time?

My cock started to fucking throb inside my suit, my hard-on grinding against my zipper. I shifted my boxer briefs, making more room for my dick so it wouldn't bust through my pants.

Me: Don't fucking tease me. I'll send a plane for you right now.
Jo: You can't have me. I'm headed to the Bahamas tomorrow night for my birthday.
Me: Your birthday? You didn't tell me ...
Jo: I'm telling you now. Now, be a good boy and wish me a happy 22nd.

Twenty-two.

I didn't know, nor had she mentioned it to me while I was in Miami.

The time on my phone showed it was a quarter past eleven. My meeting with Walter was at eight tomorrow morning. If I got on the plane now, it would be tight, but I would have just enough time to wish her a happy birthday in person and then fly back to LA to make the meeting.

I pulled up my Favorites and hit my assistant's name, listening to her answer after the second ring.

"Val, I need the plane."

"Okay, hang on one second. Let me call the pilot."

The sound of her voice told me I'd woken her. But it didn't matter; this job was twenty-four/seven, and she got paid a hefty sum to always be available for me, knowing to expect my calls at all hours.

"Jenner?" She didn't wait for me to reply before she continued, "There's a problem. Your parents are on the plane as we speak, flying to Brazil."

"They're flying ... where?" I raked my hand through my hair, trying to remember if they'd told me about this trip. "Oh fuck, that's right."

"Should I reach out to the private airlines and see if they have a plane available or look for a commercial flight?"

I was far too drunk to fuck with anything commercial, and finding another private jet could take hours—time I didn't have.

"Change of plans," I told her. "I need you to shop for a gift instead. It's for a woman, a twenty-second birthday. I'll text you the name and address."

"Do you have a preference on the type of gift?"

I stared out the window as Steven began the hike up the Hollywood Hills. "Something beautiful, something she won't forget."

"What's my budget?"

I sighed. "You don't have one. Make it memorable, Val."

"I'm on it."

I thanked her and disconnected the call and pulled up Jo's message.

Me: For the record, I just tried to fly there, so I could say those words to you in person. My parents took the jet overseas, or I'd be on my way right now.

Jo: Don't tease me, Jenner.

Me: Would you want me for your birthday?

Jo: In ways you couldn't possibly understand.

This girl did something to my cock. She taunted it, teased it; she made me want to fucking pound her in ways she couldn't possibly understand.

Seven days since I'd seen her, and even though I'd been swamped with work, I hadn't been able to get her out of my head.

I couldn't stop thinking about her body.

The only thing I wanted in this moment was to tie her to my bed and rip off that jersey with my teeth, kiss my way up those beautiful legs, and bury my mouth between them.

I wanted to rub my nose across her pussy.

I wanted her scent all over my fucking face.

I wanted her wetness in my beard and on my lips, tasting her every time I licked them.

I wanted to devour her.

I wanted to fucking savor her ...

Me: I think you're wrong about that ...
Me: Have a good birthday, gorgeous. Celebrate your ass off, but not too hard—you know how much I love that fucking ass. This moment only comes around once, so enjoy it.
Jo: Thank you. <3

Jo: Are you nuts? Jenner, I have no words right now. I'm absolutely shocked you did this for me ...
Jo: The bag is so incredibly beautiful and the special interior—I'm completely dead over it. What an amazing, beyond generous present. Please know how much I appreciate this gift and YOU. I love it. Truly. Thank you sooo, so much.

I smiled as I read the text from Jo, my lips widening even more as I viewed the picture she'd sent, showing her wearing the bag.

My assistant had texted me the receipt from Gucci, so I knew all about the three thousand dollars she had spent on Jo. But after my assistant made the purchase, I decided it wasn't enough.

It wasn't personal, the way I wanted her gift to be.

So, I'd reached out to the store and had them contact an artist, who painted Jo's name on the inside of the bag along with a small skyline of Vegas above it.

I blew up the photo to get a better look. I knew nothing about purses, but the large red crocodile-looking-skin bag looked sexy as hell on her shoulder.

Me: It looks stunning on you.

"Who's making you smile so hard?" Walter asked, returning from the restroom.

I glanced up from my phone, shoving it back into my pocket. "A business deal that just closed."

"Bullshit." He placed his napkin on his lap. "You've been in this business for far too long to get a hard-on over real estate. Plus, you've closed deals for me that have exceeded half a billion dollars, and I've never seen you smile like that. It's a woman. Who is she?"

I shook my head. "Nah ..."

"You think I don't know what a man looks like when he's in love? Come on, son. I've been around the block plenty of times in my old age. That's a smile caused by a woman—nothing else."

I was impressed that he could read me so well. Practicing law had given me this enigmatic edge. Most people had no idea what I was thinking, and I preferred it that way. Aside from my brothers—those cocky bastards who thought they knew everything—Jo was the only other person who seemed to have a way inside my head.

"She's someone I met on vacation. It's nothing serious. We live on opposite coasts, and we're in different places in our lives." I thought of her trying on her graduation gown, studying for finals that I assumed were coming up, while I sat in this meeting with my top client. Man, two different places was an understatement. "But she's a good girl, and I hear those are hard to find."

"I knew there was a *but* coming." He gripped my shoulder, squeezing it. "Take it from someone who knows. There aren't many good ones out there. When you find one, hold on to her. Put a ring on her finger and then make her a mother."

I chuckled. "Ring, children—hell, I'm not ready for that."

"You'd be surprised what love can do to a man, Jenner. One minute, you're chasing pussy into a public restroom, and the next, you're picking out baby names."

Baby names?

Fuck no. That was Ford's thing.

Buying a ring?

That was more Dominick's thing.

I was good right where I was, which was sending gifts and seeing Jo when I was in Florida.

But even if she were here and she fit into my life, would that make a difference? Would I want more?

Fuck if I knew.

"I'll take your word for it, my man." I reached inside my briefcase and pulled out the paperwork I'd prepared. "I've reviewed each of the sites you sent over, and I've put together some thoughts. Out of all the parcels in Park City, only three caught my eye. I've outlined them here"—I pointed at the sheets of paper and the notes I'd left in the margins—"but I have to say, I have a favorite."

Walter had followed through with my advice, now focusing solely on Utah for his next build-out, and he'd had his realtor scout the available lots in the area. I'd been to Park City enough times to know the locations, and with help from his accountant, we were able to run some numbers, estimates on his return of investment.

He reviewed my notes, looking up as he asked, "Do you think I need to move quickly?"

"You mean, have I heard rumors of your competition coming into the same area, scooping up one of these parcels? No. I think you're safe. Most of the high-end chains are already there and established. The boutique hotels can't afford this land. But could the Ritz sweep in and stake their claim? Sure. If that happens, I'll find out long before they make an offer, and we'll make our move."

He nodded. "I need time to think this out." He broke eye contact and waved our waitress over to order. "Scotch"—he held up two fingers, signaling one for each of us—"and make them neat." He turned back toward me.

I checked my watch. "It's not even nine in the morning." I laughed, my head instantly throbbing, the hangover present and raging. "Isn't it a little too early to celebrate?"

"I'm in the mood to drink."

I couldn't get up from the table and jump into my SUV that was waiting outside the restaurant, telling Walter to fuck off like I would if Dominick and Ford were here instead.

Walter wasn't someone I could deny for any reason.

I took a deep breath, staring at my eggs that I was having a hard time getting down. "Then, let's drink."

"Hello?" I said into my phone the moment I walked into my house, returning from a long, scotch-filled morning with Walter.

The booze was doing its job.

I'd be taking the rest of the day off, whether my schedule permitted it or not.

"Hi."

Jo.

Fuck.

I knew better than to answer without checking who was calling. It could have been a client, and I would have been really fucked, far too buzzed to speak to them in this state. But hearing her voice was a welcome surprise.

"Jo ..." I went to grab a water from the fridge and ended up with a beer, carrying it to my wall of windows that overlooked the pool and the Hills. "To what do I owe this pleasure?"

"I know I sent a text, thanking you, but it's not enough. You need to hear my voice and just how appreciative I am."

I placed my hand on the glass. "You're sweet."

"No, you're the sweet one. Jenner, oh my God, this bag." She paused. "You didn't have to send anything—I hope you know that. I certainly didn't tell you it was my birthday to score a gift."

"That's not why I sent it, trust me."

"Good. Well, it was honestly the best surprise ever. My girls can't stop gawking at it. Monica is dying of jealousy, but I've threatened her life. If she goes anywhere near it, she's toast."

I opened the door and stepped outside, needing the breeze on my face. "I'm glad you love it. That makes me happy."

"We haven't spoken since you left. Are things good? How's work? And how was Seattle?" She giggled. "I assume all must be going well. You're liquored up, and it's not even noon."

I laughed. "How the hell do you know that?"

"Really? Come on. I know you better than you think I do, Jenner. I can hear it in your voice."

Goddamn it.

My dick turned hard at the sound of my name, at her incredibly sexy voice.

But something else she had said really hit home.

She knows me.

"You're not wrong," I admitted. "It's been a long-ass morning with a client who wanted to chase his breakfast with bottomless scotch."

"The only better way to start your day would be waking up in Miami."

I took a seat on one of the lounge chairs, rubbing that thought across my forehead. "Are you sure you're not headed to LA anytime soon?"

"Why, Mr. Dalton?" Her voice had turned sassy, making me want to spank her fucking ass. "Do you want to do something extra naughty to me?"

I ground my teeth together. "You have no fucking idea."

She couldn't possibly.

First, her texts, and now, this conversation—nothing but fucking teases.

I didn't want to just spank that ass. I wanted to heal it after, rubbing circles across it with my palm.

And then I wanted to be inside of it.

"I think I do ..." She exhaled in a way that told me she was as worked up as me. "But I can't make it to LA. I have the busiest week coming up. We're leaving tonight for the Bahamas, and as soon as we get back, I have two papers due, three exams, and a concert next weekend." I could hear her smile. "You're the one with the jet. Why don't you come here?"

I didn't remember setting my beer down, but I picked it up and guzzled several sips.

Why is she so fucking irresistible?

Why am I seconds away from phoning my assistant to have her reserve the plane?

"What about your concert?" I asked. "If I came to Miami, would you skip it for me?"

I was giving her an out.

A reason to cancel this ludicrous idea. My ass staying planted in LA was far better for both of us.

"Come on, Jenner. With your connections, I'm positive you can score a ticket to the sold-out show and probably get better seats than Monica and I bought."

If I couldn't, Dominick or Max could.

Why am I even considering this?

Going to Florida would only make us closer, and that wasn't something we could fix, living so far apart. It would only make me think about her more, and she already owned half the thoughts in my fucking brain.

"Hold on," I told her, and I pulled my phone away from my face.

I checked my schedule for next weekend. I had several meetings on Friday and Monday that could be moved.

I pressed the phone back to my ear, staring at the house across from mine on the other side of the valley, trying to focus on anything but the reality of this situation.

But it wasn't going away.

It was only intensifying.

"You really want me there?" I asked.

"*Mmm.*" She breathed. "Yes."

I couldn't resist that sound.

I couldn't resist what I was going to do to her body.

I squeezed my eyes shut, bringing the beer up to my mouth and swallowing until it was gone.

This was fire.

I knew that.

And I knew, somehow, it was only going to fucking burn.

I set the empty bottle on the pool deck, and I bit into my lip, thinking of the things I was going to do to her mouth. "I'll be there."

FOURTEEN

JOANNA

"I can't come again," I gasped, trying to find air in this steamy suite when it felt like all the oxygen had been fucked out of me.

That was because Jenner's mouth was on my clit, my body so tingly from the orgasm he'd just given me.

"You can."

I didn't believe him.

I'd already had three, and I'd practically lost my voice from screaming, every part of me completely drained. Every nerve ending shouting, every limb numb.

And then there was his tongue, lapping away, urging me to find that release again.

"Oh fuck."

"Yes ... just like I said," he panted.

After spending an hour inside me, he'd barely caught his breath before his mouth dived between my legs.

And this was only the very beginning of his trip. He'd flown in this morning. It wasn't even lunchtime yet, and I was already orgasmed out. His hands, his dick, his wicked tongue—all making me feel so good.

God, this fucking man.

I couldn't get enough of him.

"Come," he demanded.

My head fell into the pillow, my back arching, my heels digging into the mattress, while my hands squeezed the blanket beneath me. "Jenner ..."

"Fucking come. Let me feel it." He moaned. "Let me taste it."

His words were like friction, bringing me to that place again—a place I didn't think I would be able to revisit because my body was so spent.

But here I was.

So aroused.

Climbing faster, the harder he licked.

His finger found its way inside me, and a bolt of pleasure shot through me, causing my knees to bend and my head to lift.

I wanted to watch his eyes turn ravenous.

I wanted to see his tongue flick my clit.

"Fuck!" I screamed.

"That's it, baby. Come on my face."

His tongue was whipping across me, his fingers thrusting, sending me so far off that edge that I was peaking, and all I had left was more screams. "Jenner!"

"Fuck yes." He switched to a horizontal pattern. "Tell me. Tell me how fucking good it feels."

His words were like air, bursting across my clit, bringing me higher with each syllable. "Your tongue ... I can't." I tried to inhale, I tried to find the words to describe what was happening inside me, but I couldn't.

I was gone, overtaken with shudders and waves of ecstasy, and he didn't let up, making sure I was riding this out.

The moment I finally stilled, he gazed up at me from between my legs. "You have no idea how fucking hot that was."

I shoved my hand through his hair, pulling the strands to lead him up my body until his lips were within range, and I kissed him, holding his face with both hands.

"Taste yourself," he whispered.

I already was, needing his mouth, his lips, his kiss to resonate this feeling.

The seal made me feel even more connected to him even though our bodies had just been intertwined.

"I missed you," I admitted when I finally pulled away.

His eyes narrowed, his hand running down my chest, between my breasts, moving around my side until he reached my lower back, and he held me against him.

There was a fight behind his pupils.

I saw it.

I felt it in his grip.

He just wasn't ready to verbalize it.

And I wasn't going to make him.

I kissed him once more and said softly, "Let's go get some food."

"I just ate."

The grittiness in his voice was extremely erotic, but I still laughed. "I mean, real food."

"I don't think anything could taste better than you."

I stared into his eyes, reading them. "Does that translate to room service? Or—"

"Room service." He pounced on top of me, holding me against the mattress, keeping my hands behind my back as he kissed and tickled my neck.

"*Mmm.*" I pushed my head back, and he licked across my throat. "Are you ever going to let me out of this room?"

"If it was up to me, no."

"What about the concert tonight?"

He kissed down to my breasts, staring up at me as he sucked my nipple into his mouth, only releasing it to say, "I could keep you so occupied that you wouldn't even remember you had tickets." He pulled that hardened bud back into his mouth and nibbled on the end, goose bumps shooting across my body.

I didn't doubt a thing he had said. Jenner had the ability to take me to a headspace where nothing mattered, except for him.

That thought was as terrifying as it was wonderful.

"You know, Monica would hunt us down, dragging us by our ears if she had to."

He came up for air, his lips now hovering above mine. "I can oddly picture that." He smiled, and it was so delicious. "Wait until you see the seats I scored for us."

My brows rose. "They certainly can't be better than The Weeknd seats you had."

"They're better."

I held in my breath. "And you got a ticket for Monica too?"

His grin grew. "You know I wouldn't leave her out."

I wasn't sure why I'd even asked; he certainly wasn't the type to make Monica sit alone.

I just couldn't help but be shocked at his generosity.

As my heart clutched, his gaze eating at me, I knew that, whatever this was, I didn't deserve him.

I closed my eyes, holding the emotion in my chest. "Thank you. I mean it." I linked my fingers with his and got up from the bed, standing by the edge. "Come with me."

"You're making me get dressed?"

"Just the opposite." I found my lip and chewed it. "I want to see what you taste like in the shower."

The seats Monica and I had purchased for Post Malone were in the middle of the third tier. We would have been closer to the ceiling than the stage. The only glimpse of him we would have been catching were on the large monitors spread throughout FTX Arena.

And then there were Jenner's seats.

Front row, kitty-corner to the center of the stage, less than twenty feet from where he was singing. There was only one view that could possibly be better, and that would be standing right next to Post.

I shivered at the thought of how much these seats cost.

There was something about concerts that Monica and I just loved. Listening to the artists, obviously, was the major part, but there was more. It was the energy in the stadium, the way our bodies automatically moved to whatever beat was playing, how it was impossible to feel anything but happiness.

Music brought us together.

And it was bringing Jenner even closer to me.

His arm never left my body; whether it was wrapped around my shoulders or waist, it was secure. His lips stayed near my cheek. His air hit my skin, over and over with each breath.

When I felt his eyes on me, I didn't look at him. I just let him stare and take me in. I let him smell my skin. I let him feel this moment between us, getting lost, like I often did when I gazed at him.

And I tried to stay just as engaged with Monica, hearing her laugh. "I feel like his sweat is about to drip on me."

Her arms were waving in the air, her body swaying.

I knew what she meant. I still couldn't believe we were this close to the stage.

But even though I was watching him sing, viewing each droplet of sweat fall down his face, I could only focus on Jenner.

I was consumed by his presence.

By his attention that was burning through me.

And I couldn't stop anticipating what it was going to feel like to say good-bye to him again. This trip wasn't supposed to happen; it'd seemed like it had taken some convincing.

I feared what next time would be like.

How intensely I would miss him.

My heart needed to prepare for it.

I cared for Jenner. I wanted a future with him. I wanted this feeling—this pulsing in my chest—to own me all the time, not just when I was physically with him.

But is it impossible?

I turned toward him, not at all surprised that his eyes were already on me.

"Music looks gorgeous on you, Jo."

My lids shut for just a second. "It's not the music."

As if he heard my thoughts, he brought his mouth to my temple, pressing his lips there, staying like that for the rest of the song.

Monica danced like there was a spotlight shining on her. The crowd held up their phones, shining their flashlights at the stage.

Jenner and I didn't move.

We stayed snug until the end of the show, our arms linked as we walked out of the stadium.

Jenner had a driver each time he was in Miami, and he was parked in the VIP area. We headed over to the SUV, and the driver held the door open for us. Monica climbed into the backseat, and when I attempted to get in, Jenner stopped me.

"I've got something planned for you," he whispered in my

ear. He then stood in the doorway of the backseat and said to Monica, "The driver is going to take you home. I want you to text us when you get there, so we know you're safe."

"You guys aren't coming?" she asked.

He shook his head and squeezed me. "I've got a little surprise for this one."

"You're so cute. I can't stand it." She slid to the end of the seat and stretched her arms across the open space to wrap them around us. "Thank you for the most incredible time. I don't know how I'll ever be able to concert without you, Jenner. You just make the whole experience so extra."

He laughed. "Thanks for being a hell of a third wheel."

"You cats have fun tonight." She snorted.

Jenner closed the door, and we watched the driver pull away.

"Are you going to tell me where we're going?" I asked as we began walking.

He kissed the top of my head—a place I was learning he liked—and he led me down the sidewalk.

This was a section of the city I knew well, and I couldn't imagine where he was taking me. We'd eaten dinner before the show, so I didn't think it was for a meal, and even though there were plenty of bars in the area, something told me we weren't headed for drinks either.

After a few blocks, his hand lowered to my back, and he turned us into a storefront, the awning one I didn't recognize, nor could I recall ever getting anything delivered from this bakery.

"Have you been here?" he asked.

I read the name again and shook my head. "Never."

He paused, holding the door handle. "I don't do this often."

I tilted my head, trying to read him. "Do what?"

"Eat dessert at midnight."

I didn't have time to ask what he meant before he opened the door. Inside, an older woman was sitting on a stool behind a long, antique-looking glass counter. A smile warmed her face the moment we walked in.

"Jenner." She rose. "Oh, honey, it's been ages."

He released me to approach her, and the two of them immediately embraced.

I could tell she was someone he had known for a long time, a motherly figure just by the way her arms wrapped around him, how she patted the back of his head.

"I didn't know you were coming into town," she said, pulling away. "Let me get a good look at you." She shook her head as she took in his face. "Always as handsome as ever." Her hand went to his cheek. "What brings you to town?" Her grin widened, her eyes flitting over to me. "Never mind. I see the reason right now." She glanced back to Jenner. "Introduce me to this lovely lady, please."

"Gloria, this is Jo. Jo, this is Brett's mom, Gloria."

Brett.

And then it clicked—his friend I'd met in Vegas.

Rather than shaking my hand, which I extended to her, she pulled me in for a hug.

"It's so wonderful to meet you." She squeezed.

I felt myself melting into her.

"It's so nice to meet you too."

Her hand circled my back before she leaned away, studying my face, like she'd done to Jenner. "What can I get you? It's my treat. Choose anything."

"Absolutely not. I'm a paying customer," Jenner said in the background. "I just wanted Jo to experience the best bakery in Miami."

A blush moved across Gloria's face. "Flattery, my boy, makes you even more charming." She nodded toward Jenner but spoke to me and said, "It's impossible to say no to this one."

I laughed. "Tell me about it."

She led me over to the display cases, the options endless.

"It's all good," Jenner said as he stood next to me. "I can say that because I've tried just about everything."

"Just like my Brett, he's got a hearty appetite."

"*Mmhmm*," I agreed but for multiple reasons. I eyed the selection that ranged from cookies to tarts, cupcakes to candies. "How do I choose when it all looks so amazing?"

Gloria moved to the back side of the counter. "Can I help?"

I glanced up, our eyes connecting, and something made me nod.

"You like desserts that are a little more on the savory side, am I right?"

"Yes. You're right."

But I had no idea how she knew that.

"I had a feeling." She reached across the counter, her fingers landing on my shoulder. "I have a suspicion you also like blueberries."

The shock that hit my chest made me laugh. "Love them."

She smiled knowingly. "I make a blueberry cake. Some call it a doughnut; some refer to it as pie. I think of it as cake because it's more savory than sweet." She slid the glass aside just enough that she could slip her fingers inside the case. With a pair of tongs, she picked up a piece of the cake and set it on a plate, adding a fork. "See if you like it."

I cut off a small sliver of the corner. "Oh my God," I said from behind my hand as I chewed, the flavors of the dense cake bursting on my tongue. "This is exceptional."

"I thought you'd like it."

She took out several more pieces and added them to a box, closing the lid. "And for you, my dear boy, I'm going to give you a half-moon cookie. I know you love the combination of flavors and some chocolate-coconut fudge."

"Coconut?" I asked, looking at Jenner, surprised that was his flavor of choice.

"Trust me," he said, "you've never had anything like it in your life."

She placed several squares of fudge along with a few cookies into a separate box, placing it on top of mine, and she handed both to Jenner.

He reached into his pocket, and she put her hand up in the air.

"Don't you even think about it. You know your money is no good here." She eyed him. "I mean it." She came over to our side of the counter and put her arms around him, whispering something I couldn't hear. "Now, get out of here," she said as she pulled back. "And go give that son of mine and his gorgeous fiancée a giant hug and tell them to come down here and visit their mama."

"You know I will."

She turned toward me, her hug even tighter than before. "Just be patient, my girl. For some, it takes a long time before they see the sun, but when they do, they hold on to the rays forever." She winked at me as we separated.

Her words caught me completely off guard.

How does she know?

Jenner's hand went to my lower back, and he led me to the door. "Gloria, always a pleasure. We'll see you soon."

She looked at me when she said, "Don't be a stranger, darling."

I waved right before we walked out, the air from outside

filling my lungs, like I hadn't breathed the entire time I was in there.

"What just happened?" I asked, a few paces from her shop.

"What do you mean?"

It took me a moment to steady my thoughts. "I feel like I just left a psychic and got a reading of my future."

He chuckled. "She's great, isn't she?"

I reached for his hand that was resting behind my back. "She's more than great. There's something uniquely special about her." I dug harder, trying to put my finger on it. "It truly feels like she was reading my mind."

"She reads all of our minds, Jo."

His eyes told me he wasn't being facetious at all.

And instead of asking how, since I was sure he wouldn't know, I focused on, "It's midnight, Jenner. Why is she there? Alone? Why doesn't she have an assistant or helper or something?"

He sighed, resting his arm over my shoulders but keeping our fingers linked. "Brett's been trying to make that happen for years. She doesn't want help and won't accept it. And she stays open for the late crowd because she feels like that's when their sweet tooth is the strongest." He looked down at me. "She's been in business for more than twenty years. She says people count on her to be there."

I could see that. Hell, I could feel it.

"She has a superpower—she learns people; she caters to them in a way I've never witnessed before."

"She's certainly not doing it for the money. Her husband is one of the top financial advisers in Miami, and her son has more cash than he'll ever be able to spend." He kissed the top of my head. "For her, it's all about the people."

When we reached the end of the block, pausing at the Stop

sign, I asked, "Should we take this back to the hotel to eat?" I glanced down the street, wondering if the SUV was going to come and fetch us.

He tucked a piece of hair behind my ear. A sentiment that didn't go unnoticed. "I thought we could stay around here and eat it by the water."

My heart throbbed. "I would love that."

We went across the street and through the park, choosing a bench right along the ocean, immediately greeted by the sound of the waves.

He handed me my box, and we opened them, the scent of the blueberry cake making my eyes close and my mouth water.

"Try this." He held a piece of the fudge in front of my mouth. "I don't even like coconut, but I get it every time I'm here."

I felt his eyes on me as I leaned forward, surrounding the corner with my lips, the sweetness hitting me the moment I bit down. "Wow."

He was right; the coconut wasn't gritty. It was just a flavor that was added into the chocolate. And the fudge was creamy, almost light and flaky, a texture I'd never had before.

"This is seriously divine."

"Now, try the cookie."

I smiled. "I've had half-moon cookies before."

"Not like this one." He placed it near my lips. "I can promise you that."

The cookie was the size of my palm—the base chocolate with a cake texture, the icing on top in both vanilla and chocolate. When I nibbled off the edge, I quickly learned this wasn't as sweet as the fudge. But it was rich and decadent, the cookie a heavy flavor despite the consistency being light, and the frosting wasn't sugary, like I had expected.

"My God," I groaned. "Does this woman make anything that doesn't taste like heaven?"

"Now, you understand."

I took out a piece of my cake, popping some into my mouth. It tasted even better than it had in her store. "I can't get over this." I checked out the remaining slices in the box, looking for something dazzling on top—fairy dust, diamonds, anything that would explain where this flavor came from.

But it was just ingredients, baked to perfection.

"How often does Brett come here to see her?"

He swallowed and chewed off some cookie. "All the time, but if it were up to her, he would live here again."

"Again?"

Jenner explained how Brett's agency had started in Miami and how he'd opened an office in LA when he started dating James. I could understand the desire to relocate if you were dating a Hollywood star, but having lived in both cities, Miami took precedence, in my opinion.

The taste of South Florida just couldn't be beat.

And Gloria didn't have a franchise in LA.

"It's so nice that you make an effort to see her when you're here."

"I didn't visit her last time, and I felt guilty about it." He laughed. "And Brett gave me a boatload of shit for not stopping in."

I took out another piece, moaning through the bite. "You made up for it."

He stared at me, still. "She got to meet you."

I didn't know how to respond, so I said nothing. I just let the words hang in the air, listening to them repeat in my mind.

Feeling them move into my heart.

"What did she say to you?" I set the box on my lap. "You know, when she whispered in your ear?"

His eyelids narrowed, his tongue swiping across his bottom lip. "Why don't you tell me what she said to you?"

I smiled. He was such a lawyer. "How do you know she told me anything at all?"

A chill moved across my body when he said, "Because I know ..."

FIFTEEN

JENNER

"We're here again," I said, glancing at Jo across the front seat of her car, parked in the lot of Miami's private airport.

She took off her seat belt and turned toward me. "I like the picking-up part. Not the dropping-off part."

The weekend had ended much faster than I'd anticipated, and we'd had a hell of a time together.

Each visit, things got better.

And the truth was, I wasn't excited about my departure either.

I didn't know what that meant, but I couldn't spend too much time focusing on it because there was nothing I could do to change the reality of our situation.

Every time we were together, I saw the potential of what we could be.

Every time I left, it reinforced why this, long-term, would be far too hard to maintain.

"Come on," I said, squeezing her leg, encouraging her to get out.

I moved over to the trunk, and she hit the button to open it. I grabbed my suitcase, and once the wheels hit the ground, I released the handle and wrapped my arms around her, holding her to my chest. I pressed my lips against her head, breathing her in.

"Is this good-bye?"

I knew what she was asking.

I just didn't know if I could give her an answer.

So, I gave her the truth. "I hope not." And I held her face with both hands and kissed her.

We stayed pressed together, her air mixing with mine, until I pulled away. There was emotion in her eyes that I couldn't miss.

That I didn't want to see.

That I didn't want to be the cause of.

Goddamn it.

I couldn't walk away and have this be the final memory.

I lowered my hands to her neck and tilted her face up. "You'd better eat that last piece of blueberry cake for breakfast."

A smile tugged at those gorgeous lips, and she giggled.

That was what I needed to see.

To hear.

To feel as her body vibrated against mine.

"Already planning on it."

"I would be incredibly disappointed otherwise ... so would Gloria."

She shook her head, staring at me. "Jenner ..."

When she wrapped her arms around my neck, I hugged her tighter this time, rubbing across her shoulders and down her back.

"I know," I whispered.

I cupped her cheeks, aiming her face up at mine, allowing me to keep her close, to direct her to my mouth.

To give those stunning lips as much pressure as I wanted.

The moment I pulled away, the war returned to her eyes.

The passion. The hunger. The sadness.

I found her hand and squeezed it, my other fingers now clinging to the handle of my suitcase, and I brought those beautiful black nails up to my lips and kissed them, giving one last brush to the side of her cheek before I took a step back.

And then another.

"You're not going to say good-bye?"

"Do you want me to?"

She shook her head, pressing her fingers to her heart. "God, no."

I paused for just a second, taking her in, and then I lifted my hand in a wave and walked through the door of the building.

The staff immediately greeted me, taking my suitcase, giving me a chance to turn around to look through the tinted glass door.

But I didn't.

I knew better.

"Heard you saw my mom," Brett said from across the table.

Now that we had all finally returned to LA—Brett had visited James on set, Dominick and Kendall had escaped to Cabo, Ford had taken Everly to Disney, and I had been in Miami—we met up for our weekly dinner.

I surrounded my scotch with both hands, hoping the conversation would die here. "I did."

But I knew it wouldn't.

Their asses had become extremely nosy when it came to what was happening between Jo and me.

"And?" Brett inquired.

"And what, motherfucker? I went to your mom's shop, I got a cookie and some fudge, I tried to pay her, she wouldn't let me, and I left."

"Why so many *I*'s in that sentence?" Brett asked. "Shouldn't it be *we*?"

Every eye at this table was on me.

They all knew I had been in Miami to see Jo.

It wasn't a secret.

I wasn't playing a pronoun game. I was just avoiding the conversation.

"Why tell you something you already know?"

Brett laughed. "I see what's happening here. You're hoping by avoiding the topic altogether, we're going to let it go and that we're not going to point out that you've now made two trips to Miami to see a girl you don't want to have a relationship with."

I drained my glass, hoping the waitress would appear any second so I could order another one. "That hasn't changed."

"Really?" Ford asked.

"Really," I answered.

"Bullshit," Dominick barked. "I don't believe you."

I glanced at my older brother. "I'm not lying. I don't have any more trips planned to see her."

"Yet," Brett chimed in.

Fuck me, they were relentless.

"Long-distance is not for me, and even though she's from LA, I don't see her moving here anytime soon. How many times have I told you guys that?" I looked down at my plate, at the bits of batter the calamari had left behind. "There's no reason to drag this out if the ending isn't going to change."

"So, you're going to let a good thing go?" Ford said.

I looked at him and said, "How do you know she's a good thing?"

"Mom says she's a hell of a good thing," Brett replied.

All of them were smiling, nodding, and I knew those assholes had had a conversation behind my back. The moment Gloria had met Jo, she'd probably sent Brett a message, and he had thrown the guys into a group chat to talk about it.

"Listen," I started, "you can lay it on as thick as you want, but it's not going to change anything, so back the fuck off."

"Because you backed off when it came to Kendall?" Dominick said. "How many conversations did we have when I didn't want to date my client's sister?"

"Endless," Ford groaned.

"Do you think, because it's you, this is going to be any different?" Dominick continued. "I don't think so, buddy."

"Why are you pushing so hard for her?" I asked everyone at the table.

"Because you're happy," Brett said. "And I haven't seen you like this in a long time. Sure, travel puts a fucking smile on your face. Sure, you like practicing law and closing million-dollar—hell, billion-dollar deals. But it's not enough, Jenner. Money isn't enough for any of us." He stopped to look at each person around the table. "Guys like us, we need more; we need something we can't get from business ventures, and that's someone to share it with." He nodded toward me. "You know that. And if you don't, you're a fucking moron."

I stayed silent while I processed his words and finally added, "My situation is different."

"How so, my man?" Brett asked. "When James and I got together, I was living in Miami—you know that. Things weren't easy for us, but we made it work. My boys—Jack, Max, hell, even Scarlett—none of them had it easy with their relationships either, distance a factor with each one. And you know

Dominick's deal; it was going to take a fucking unicorn to get him to settle down, and Kendall turned out to be one." He took a drink from his tumbler. "What I'm saying is, we've all been there, buddy. We've all experienced our fair share of shit."

"You're right," I agreed, running each of their stories through my head. "I'm definitely not denying that."

"But it changes nothing—is that what you're saying?" Dominick asked.

I shook my head, sighing. "I don't know ... I just don't fucking know. And I don't even have the time to think about it. My schedule is about to take me on the road, and none of those stops are near Florida."

"What's preventing her from coming to you?" Ford asked.

I laughed. "School. Finals. Graduation. Remember, she's a pup."

"Damn, dude," Dominick exhaled. "I keep forgetting how young she is."

And that had been one of my main points, but they kept dismissing it.

"But she won't be in school for much longer," Brett voiced. "Graduation is in, what"—he took out his phone and looked at the screen—"six weeks or less?"

I nodded. "Yeah, something like that."

"It'll be interesting to see what happens when she's not chained to Miami—where she'll choose to end up," Dominick said.

I thought the same, but I wasn't going to mention that to Jo. I didn't want to influence her decision. I didn't want to put any pressure on her. I wanted her to decide on her own.

And even though home was LA, it didn't sound like she had any intentions of returning.

"Who wants to place a bet?" Ford asked.

No fucking way. This wasn't happening on my watch.

I put my hand up in the air. "If you want to bet on the outcome of my life, do it behind my back, but I'm certainly not going to sit here and listen to the wagers you guys are willing to risk."

"Fair enough," Ford said, grinning at the other boys.

"I'll start the group text right now," Dominick added.

"A bunch of fucking dickheads," I barked at all of them.

Jesus, it was going to be a long fucking night.

Me: How many times have you been back to Gloria's?

Jo: Ha! I'm not going to lie ... it's been tempting.

Jo: It's good to hear from you, Jenner.

Me: I'm in Manhattan for business, flying to Dallas tomorrow, and then onto San Fran.

Jo: My forever wanderlust. Must be magical to see so much in such a short time.

Me: I've seen boardrooms and conference tables and the view from my hotel.

Jo: It's too bad none of those stops are taking you south.

Me: Will you be making any trips home after graduation?

Jo: Don't know. Probably not. I have to plan my next move—remember, that whole job thing? ;)

I stared at the screen. So many thoughts were filling my head, so many replies I wanted to type.

Nothing felt right.

Nothing felt worthy.

Jo: I've missed you.

And then those three words came across my phone.

Ones that had so much meaning.

Ones that resonated so hard because I felt the same.

Damn it, Jo.

Jo: I have to run into class ... I'll talk to you soon.

She ended her text with an emoji. The face with puckered lips and a red heart coming from the mouth.

She was sending a kiss.

And, fuck, I felt it.

SIXTEEN

JOANNA

"I'm losing him," I said to Monica as I crawled onto her bed, snuggling up next to her, our feet matching in the same fuzzy pink socks.

"Impossible."

The emotion in my chest caused everything to tighten. "Not impossible. We haven't had a real conversation in two weeks. Just some awkward text exchanges."

"He's busy, right?" She set her textbook on her nightstand. "Didn't you say he's been traveling nonstop for work?"

"Yeah, his Instagram shows a different location almost every day."

"So, that's it, babe." She tucked a chunk of my hair behind my ear. "He's so occupied; he doesn't even know what city he's waking up in."

"But, Monica ..." I paused, the emotion now sliding into my throat. "Why doesn't he call me before he goes to bed? I mean, the man does sleep at some point. Why doesn't he phone me when he wakes up? If he cared, wouldn't he do at least one of those things?" I fought the tears from coming into my eyes. "Wouldn't he want to hear my voice?"

"Has he ever called during either of those times?"

I shook my head.

She rubbed her toes over mine. "So, he's not a caller. We can forgive him for that, can't we?"

"Or maybe he's just not as into me as I'm into him."

Oh God.

This was so hard.

So many layers, and each one ached in a different way.

She turned toward me and said, "You don't know that. In fact, my gut tells me he's very into you."

"Nope." I held in my breath. "I can feel the change."

"What did Gloria tell you?" She didn't wait for me to respond when she added, "That you have to be patient, so why don't you listen to the woman? She knows all the things. I don't know why you're doubting her."

When we had left her bakery and sat by the water to eat, I had felt so much hope from her words.

But now, that hope was gone.

What happened?

Where did he go?

How did I lose him?

"Call him," Monica said, pulling me from my thoughts. "Or even better, surprise him in LA. You're due for a visit home anyway. God, it's been ages since you've been back."

"How?" I tucked my knees against my chest. "I have an exam Monday morning, bright and early."

"Babe, tomorrow is Friday. You're done with class at what, two? Jump on a plane at three or four. That gives you Friday night, Saturday night, and take a late afternoon flight back on Sunday."

I rested my chin on top of my knees. "I don't even know if he's going to be in LA this weekend."

She lifted my phone off my lap and held it out to me. "There's only one way to find out."

I took it from her, staring at the screen.

Can I pull this off?

Is it even the right thing to do?

As I glanced up, Monica said, "Stop thinking about it and start typing."

She was right.

I found the last text we'd exchanged, my thumbs tapping the screen to work on a message.

Me: Tell me you have something amazing planned for this weekend? I want to live vicariously through your fun, extravagant life while I'm buried in books and papers and exams. Sigh.

Jenner: You're almost at the end, not much longer now.

Me: You want to tell that to the bags under my eyes? They're getting darker and deeper every day, LOL.

Jenner: The last picture you posted on Instagram had no bags—unless we're talking about the Gucci you had on your arm. You look gorgeous, Jo. I'm positive you do right now as well.

"I love him," Monica said as she read over my shoulder. "Like, *looove* him."

I glanced at her. "He didn't take the bait."

"He will. Keep going."

Me: You're sweet. Thank you. I've been admiring your Sedona pics. I've never been. Is it even more beautiful in person?

Jenner: For sure. My phone barely captured the beauty. You need to go. You would love it. But I've got to say, it feels good as hell to be back. It's been a long stretch of travel.

Me: I never thought I'd ever hear you say that.

Jenner: Even a wanderlust—isn't that what you call me?—needs to plant his ass home every once in a while.

Me: Does that mean a Dodgers game and some Nobu on Saturday? ;)

Jenner: I like the way you think.

Me: I'm glad home is being good to you and you're getting what you need right now. Enjoy, Jenner.

Jenner: Get some studying done ... LA misses you.

"And he does too. Trust me," Monica said. "He would give up his left nut to have you there right now."

"You're nuts—"

"Oh, babe, you haven't seen anything yet," she said, interrupting me and grabbing the phone from my hands. She smiled the whole time she pressed the screen, eventually turning it toward me to show me what she had done.

"You didn't just purchase a plane ticket on my phone?"

"Wasn't that the whole point in texting him?" She laughed. "My, my, a little convo with Jenner, and you've suddenly forgotten our fabulous plan."

I felt my eyes widen. "So, I'm flying to LA? Tomorrow?"

She nodded toward her door. "Go pack."

Surprising Jenner wasn't as easy as I'd hoped because, as it turned out, I didn't have his address, and Google wasn't giving it up. My only option was to ask someone for it, which meant I had to reach out to one of his brothers. Dominick was the easiest to find, his profile coming right up on Instagram.

I was so hesitant to send that message.

Maybe Jenner had a life in LA that I knew nothing about. Maybe I was on the verge of walking into an avalanche.

Maybe he wouldn't want me there.

But as Monica had put it, the only way I'd ever know was if I tried, so I sent Dominick a quick note and received a reply almost immediately. He gave me the address and gate code that would gain me access to Jenner's front door. He'd even asked for my flight information and promised Jenner would be home.

As the ride-share drove me to his street, part of me didn't know if this was a good idea, but I still had the car drop me off a block before his house, so his camera wouldn't alert him that there was a car outside. And I still tiptoed to his callbox and quickly pressed the numbers that would open the gate.

I gripped the handle of my suitcase and hurried up to his door, pressing the bell, knowing if he checked the feed from the camera facing me, the secret would be out.

I knew he had, but he still opened the door with the biggest smile on his face.

His eyes traveled the length of me, his teeth finding their way into his lip. "What are you doing here, gorgeous?"

I melted from the way he was gazing at me, flutters exploding in my chest.

"I was in the area." I smiled. "So, I thought I'd stop by."

"Get over here."

God, that sexy voice was something I'd missed.

The moment I was within reach, he wrapped his arms around me and hauled me against his body, his lips instantly slamming onto mine. His kiss was passionate, almost needy. I responded the same way, desperate for his heat, his intensity.

Needing him more than anything.

He finally pulled away, holding my face as he asked, "How

long do I have you for?" He glanced at my suitcase, his stare turning back to me. "More than a night, I hope?"

"I fly back Sunday afternoon."

"The whole weekend," he growled. "Do I have to share you with anyone?"

He was asking about my family, and a pang of guilt hit my stomach.

They didn't even know I was here, and that was so wrong of me. But if I told them, they would want every second of me, and I would have no time left for Jenner.

I couldn't let that happen—not for this trip.

But what made the guilt a tiny bit better was that I would be seeing everyone at graduation, and that was coming up very soon.

"No," I admitted. "You have me all to yourself for the next two nights. And that"—I pointed at my suitcase—"is full of lingerie, so what do you plan on doing with me?"

The look that crossed his face told me he was seconds away from ripping off my clothes.

"One thing is for sure." He lifted me into the air, my legs wrapping around his waist. "I'm not going to waste a fucking second."

My eyes closed as his mouth found mine, and as we moved, I lifted his T-shirt over his head, knowing the second we landed, I was going to pull down his gray sweats, my fingers needing to feel his skin.

But we didn't land.

He held me against a wall, tearing at my clothes, tossing them to the floor until he got me naked. My bare back was pressed to the paint, his lips devouring my neck and cheeks, sweeping as low as my nipples.

I raked my hand through his hair. "Jenner ..." I moaned.

I couldn't find my breath.

I didn't want to.

Getting lost in him was the only way I wanted to spend this weekend—the whole reason I'd flown across the country.

"You feel so good."

He was touching my pussy, rubbing up and down my clit, spreading my wetness, before two of his fingers entered me.

My head banged against the wall, gripping his shoulders, the heat from his skin burning me.

I would never get used to his warmth.

It was now something I thought about so often.

Something I craved.

The way it lit my body, the way it caused such a fire.

Especially when he added a third finger, arching them toward my G-spot.

"Fuck," I cried. "Yes!"

I needed more.

I needed him.

"Fuck me," I begged.

We were moving again, and I suddenly felt a counter beneath me, realizing we were in his kitchen. Using my feet, I dropped his sweatpants to his ankles. Now that nothing separated us, I expected him to thrust inside me.

But that didn't happen.

His mouth found me instead.

Once he bent my knees and spread my legs over the stone, he began to feed on me. He licked my clit, fingering me, pinching my nipples. He wasn't going slow, teasing me like he'd done in the past.

This was fast.

Hard.

Dominant licks that had one purpose.

To make me scream.

And I was doing just that, unable to hold in my moans, unable to stop my legs from shaking.

I gripped the edge of the counter with one hand, pulling his hair with the other. "*Yesss!*" I shouted. "Your fucking tongue."

I couldn't stop the orgasm.

His mouth, his fingers, causing the friction I needed.

And within a few more flicks, I was squirming over the countertop. "Jenner!" I tugged his short strands, rocking my hips forward, my stomach shuddering from the waves that flooded through me. "Oh God."

When I finally stilled, he stood, licking me off his lips. "Jesus ..." He paused, shaking his head. "Watching you come is so fucking sexy."

His hair was ruffled because of me.

His body was ripped.

His cock so hard that the bead at the tip was ready to drip.

"I can't get enough of you."

It was like he was reading my thoughts.

My feelings identical.

And the truth was, I didn't want him to be able to get enough of me.

I wanted him to want me.

I wanted him to need me.

I especially wanted him to crave me.

"Show me, Jenner."

His finger landed on my lips, one that had been inside me, the wetness still there. "Don't move."

He left me on the counter, and when he returned a few seconds later, he was lifting a foil packet toward his mouth, tearing the corner with his teeth. Once the rubber was in his hand, he pumped his cock a few times and said, "Suck it."

I couldn't do that from this position, so I slid off, landing on my feet, and knelt on his kitchen floor.

The moment I had his cock in my hand, I moaned, "God, I missed this."

And I did.

Every time I fingered myself, I thought of his dick.

Every time I pressed my vibrator against my clit, I thought of his mouth.

Jenner was who I fantasized about.

He was the man of my dreams.

And now, as I licked around his crown, tasting the sweet sexiness of his skin, swallowing the drop of pre-cum, those dreams were coming true.

But I needed more.

I surrounded his head, sucking the tip.

"*Yesss*," he hissed. "Fuck."

An urgency had been building inside me since the flight over, and his throbbing hard-on told me he wanted this as much as I did. There was no reason to tease, to take my time. It was all about pleasure at this point.

My hand dropped to his base, meeting my lips in the middle, and I bobbed over the top of him.

Up and down.

I swiveled around his crown with my tongue, diving down to the center of him and back up. With each plunge, he gripped my hair, guiding me deeper.

"Oh fuck," he moaned. "That's it."

There was nothing hotter than this view, than to look up at Jenner from this angle, past his etched muscles and patches of hair to a face that was so incredibly handsome.

And an expression that was filled with pleasure.

Pleasure I was giving him.

I couldn't handle it.

Our eyes connected, his gaze almost rabid, his hips moving with me, every exhale ending in a moan.

All because of me.

Because of my mouth.

"Come here," he ordered, and he pulled me up and placed me back on the counter.

The moment I landed, he rolled the condom on and instantly buried his cock inside me in one quick, hard, satisfying thrust.

"Jenner!"

The fullness was overwhelming in the best possible way.

"You're so fucking tight." He moaned. "Jesus, Jo ... your pussy."

I dug my nails into his shoulders, wrapping my arms around them, holding him tightly against me. "Harder." I urged him deeper, my body spreading for him. "Fuck me harder."

He listened.

He gave me what I wanted.

"Goddamn it, you feel good." He kissed me. "Has your cunt been waiting for this?" His hand lowered, his thumb now brushing my clit. "Waiting for my cock to fill it?" He gently pinched the top, holding it between his fingers. "You're so fucking wet; I could make you come in seconds." He rubbed a little faster. "Is that what you want, Jo? For me to make you come?"

My head tilted back as the climb took hold. "Yes."

The pad of his finger flicked across my clit, sending a hard surge through me. "Tell me how badly you want it." He did it again. "How badly you want me."

My knees bent, my toes curving around the edge of the counter. This new position let him in even deeper. "Jenner ... all I can think about is your cock." I started to shake, the feeling taking over. The fullness. The desire. "I need it." I gasped as he hit that spot so far inside me. "I need you."

He leaned in closer, his lips now by my ear. "Do you want

to come?" He nibbled on my lobe. "Do you want my cock to make you scream so loud that you can't fucking breathe?"

My nails found his skin and stabbed—a reaction to his power, his strength.

His pounding.

"Oh God, Jenner, yes."

His mouth was on my neck, his other hand so busy around my body that I couldn't keep track of its location—my stomach, my nipples, reaching around to grip the side of my ass.

"I should punish you for taking so long to visit me."

If this was a punishment, I would gladly take it every day.

I just didn't want him to stop.

"But your body is showing me how remorseful you are."

He lifted me off the counter and carried me to the couch, bending me over the back of it so my face rested on the seat cushion and my stomach arched over the top. Before I had a chance to even inhale, he was plunging into me.

"*Ahhh!*"

The placement made his massive cock feel even larger.

He reached underneath me, rubbing my clit as he lunged into me, my body picking up right where it had left off.

The build was sparking.

Air completely leaving my lungs when I moaned, "Fuck ... Jenner."

"I don't know how you could feel tighter, but you do."

The only thing I could focus on was his strokes—they consumed me—and the only thing that brought me back to the moment was a hard slap on my ass. A warm tingle followed once I got over the initial jump, causing my back to arch, my butt to point higher in the air.

"You liked that."

I wasn't surprised he could tell. I was pushing my cheeks

into him, my pussy pulsing around his dick, anticipating when he would do it again.

"You want more?"

My skin still stung.

But the slight gust of pain was unexpected and a welcome combination.

"Yes."

He circled my hair around his fist, pulling it so my head lifted off the cushion. "Do you want more, Jo?"

I glanced over my shoulder, giving him my eyes. "Yes." My voice turned even needier, adding, "Lots more."

That earned me another slap, this one on the other side of my ass, sending the heat even higher through me, even more so as he rubbed my clit.

"Jenner!"

This man knew my body like it was his own. He knew how to make me feel sensations I'd never experienced. He knew how to send me so far over the edge that I couldn't return.

That was where I was now—dangling, seconds away, my stomach trying to hold off before the peak came blasting in, exploding, and I was shuddering over the back of the couch.

"*Yesss!*"

"Fuck yes," he roared.

I gripped the pillow, squeezing the cushion into my fingers, holding on because it was the only thing I could do while he slammed into me.

"Fucking come!"

And I was.

I couldn't stop.

The tightening in my muscles, the bursting in my clit—none of it was letting up, and when it finally did, my body reaching the bottom of this long climb, he was pulling out of me. He walked us to the other side of the couch and sat down, turning me around before he set me on his lap.

Reverse cowgirl.

Something I'd never done.

Something I was most definitely going to do right now.

His lips pressed on the outer edge of my ear where he growled, "Fucking ride me."

I bent my knees onto the couch, holding his legs to gain balance. And while I aimed his tip to my pussy, slowly lowering, his hands cupped my breasts.

"Fuck yes," he breathed. "Ride that cock."

He was kneading my nipples, and the pressure got stronger as I rose, increasing even harder as I lowered. There was something about this angle that felt like he was at the end of me, hitting a spot even deeper than before.

I couldn't take a breath.

I was at this overwhelming capacity, and I kept him right there, circling my hips, the tip now rotating inside me.

"Do you feel that?"

All I could do was moan.

"How does it feel when my fucking cock hits it?"

He still spoke to the back of my ear, each word making me quiver.

"I ... can't."

That was all I had, but he seemed to accept it because he said, "Don't let up, Jo. I want you to come just like this."

I wasn't far from that.

He swiped his finger across my clit.

"Oh fuck!" I gasped.

As I lifted off him, gliding up to his tip, he bounced his hips, giving me short, hard thrusts, flicking my clit like his fingers were his tongue.

"Someone's getting so fucking close."

I was so overtaken by these swirls inside my body that my back fell against his chest. But I didn't stop moving. I used his muscles to push off, to grind over him.

Like this was a dance.

His breaths were my music; his fingers were my beat, each tugging at my orgasm.

"Make me come, Jo."

And his words were my fuel.

I held his thighs, sliding to his tip and then burying his dick to the base. With each dip, I moved faster. Pleasure was spreading through me and through him, so obvious in his moans.

"You're getting tighter." His fingers bit into me. "You're going to fucking come again."

Wanting him to feel as good as me, I turned my hips and used my feet, lifting myself up, rocking against him. When he bit the back of my neck, his exhales turning to grunts, I knew he was close.

"Come with me."

The orgasm was already there.

Even more so when two of his fingers started thrumming over my clit in the most achingly erotic way.

"Oh fuck!" I swallowed, sucking in more air. "Jenner!" The tingles were taking over my movements, drawing each one out, causing me to shake so hard that I was bucking over his cock. "Yes!"

"Milk it."

I shuddered.

"I want your fucking cunt to milk my cock."

As we moved together, I screamed, the intensity peaking, and I turned even louder when I felt him lose it, his hips rearing back to plow into me, his fingers biting my skin.

"Ah fuck." His arm wrapped across my chest. "Take it. Take my fucking cum."

I rode through the rest of his orgasm and mine, and when we both stilled, my legs straightened, collapsing all my weight on top of him.

His other arm crossed my chest, and he held me against him. He kissed the back of my neck, his lips stalling on my cheek. "I'll never get tired of your screaming, Jo. Damn it, it's my favorite sound." He turned my face, our lips meeting. "You can start my weekend that way anytime you want."

It was an invitation.

One that made me smile.

"Anytime?"

He nodded, his stare owning me. "If it comes with a greeting like that, yes."

SEVENTEEN

JENNER

Jo and I got into my car without a plan. We were hungry, and the only way we were going to stop devouring each other was if we left my house. So, I just started driving, a part of me knowing where I was going to take her. I'd thought of the destination while we were in the shower, rubbing soap over her fucking amazing body, weighing the different options.

Only one place seemed right.

She knew LA. She'd grown up here. If she was going to return to the West Coast, it was because she wanted to be here, not because of a place I had shown her.

What we needed was a space where we could listen to each other.

But we needed food to do that as well, so I pulled up to the front of the restaurant and shifted into park.

"Nobu?" She laughed, and I remembered she'd mentioned this place in her text. "Of course we're here; it's so you." She smiled. "And so delicious."

"I'm just running in." I opened my door. "It's going to take me a minute. Stay put, all right?"

She nodded, and I left the car running and hurried inside, immediately greeted by the hostess.

"Jenner, hi," Alyssa said, leaning forward across the desk in her low-cut dress. "It's a little early for you, no? I usually don't get to see you until way past sunset."

"Alyssa ..." The only negative of sleeping with the hostess of my favorite restaurant was having to see her every time I came in. "I'm in a rush. Any way I can place an order and you can have the guys quickly put it together?" I reached into my wallet and pulled out my credit card and a hundred-dollar bill, slipping both in her hand.

She glanced down at her palm, a grin moving across her face. "I'm sure I can work my magic. What do you want?"

Because I came here so much, I knew the menu by heart. I grabbed a piece of paper from the top of the desk and a pen, and I jotted down my order.

She reviewed it and said, "I'll be back."

While I waited, I took out my phone, scanning through the messages that had come in.

Dominick: How do you like your surprise?
Me: You're behind this? Jesus, I couldn't figure out why you were so adamant about where I was headed after work or how she got to my front door. Now, it makes sense.
Dominick: Why are you texting me? Shouldn't you be busy as hell right now?
Me: I'm picking up food and taking her on a little adventure.
Dominick: Stop ... you sound like a man in love.
Me: Not this again.
Dominick: Just stating the obvious, buddy. Have fun.

"Here you go, Jenner," Alyssa said.

I shoved my phone into my pocket and signed the receipt,

taking my credit card from her and the two large bags. "I appreciate this, Alyssa."

"My pleasure," she sang.

I hurried out the door before she could say another word and placed the bags in the back of my car before I got into the driver's seat.

"Food to go," Jo said. "This keeps getting more interesting."

I rolled down our windows, letting the breeze in, and I put my hand on her thigh as I started the drive. There was always traffic along this route, but because of the time, we missed the big rush and got here faster than normal, the scent of the ocean filling the car as I pulled into the driveway.

Jo looked at the large three-story home through the windshield. "Your parents' house?"

"Yes."

"Man"—she shook her head—"they have exquisite taste." She slowly gazed at me. "I'm so happy you brought me here."

"You haven't even seen the house yet."

"It's the thought ..."

I squeezed her leg, giving her a quick kiss, and said, "Come on. We have a ton of sushi to eat."

I got the bags from the back of the car, and she followed me to the front, where I typed in a code, the door unlocking to allow us inside. As we made our way through, I grabbed a bottle of red from the large glass wine room my parents had built in the living room. Once I had an opener and two glasses, I stopped at the closet to get a blanket before we made our way outside. We walked across the large deck and down the stairs that ended in the sand. Since it was high tide, I set everything a few feet from the water, giving us enough space so we wouldn't have to move if it grew any closer.

"Had I known you were coming, I would have done this differently," I told her.

"Differently?" With the blanket down and the containers now spread about, the chopsticks and napkins next to them, she began to take off all the lids. "How so?"

I lifted the lip of the metal seal, pulling it off the wine bottle. "There are companies that do these kinds of spreads, and they're a hell of a lot better at it than I am. I would have hired one."

She clasped my arm as I pulled out the cork. "Stop. This couldn't be more perfect."

"You're sweet."

"Maybe, but I'm serious, Jenner." A smile warmed her face. "I love this so much."

I needed to taste her.

I held the bottle to the side and leaned forward, halting inches from her lips. The breeze was blowing through her hair, her long strands tickling my face. I cupped her cheek, holding her steady, the same wind sending me her perfume. Her fall scent of cinnamon and pumpkin mixed with the salty air, the combination so fucking perfect.

"Jo ..." I whispered, my eyes closing, breathing her in. I stayed like that for just a few beats, finally connecting us. "*Mmm*," I growled, the flavor of her lips even more enticing. "Fuck me, you're dangerous."

She laughed. "That's what I've been saying about you since we met."

I released her and poured the wine into two glasses.

"What should we toast to?" she asked, holding hers up in the air. "Oh wait, I know." Her large Gucci bag wasn't far from where she was sitting, and she reached inside and pulled out a small box. "How about to the most incredible dessert we've ever had?"

I chuckled as I looked at the familiar packaging. "Is that what I think it is?"

"You mean, did I stop by the bakery to get you a half-moon cookie and some chocolate-coconut fudge?" She winked. "Maybe."

"You fucking didn't."

"Gloria says hello." She clinked her glass against mine and took a drink. "I have to admit, seeing you smile is one of my favorite things ever."

I held the glass against the blanket, not bringing it up to my lips. "I can't believe you went there for me."

And I couldn't believe she'd come all the way to LA, knowing that with school winding down, she had a lot of shit on her plate.

"I know how much you enjoy her baking," she said, using her fingers to pop a piece of sushi into her mouth. "It was the least I could do."

I ran my hand across her calf, pulling her foot onto my lap. "Thank you."

She nodded and took another bite. "Jenner, the house is as beautiful as I envisioned." Her stare shifted up to the glass windows that aligned the back of the home. "I remember when we talked about it, and I had this picture in my head—this is it." Her gaze returned to me. "It's unfortunate you can't unplug here, that your parents don't let you."

I sighed, reaching for a set of chopsticks to pick up the nigiri. "They have no problem doing that when they come on the weekends. My father goes on bike rides, and my mother walks the beach. Their chef prepares them three meals a day, and they eat up there"—I pointed at the patio—"where they watch the waves between bites." I chewed the savory tuna belly and took a drink of wine. "But when we're here as a family, it's all business."

"I can see how your parents can unwind here." She stared out at the beach. "It's so gorgeous. Magical even." She lifted her set of chopsticks and took a few pieces of the yellowtail sashimi that was peppered with jalapeño. "It's funny; I spent tons of time in Malibu as a kid, even as a teenager. When my friends and I turned old enough to drive, we'd come here every weekend. I didn't appreciate it then. It was just a beach, nothing special—water, sand, sun. But now, it's something." Her eyes were on me. "Or maybe it's just being here with you."

I observed her taking a deep breath.

"Can I ask you something?"

I slipped off her shoe, rubbing the back of her foot. "Of course."

"How many women have you brought here?"

I kneaded my knuckles into her arch. "None."

"Seriously?" She tilted her head. "Not a single one?"

"No."

I watched that news settle into her, hit her in a way she wasn't expecting.

"And to be honest, a woman has never stayed the weekend at my house." I licked across my bottom lip. "And they certainly don't have the code to my gate." I could see her thoughts when I continued, "Does this keep getting more interesting?"

"Yep." She took a sip. "That's kind of an understatement."

The breeze fed me more of her scent right before I said, "You're different, Jo."

Admitting that out loud wasn't as hard as I'd thought. Maybe that was because I'd been thinking it for so long, fighting those words every time they tried to resonate.

She wedged her wine into the sand, leaving the chopsticks in the container. "I've never been different before."

"I can tell you don't want to be ordinary. You haven't since the moment I met you."

"Because I'm the fool who went up to your suite ten minutes after meeting you. You're right; that's hardly ordinary."

I squeezed her toes, punishing her for that wicked statement. "Because you showed me who you really are. I couldn't fucking resist you, and I charmed you into sleeping with me."

She grinned. "Is that what went down?"

"Yes." I pulled her foot until she was close enough to pick up and put on my lap, wrapping my arms around her. "We both know I didn't give you a choice. You were either walking up to my room or I was carrying you."

She leaned her back into my chest, and I could hear the smile in her breathing.

We stayed quiet for several moments until she said, "Would you ever buy a place out here? Somewhere to slow down—you know, a space that forces you to unplug?"

"The air is my second home. I would hate to think I'd have to come back to the same place all the time, month after month, when there are so many spots I still want to visit."

"Ah, but you're looking at it all wrong." She nuzzled her face against my neck. "This wouldn't be travel. This would be an escape. Hotels are fabulous, but they don't feel like home. This is somewhere that can comfort you, that will give you the extras, like the fuzzy, warm robe you take the time to put on after your shower, the high-end cookware you use to make yourself a meal, the hardcover you finally find the time to sit back and read. Then, after a couple days, you hop on the plane and travel like normal."

The idea of a second home wasn't foreign. Dominick had an investment property. My parents had several. I certainly saw the attraction and had considered it in the past.

I pressed my lips against the top of her head. "The only thing is, if I don't go to the house often enough, I'd feel like I was cheating on her ... and we already know I have a problem with commitment."

She shook her head. "I can't with you ..."

I held her tighter, staring out onto the ocean. "This is beautiful, but it's not a view I'd want."

"What sight would you rather have outside your windows?"

"The mountains." That was the scenery I often saw in my mind—the lush hills, covered in fresh snow or fall foliage, the fresh air. "Park City."

"Utah is your special place, huh?"

There was something about Jo's scent that reminded me of that town. "I've been many, many times. It never gets old. I never get tired of it. In fact, I almost crave going there. Have you been?"

"No."

I exhaled. "There's nothing like it."

"Then, you need to go house shopping if you love it there so much."

I laughed, but interestingly enough, she could be onto something. Even if it was just for investment purposes, it wouldn't necessarily be a bad idea to add a home to my portfolio. The interest a deduction my accountant would appreciate. A place to crash during Walter's build-out, which I'd be visiting almost monthly during construction.

"I'm going to be doing some business there very soon," I told her. "Maybe I'll look at some places while I'm out there."

"Perfect idea."

I turned her face, giving me access to her eyes. "Why are you so for this?"

She ran her hand over my cheek. "I can't pretend to know what your days are like and the stress that's involved with your job. But I can hear it in your voice, and I can see it in your eyes. Everyone needs a moment to catch their breath, Jenner. Even you. You say you do that in the air and when you travel, that you separate yourself from work"—her fingers rubbed under my chin—"but part of me really doubts that. I get the feeling you maximize the plane's Wi-Fi until the second you land. Even right now, there's something on your mind."

She saw right through every shield.

But work wasn't the only thing on my mind.

At this moment, Jo was what I couldn't get out of my head, taking up more space than I had ever allowed.

"And you think I'd be able to shut that all off if I had a second house?"

"If it was a designated area for that, yes. You would have to make a conscious effort, like putting it on your calendar, because unplugging doesn't come naturally to you."

Her hand lowered to my heart when I said, "You think you have me all figured out."

"I know you better than you think I do." Her lips tugged but didn't make it into a full smile. "You might think you're so much older than me, but you're only in your early thirties, and burnout is a real thing—I've witnessed it firsthand. Don't let it happen to you, where you start resenting law."

When she lifted her fingers, I kissed them. "Are you worried about me?"

"I just want you to be the best version of yourself." She adjusted her position across my lap, her stare intensifying once she settled. "To make that happen, we all need to make improvements in our life—myself most definitely included. If yours is a mental vacation that's going to cost you a few million, something tells me you can afford it."

"The best version of yourself."

A woman had never said that to me before.

They were gone before they ever had the chance.

But was Jo staring at the best version of me?

I'd accomplished a hell of a lot over my career. I had financial freedom—something I'd never dreamed of achieving this young. I had a roster of clients who made my competition seethe in jealousy. One of the top law firms in the country would one day be handed to my brothers and me. I'd seen so many parts of the world that I had connections in almost every country.

But there was one area where I lacked.

One part of my life that my brothers and friends always gave me shit about.

I didn't have anyone to share my success with.

With my hand now cupping her cheek, I whispered, "You're right. About all of it."

"I know." She laced her fingers through mine. "And I know that wasn't easy for you to say."

I gazed at her lips, an aching hunger working its way through me.

I didn't just want to kiss them.

I wanted to be able to stare at them every day.

I wanted to know they belonged to only me.

"Say what else is on your mind, Jenner."

I raked my other hand through her hair. Her blue eyes were screaming like usual, but the color seemed even louder right now.

"You, Jo." I traced a line down her mouth. "You're on my mind ... and it doesn't seem like you're leaving."

She took a long, deep breath. "Do you want me to?"

Now, both hands were on her cheeks, locking her on my lap. "No."

EIGHTEEN

JOANNA

"Babe, why are you crying?" Monica said the moment I walked into her room, the textbook falling from her hands as she extended her arms in the air. "Come here. Hug me?"

I took a seat next to her on the edge of the bed. "I got it, Mon."

Her eyes widened. "Your period? Your final GPA? Help a girl out. What are you talking about?"

"The job—not the one at the gym or with the art dealer. I'm talking about *the* job. The one I've been hoping for. The one I didn't think I had a chance in getting because I'd heard nothing and then *bam*."

A softness spread over her face as the realization hit her. "The job, *job*?"

A tear dripped into my mouth as I nodded.

"Oh my God, Jo." She pulled me into her arms, hugging me. "I knew it was just a matter of time before it was yours." She released me but gripped both of my hands. "You got it, babe, like you really got it." There was as much emotion in her eyes as there was in mine. "I know what this means to you."

And she did. She was the only person I'd talked to about this.

The only person who knew how badly it would hurt if it didn't come through.

The only person who knew that this was my dream.

"I can't believe it," I whispered, the emotion clogging my throat, my chest aching from the news. "I seriously can't believe it, Monica."

She squeezed harder. "I can. You've worked your ass off for this. You deserve it." She wiped one of my tears away. "When do you start?"

"Two weeks." My lips pulled into a smile. The stress of that time frame and everything I needed to do was hitting me in a whole different way. "Which means I have fourteen days to find a place to live and move to LA and"—I paused as I shook her hands—"convince you to move with me."

"Me?" She huffed. "LA?"

"You can't honestly think I'm going across the country without you ..." I waited for her to reply, and she didn't. "Besides, the queen of fashion needs to be in LA, where all the celebrities live. Think of the jobs you could score with some of the established stylists and designers. Mon, you'd kill it out there."

She turned her head, giving me her profile. "Oh God, my heart." She swallowed. "Is this really happening? Or am I going to wake up and realize it was all a dream?"

"Oh, it's happening and probably a little faster than either of us would like." I took a breath, the tightening pushing the emotion away. "We need to book movers and find a place to live and—the list is endless."

And that was only the logistics of relocating.

The job itself created a whole separate list of things I needed to do, one that involved many promises, along with a test that I still needed to pass.

It would be easier to take the position at the gallery or the gym. At least there, I knew what to expect. I would almost be my own boss.

I could stay in Miami.

But neither of those positions would make me happy.

They weren't what I had been working so hard for.

And they wouldn't bring me any closer to Jenner.

Jenner ...

Oh God.

I shook my head, returning to the moment, clenching my best friend's hands. "So, it's a yes? You're coming with me to LA?"

She bounced on the mattress. "Hell yes." And then she sighed as she added, "But how am I going to afford the rent? Miami is expensive enough. LA is even worse."

"We'll figure it out." I nodded at the Starbucks cup sitting on her nightstand. "And we'll get you a fancy espresso machine to save you the ten dollars a day."

Her eyes grew. "Wait. That's how much coffee is there?"

I laughed and rested down next to her, our heads touching as we shared a pillow. "I can't believe we graduated, like, four seconds ago, and now, this is all unfolding."

"I can't either," she said.

My parents had only left a little while ago, the whole weekend a whirlwind of family and friends and celebrating, partying and tons of food.

The only thing missing was Jenner.

For many different reasons, I hadn't invited him to come. The timing just wasn't right for him to be here and to hang with my whole family. And knowing he had to go to London for a business trip made the decision even easier on me. But the lack of an invite hadn't stopped him from sending an amazingly thoughtful gift.

A suitcase from Louis Vuitton.

Maybe the wanderlust in him wanted me to join him on the road.

Maybe he just wanted me to travel in style.

Or maybe he was hoping I was going to pack up that suitcase and move to California.

Whatever his reasoning was, he'd kept it to himself, and I lavished him in every kind of thank-you I could think of—FaceTime sex, texts, and several phone calls.

"So, how does this work?" Monica asked. "Do we find an apartment online? And then book movers?"

My girl was from Florida, only thirty minutes away from here, but had lived in the dorms her freshman year to get the whole college experience. That was how we'd met. The only other time she'd moved was when we got our apartment sophomore year, and we'd lived here ever since.

"It would probably be easier and more cost-effective if we sold the big things, like our couch and beds, and just bought new stuff there. Then, we can—"

My voice cut off as my phone chimed from my back pocket. I lifted my butt off the bed to grab it, reading the message on the screen.

Jenner: I want to show you Utah. How about you meet me there next week? I'm going for work, but I'll extend the trip, and it can just be you, me, and the mountains for a few days.

My heart clenched as I read his message for a second time.

And a third.

He was asking me to go on a vacation with him?

To the place that meant the most to him, to the place where he was even thinking about buying a second home.

My hands shook as Monica tugged my arm, pulling at the phone so she could see the screen.

"That man is so irresistible; I can't stand it," she said. "First, luggage. Now, a trip." She leaned up on her elbow to look at me. "You know how huge this is, don't you? He's taking things to the next level."

"I don't know about that," I whispered. I felt her eyes boring through me, so I turned my head to face her. "But yes"—I swallowed—"it's huge."

She stared at me silently. "Isn't this what you want? More from Mr. Delicious? He must be losing his mind over you moving to LA."

"He doesn't know."

"What? You haven't told him?"

I took a deep breath, and just as I was exhaling, her hand went to my shoulder, shaking me.

"Girl, this is what you've been waiting for—for the two of you to be in the same city. Why aren't you calling him right now and screaming the news?"

My chest was so tight; I was having a hard time breathing. "I just found out, Mon. You're the first person I wanted to tell."

"And you don't want to tell Jenner?"

I swallowed again, my throat even tighter this time. "Of course I do." I pushed against my chest, trying to loosen it. "Maybe I'll wait until Utah and surprise him with it."

"I can see it now ..." Her eyes closed, and she continued, "The mountains in the background, the two of you cuddling close, the news trickling into his ear, and then the biggest smile on his face before he grabs you and lays one on you." Her lids opened, and she looked at me. "Okay, I approve. That's the perfect time to tell him."

"I like the plan," I said, sitting up, my feet falling to the floor. "Now, I need to go be productive and find us a place to live."

"Don't forget, you need to shower too. The girls are coming over soon, and we're heading to South Beach tonight."

I nodded. "Right." I moved over to her doorway. "You know, on second thought, I'm going to run out for a little bit. Don't worry; I'll be back in time."

Her brows rose. "You're leaving?" When I didn't immediately answer, she added, "Where's all the weirdness coming from?"

I shook my head. "Nowhere. I'm not acting weird. I'm fine, really." I paused. "I'm just suddenly very overwhelmed with all the things." I forced a smile. "I'll be back, and then we can celebrate all this epic news."

"I'm just as overwhelmed. I get it, babe, but I promise, this is going to be amazing. This is what you've wanted—what you've *always* wanted—and now, you'll have Jenner and me by your side."

"You're right."

I couldn't say any more.

So, I lifted my hand and waved and grabbed my keys on the way out. In my head, I told myself I was just going to get some treats for my friends tonight.

But I knew that wasn't the reason I was driving to the bakery.

The truth was, I needed to talk to Gloria.

And I swore she could sense that the moment I walked through her door.

"Jo," she said, looking up from the newspaper she was reading. "It's so nice to see you. How did graduation go?"

The last time I had been here, buying Jenner some fudge before my trip to LA, I'd updated her on school.

But I couldn't even imagine talking about that now.

As I got closer, the lines etched in her forehead grew deeper, and her eyes turned worrisome.

I stopped at the counter, placing my hands on the glass.

She immediately placed her palms on top of my hands. "That boy doesn't get many surprises in his life. You showing up to LA was one."

I tried to breathe. "Yes." I attempted a smile despite how I was feeling. "We really had the best time."

"I know." She stayed quiet as she watched me, her thumbs grazing my skin. "He's about to be in for another surprise ... isn't he?" Her hands rose to my forearms, clasping them. "Oh, honey ..."

NINETEEN

JENNER

"You saved the best for last," I said to Walter as we climbed into the SUV, the driver bringing us to the final lot in Park City. "I think you're going to love this one."

Walter had narrowed his search down to three pieces of land—ironically, the same ones that I'd chosen for him. There was absolutely nothing wrong with the two we had already seen today. They were beautiful, but they weren't built on the edge of a mountain like the one we were approaching.

This one had something the others didn't.

This had a factor that was beyond wow.

"You think I'll like it more than the last two?" he inquired.

I nodded. "Much more."

Walter opened the folder in his hand, pulling out the specs. "It's also thirty percent higher than the others."

"And well worth it."

The SUV began to slow as we approached.

Walter glanced up as he said, "When you add in the cost of the build-out, that would make this one of my most expensive properties. Not to mention, the amenities we're going to offer, which increases things another twenty percent."

"Amenities that will make you outshine your competition."

I'd reviewed his preliminary plans and made several suggestions of my own, knowing how much they would add financially. I also knew they would make his hotel more enticing than the others in the area, appealing to vacationers who came to this section of the country.

"Like I said, Walter, it's all going to pay off." I nodded toward the window, the view of the lot directly outside. "Can you picture it?"

He stared through the glass for several moments. "God, that's a beauty." He exhaled, shaking his head. "The pictures didn't do it justice." His eyes connected with mine. "You're right."

"Come on. You need to walk the grounds to fully appreciate this space."

We climbed out and moved to the side of the road, peering over the edge of the cliff that showed the road we'd taken to get up here.

"Envision this in the fall and winter," I said to him. "Everything bursting in color and then covered in white."

"A goddamn winter wonderland."

I chuckled. "With several two-bedroom penthouses that'll each get you upward of five thousand a night."

"Music to my fucking ears." He turned, walking toward the center of the massive lot. "This one has it all over the other two."

Even though the land was covered in trees, which would be quite the undertaking to get it all leveled and paved, it was obvious how special this property was.

"Imagine the building protruding out the side of this mountain"—I pointed toward the rock where the base of the hotel would sit—"shaped in a way where every room would have a view of this magnificent landscape."

"What else do you see?"

We'd played this game before; therefore, I knew how it worked. Walter wanted my vision beyond a legal standpoint, and he paid me a heavy sum for it.

"I see fire being the main element, mountain-chic decor. The scent of s'mores the moment you walk into the lobby with the crackling of wood thrumming in the background. When they enter their rooms, I want them to feel like they're in a high-end cabin with heated floors and gas fireplaces, bedding that doesn't just tuck them in but cuddles them." I paused, thinking of my conversation with Jo. "This hotel isn't just going to be a place where they come and ski. It's going to be a place where they come to reset and unplug. Where they find themselves ..."

The sound of tires spinning across the rocky gravel drowned out my voice, and I turned to the SUV that was pulling up a few feet away.

Walter looked at me and said, "My guest has arrived."

"The realtor?"

Since this was our first walk-through, Walter hadn't wanted the realtor to come with us.

He didn't want to be sold.

He wanted to make a decision and then call in the realtor to draw up the paperwork.

"No, it's my newest employee," he said. "I asked her to join us. She just flew in."

The driver got out and opened the door to the backseat.

There were too many trees blocking the space between us, but I saw a pair of high heels hit the ground and the sound of the door shutting. As she moved past the tall, thick trunks, I could see lean legs and a trim waist, tits that weren't any bigger than my hands. Long black hair that trickled past her shoulders, hitting her elbows as she walked.

I held my fucking breath as she turned at the path, a feeling blasting through my stomach when she faced us.

A feeling I hadn't at all been prepared for.

My stare moved up her face—her perfect, pouty lips and eyes that were screaming blue, now connected with mine.

Jo.

What the hell is she doing here?

The Gucci bag that I'd given to her dangled on her shoulder, and she gripped it as she came over to us.

If anyone looked at her in this moment, they would see confidence, charisma. A woman who was about to blow our minds with whatever came out of her mouth.

But I knew that smile that was lifting across her lips. It was her timid, uncertain expression. She wore it whenever we talked about us and whenever we were outside the airport, one of us flying home.

Something is going on here, something I haven't figured out yet.

If Jo had landed a job, why hadn't she told me?

Working for Walter was a hell of an accomplishment. The hires I'd met in the past weren't recent college graduates. Walter looked for experience, in-depth knowledge of the market, employees who could escalate his brand. He didn't want numbers on his team; he wanted quality.

Not that Jo wasn't capable of bringing that, but she didn't have the real-world experience that he was usually after.

I certainly wasn't going to let my largest client know I had a thing with his newest employee. He knew how much I slept around. I didn't want him to think she was someone I'd fucked in a restroom. That wouldn't help her career or her longevity at Spade Hotels.

So, when she came to a stop, standing between Walter and me, I said to Walter, "Are you going to introduce me?"

He looked at Jo and put his arm around her shoulders, grinning at her in a way that made my fucking stomach hurt. Touching her in a way that made me question everything I was witnessing.

He finally looked at me, his smile even larger now. "Jenner, I don't believe you've ever met Joanna ..."

Joanna?

The hurt in my stomach was still there.

But so was a deep churning, one that circled with fucking claws.

Especially as she gazed at me, our eyes fucking locking, the pain increasing tenfold.

Walter's grip strengthened around her, the movement causing Jo's shoulders to shake as he added, "My daughter."

TWENTY

JOANNA

As I watched Jenner register the news, my stomach caught on fire. I reached into the pockets of my jacket, putting pressure on my navel just so I wouldn't throw up.

I didn't know what I had been thinking. I should have found a way to tell him sooner.

And I'd wanted to. Every time we were together, the guilt had nagged at me.

But it was easier to just keep going, to keep him in the dark, especially since we weren't in a relationship, and I didn't know if we would ever be in one. And then my trip to LA happened and things between us started to change. The trip brought us closer together, and the guilt thickened.

I didn't want to ambush Jenner.

Not like this.

I was going to tell him when I flew to Utah tomorrow, breaking everything down, sharing that my father had finally offered me a position. But Dad had called this morning, saying he needed me to meet him in Utah, and I knew he was going there with Jenner. Once I hung up with him, I tried to find my breath and the courage to call Jenner and do the right thing, warning him so this wouldn't happen.

When I finally made that call, he didn't answer.

He had already been flying with my father.

And, now, as we stood here, Jenner's eyes were boring through me.

His posture stiff, his expression agitated.

His hands clenching, like he was dreaming about the moment he was going to spank me.

Oh God.

"Joanna, I want you to meet Jenner Dalton," my father said, continuing the introductions. "Jenner's the best attorney in the country—and I know that for a fact. I've gone through plenty of them over the years."

Jenner's hand extended through the air, and mine did as well, meeting him in the middle.

He didn't gentle his grip; he didn't lower the intensity of his gaze. "It's nice to meet you, *Joanna*."

He emphasized my name, like it was a slap across the face.

I deserved that.

I deserved even more.

"Likewise," I responded. "But please, call me Jo. My parents are the only ones who call me Joanna."

"And pumpkin," my father added.

Trying to make light of the situation, I laughed. "That might be pushing it a little too far, Dad."

"Jo, then ..." Jenner said, releasing me but his stare didn't.

It stayed on me.

It owned me.

It ... punished me.

My father held my shoulders even tighter, shifting me so he could look at my face. "Jenner, this is my pride and joy right here. She just graduated from the University of Miami a few weeks ago with honors, a dual degree in marketing and business."

"Congratulations," Jenner said. "That's quite an accomplishment."

He was flat as he spoke, a robot moving through the necessary motions.

Meanwhile, my body hummed with anxiety.

"She's worked her tail off to earn a position at my company," my father said. "Her first assignment—or first test, I should say—is to assess the potential of our newest property. With all the money millennials are inheriting, kids her age are traveling as much as you and your friends, Jenner; therefore, Joanna's opinion, in this current market, is as valuable as yours."

Even though my father was bragging about me, he was drawing a line between our ages.

I felt like a child, sitting at the kids' table.

As I focused on Jenner, I was sure he was thinking the same thing.

In fact, I was sure he was thinking many things.

Each layer showed in his expression.

And each one made me want to die.

"Joanna, you've been to enough of my properties to know what best represents my brand," my father said. "Why don't you tell us what you think of this lot?"

I'd spent the entire plane ride studying the three properties my father had chosen along with all the other high-end hotels in the area. I knew the facts. I knew what was right in front of me.

This was the moment where I left the kids' table and proved my worth.

I looked away from Jenner, his stare not helping my nerves, and I moved out from under my father's arm, glancing through the dense trees in every direction.

"I'm basing my opinion on the photographs that you sent over since I haven't seen the other two properties in person, but from the pictures, I have to say, this piece of land is certainly the best." I walked a little farther toward the road, hearing the men follow behind me.

"For one, the elevation is outstanding. According to the city's property records, no other hotel in the area is as high as this. People of all ages—millennials, baby boomers—we like height; we like views. We like to feel as though we're on top of the world."

I scanned the vast peaks that surrounded us, the way the valleys dipped, the mountain range that extended as far as the eye could see. "Now, if we're talking structure, your competition leans toward boring, traditional, block-style facades that blend with the landscape of the town. Of course, they're not built into the side of a mountain, so their base is already bland. Not us. There's an expected level of luxury and uniqueness with the Spade brand, and having viewed the preliminary specs, I see that in the exterior of the building, and I know I'll feel that in the interior."

I took several more steps, standing at the edge now. "All the places to currently stay, the large and boutique-style hotels, are down there, Dad—I'm sorry, Walter." I pointed over the cliff. "But you're up here, seven thousand feet above sea level. As for the other two properties you're interested in, they don't have that advantage. They're beautiful in their own way, but they're average."

I took a final scan of the area. "Not a single thing about this strip of land is average. It screams wealth and exclusivity. It has the most breathtaking views, and it doesn't just bring vacationers to the mountains; it puts them directly on one. And that, in my opinion, is why this is the one."

The men stayed quiet, as though they were processing what I had just voiced.

Eventually, my father looked at Jenner and said, "She's going to be good, isn't she?"

"She already is," Jenner replied.

"If you want to fly with me to LA, the jet can then take you back to Miami," my father said to me as the SUV parked outside the private airport terminal.

My dad was looking at me from the front seat while I sat in the back, next to Jenner, whose eyes had avoided me the entire drive over here.

"No, thank you, Dad. I booked a commercial flight home."

The flight just wasn't scheduled to take off today ... or tomorrow.

A detail my father definitely didn't need to know about.

"What about you?" my father said to Jenner. "Are you still planning on looking at houses tomorrow?"

Jenner nodded. "I meet with the realtor in the morning."

"Then, I'll see the both of you in LA." He glanced at me. "The move is still on schedule, about a week away?"

"Yes." My heart clenched as I realized Jenner was now learning about my relocation. This wasn't the way I'd wanted him to find out, but since I couldn't stop my father from talking about it, I leaned forward and kissed him good-bye. "Monica and I have all the details worked out. There's no reason why I shouldn't be able to report to the office on the date we agreed on."

"Excellent," he replied. "Text me when you get home. I love you." He glanced at Jenner, shaking his hand. "Good luck on the house search." And then he got out and walked into the terminal.

The driver slipped back into the car once he closed Dad's door and said to us, "Where can I bring you?"

Silence simmered between us, and I slowly gazed at Jenner. "We need to talk."

Air huffed from his mouth. "You think?" He glanced away from me and gave the driver the name of his hotel.

As soon as the SUV started moving, I couldn't handle just the sound of the road. I needed Jenner to understand. I needed to at least explain myself.

I turned my body toward him, reaching for his hand. "Jenner ..."

He glared at me. "Not now."

He wanted to wait until we were alone to have this conversation.

I could respect that.

But that didn't mean it was easy, staying quiet the rest of the ride until we pulled up to the entrance of the hotel. He waited for the driver to unload his suitcase, and once Jenner was gripping the handle, he walked into the lobby. My stomach ached as I stood behind him at the front desk, especially when he requested only one room key.

He said nothing as he walked by me on the way to the elevator, but I followed him inside, waiting for his eyes to land on me.

But they didn't.

He wouldn't even glance in my direction.

The door slid open at the fifth floor, and we walked down the hallway to his suite. The moment he stepped in, he left his suitcase right by the door and went over to the minibar.

He had a few gulps of whiskey down his throat when he finally faced me. His back was pressed against the counter. He looked so incredibly handsome in his black suit, but it was his eyes that haunted me.

That made the tears instantly want to flow.

His chest rose and fell several times, moving so fast when he said, "Did you know?"

I dropped my Gucci bag into the nearest chair, holding the hard, sturdy wooden back. "Not at first."

His teeth ground together. "When did it dawn on you?"

My eyes burned from trying to hold back the tears, my throat on fire as I swallowed. "Lawyer, LA, Jenner—I put it together."

"So, you fucking knew ..."

"Jenner—"

"You lied to me."

"No." I shook my head. "I just didn't tell you, but I wanted to—"

"What the fuck is the difference?"

My heart was beating so fast that I was having a hard time talking, but I needed to get the words out, and I needed to get my shit together. Now more than ever.

I took a deep breath and said, "Please listen to me. Let me explain myself."

I didn't know how much longer my knees were going to support me, so I walked over to the large bed and sat on the edge, gripping the blanket between both hands.

"My father has spoken about you before, brief mentions where he would discuss projects you two were completing together, but that's it, nothing more. You have a memorable name, and while we were chatting in the sportsbook, I assumed it was you. But to be honest, I was already so invested at that point that I certainly wasn't going to ruin the moment and tell you who I was and derail the chemistry exploding between us. And then we were suddenly hanging out nonstop in Vegas, and the opportunity sort of got lost. I didn't expect to hear from you once I got back to Miami." I took several deep breaths, remembering the pain I'd felt when I left his room, when I'd cried in Monica's arms. "But you came to visit, and things started to progress and—"

"And you should have fucking told me." He took a drink. "During any of those moments—either of my trips to Miami, when you came to LA, when I took you to my fucking parents' house—you should have said who you are." He ran his hand through his hair. "Do you realize your father is my largest client? Do you know what he would do to me if he knew I was fucking his daughter?"

Fucking his daughter.

A description that was so cold.

So emotionless.

"I should have told you," I admitted, squeezing the comforter so hard that I swore the down was giving me rug burn. "I'm sorry. I wish you hadn't found out this way. I wish you hadn't been in the air this morning when I tried to call you and tell you, but I can't change how this all went down." I fought my eyes, refusing to let them drip, negotiating with my chest to let up a little.

"But if I'm really being honest, I don't know that I would have told you in Vegas even if I could do this all over because then you never would have slept with me, and then I never would have known what this feels like." My voice softened. "What you feel like. What it's like to be in l—"

"Don't say it."

It felt like he'd cut off all my air.

My lungs wheezing for more.

"Don't even think it, Jo, because those days are gone." He downed the rest of his glass and reached into the fridge for another bottle. He poured it into his tumbler and held it against his chest, not too far from his lips. "You're Walter's daughter. You're so fucking off-limits—on a level I don't think you can even understand. What happened between us, whatever was starting, it's over."

"What?" My stomach was stabbing, to the point where I knew I was going to be sick. "Because I didn't tell you?"

"Because your last name is Spade." He laughed, although I could tell he didn't think this was funny. "Why the hell do you have Jo Cartwright on your Instagram account? Did you change it just for me, so I wouldn't figure it out?"

He really thought I was a liar.

That I would go to any lengths to manipulate him.

"Cartwright is my middle name, which is my mother's maiden name, and what I prefer to go by. Spade comes with attention, with assumptions, and I don't want to be the next Paris Hilton, Jenner. I wanted to go to college across the country and fit in just like everyone else."

It took him several seconds to respond, and when he did, he said, "Your humbleness changes nothing. You still didn't tell me who you were, who your father was. And now that you work for Spade Hotels, you're my client too."

"I'm just in entry-level marketing. I'm not your client, and we won't be working together."

"Aren't you here in Utah?"

I released the bed to push against my chest, hoping the pressure would stop my heart from breaking. "Yes."

"Are you going to be assisting your father with the build-out?"

I nodded.

"Then, we're working together."

I let the news pulse through me, my body reacting in so many different ways that I didn't know whether to cover my face or look for a trash can. But before I did anything, I needed to get this out. "I was going to tell you tomorrow, when I flew in. I had the whole thing planned out in my head—how I was going to explain Vegas, how I was going to surprise you with my move to LA." My head dropped, and I stared at the carpet. "I knew you were going to be angry. I knew it was going to cause a fight." I finally glanced up. "But I didn't expect this."

He sat in one of the chairs and crossed his legs. He was closer than before, but he still felt a mile away. "I don't think you understand the relationship I have with your father. I've worked with him since the start of my career. He was one of my very first clients. We don't have a personal relationship, meaning we don't travel together, I don't meet the women he dates, nor did I know much about you other than the few times he's referred to his daughter—his pride and joy, Joanna—but I respect him." His legs uncrossed, his hands and the whiskey resting between them as he exhaled. "I wouldn't do anything to jeopardize the trust he has in me."

I sucked in a mouthful of air. "Do you think that would happen if he found out about us? That he would ... fire you?"

He chuckled. "You're kidding, right?" He was looking at me like I was an alien. "Jo, do you not understand how this works? You don't fuck your client's daughter, especially when she's only twenty-two years old and still in college. I make decisions regarding your father's business, his investments, his wealth. I have access to his confidential records, things only he and I know. If he found out what I did—what we did—the trust would be gone."

"I'll make this right—"

"You can't. It's not even an option. You're just going to report to his LA office as planned and never tell him what happened between us, and we're just going to move on as though nothing ever did."

My hand returned to the bed. "That's it?" My stomach

flipped, threatening to empty. "That's the end of us? You're just going to cut things off like I never mattered?"

"That's not fair."

"Neither is this." Tears were at the rims of my eyes, and my lips wouldn't stop shaking. "I care about you, Jenner. So much so that I rented an apartment fifteen minutes from your house just so I could be close. I begged my father for a job when he wanted me to have a few years of experience under my belt. I had dreams of us being together—"

"And those died the moment I found out who you really are." He stared at me like he didn't recognize me. "I realize we never made a commitment to each other, but since your trip to LA, things have been different between us. I've been entertaining the ways we could make this work." His voice lowered, turning even grittier when he said, "And now, that's impossible."

I didn't stop the tears.

I let them drip.

I could only be strong up until a point, and his words had sent me far over that edge.

Still wearing my jacket, I held the sleeves to the bottom of my eyes, catching the makeup that wanted to run. "Jenner ..." I wiped my mouth, my spit turning so thick. "I'm not the girl who follows a guy up to his hotel room minutes after meeting him. I've slept with three people my entire life, including you, and the other two were long-term relationships. But the way you've made me feel since Vegas"—I stopped to inhale, to search for a way to describe this feeling—"is nothing I've ever experienced before. I'm completely lost when it comes to you—lost in feelings, lost in sensations, lost in hopes, in wants and desires. I didn't do this to hurt you or to hurt us. All I've wanted is for us to be together, and I thought moving to LA, like I am, would make that come true."

My heart throbbed as he stared at me, saying nothing.

My confession wasn't enough.

I needed to do more.

"I did this all wrong," I continued. "I should have tried harder to confess the truth to you. I should have fought through it no matter how difficult it was. But, God, this can't be the end of us ..."

His silence ate at me.

I couldn't handle another second of it.

"There has to be a way we can salvage—"

He nodded toward the door. "I think you should go."

What?

He wanted me to ... go?

I couldn't believe what I was hearing.

Or the coldness I was seeing on his face.

How he had no desire to fix this, to work it out with my father, to find a way for us to be together.

I didn't believe this was what he truly wanted.

"Jenner ..."

He stood and moved back to the bar, refilling his glass. When he turned around, his expression was even harder than before. It was etched in ice. "This is irreparable, Jo. It doesn't matter what you say ... it'll never work."

A stillness moved through me that was worse than the silence.

This was pain.

An ache.

Like the darkness of a sky seconds before a storm.

I didn't want to humiliate myself, begging if he saw no hope.

Clearly, I was the only person in this room who wanted a relationship, a future together.

My truth meant nothing.

I meant nothing to him.

I stood and grabbed my bag and moved over to the door, holding the knob. I felt his eyes on my back, and I turned around, facing him. Bile was rising from my stomach and going up my throat, the realization hitting me again as his stare turned even frostier.

"Good-bye, Jenner."

I let the door shut behind me as I hurried into the elevator and reached into my purse. I'd left Miami without any luggage, knowing I wouldn't be able to hide it from my father since I'd told him I was flying right home, so I weeded through the few things I'd thrown in here—my toothbrush, extra panties, my makeup—and found my phone.

I needed to get the hell out of Utah, to change my flight, to order a car that would take me to the airport.

But I could barely think, and I didn't even know where to start.

I opened the app to get a car, scheduling one to pick me up outside. While I waited for it to arrive, I called Monica, and she answered after the second ring.

"Why on earth are you calling me? Shouldn't you be in bed—"

"Mon ..." My chin quivered, more tears spilling over my lids at the sound of my best friend's voice. "We're done. Over." I found my sunglasses in my bag and threw them on over my face, trying to hide from the arriving guests. "He wants nothing to do with me."

"*What?*"

I took a deep breath, staring at the mountains around me. "I have something I need to tell you ..."

Not even Monica knew the truth.

The only person who did was Gloria. I'd confessed everything to her when I returned to her shop the day Dad had offered me the job. I needed advice, guidance, and she had given it to me.

But before I told my best girl, I'd needed to tell Jenner first.

And now that he knew, it was time to relive it all over again.

"Jenner is my father's attorney," I said into the phone. "I figured that out shortly after I met him in Vegas ... before we slept together ... and I didn't tell him."

"Wait a second. I need to process." She paused. "So, you knew him this whole time?" She gasped. "And he just pieced it all together, didn't he? Because he's in Utah with your father and you showed up and—oh my God."

I wiped the tears off my chin. "Yep."

"Did it go as badly as I think it did?"

"Worse."

"Babe ..."

I swallowed the acid down my throat. "Don't hate me, Mon. I know I should have told you. I know I should have told him. I fucked up. It's all my fault."

She said nothing for several seconds and then, "Are you on your way home?"

"Yes."

"You need to get to me as fast as you can."

I saw the car pull up, and I waved to the driver. "So you can kick my ass?"

"No, Jo. So I can hug you."

TWENTY-ONE

JENNER

"You're fucking kidding me," Dominick said from the other side of his desk. "Jo is Walter's daughter?" His eyes went wide, his head shaking. "How the hell didn't you figure that out?"

"Jo Cartwright is what's listed on her Instagram. I assumed that was her last name. Turns out, it's her middle name, and I'm the fucking moron who didn't ask her." I dropped my hands on the armrests, exhaling so loud. "If Walter finds out the things I've done to her ..." My neck tilted back, I closed my eyes, imagining the scene that would go down if he got wind that I'd tied Jo to my fucking bed. "He'd hang me by the goddamn balls."

"Especially if he knew your history with chicks." He eyed me. "Oh fuck, he does, doesn't he?"

I remembered a dinner we'd had where he asked if there was a skirt in LA I hadn't looked under. "Yeah ... he does."

"Fuck." Dominick shifted in his seat, adjusting his dick, like he was protecting his own balls. "Is she going to tell him?"

"Her father? Hell no. There's no reason to say anything to him. We're done."

He lifted his coffee off his desk, watching me as he drank. "You said you two will be working together now?"

"On the Utah build-out, but once that ends, I don't know if our paths will cross." I clasped my hands behind my head, using my palms as a pillow. "Did I forget to mention she's moving to LA? Fifteen minutes from my place."

"Everything you wanted but wouldn't admit." He continued to stare at me. "But still, there has to be a way to make this work."

I laughed.

In fact, I laughed so fucking hard that I almost rocked out of my chair. "What are you smoking?" I halted, waiting for him to change his mind. When he didn't, I added, "Do you honestly think I can go to Walter, who pays me millions a year, and tell him I've been fucking his daughter, and now, I want to date her?"

He took a deep breath. "I don't think I'd put it like that ..."

"How would you put it, then?"

His stare moved to the top of his coffee. "I don't know, but if I wanted to be with her—like I suspect you do—then I'd figure out a way." His gaze returned to me. "I'm just having a hard time accepting that you two are finished."

"We are, trust me." I stood from his chair and walked to his office door, sighing. "And it's too fucking bad because I'm really going to miss that girl."

Jo: It's been four days ... can we talk?

Me: What is there to talk about?

Jo: Us.

Me: There is no us, Jo.

Jo: It hurts so bad to read those words. I can't believe you can dismiss me so easily.

Me: There's no dismissing. I'm just accepting the reality that we can't be together.

Jo: But we can. If you care about me as much as I care about you, then we'll find a way.

Me: We both know that's not possible.

Jo: No, that's what you believe. I believe in us.

My fingers hovered above the screen as I stared at her reply.

She thought I didn't care, that I didn't want her.

That I didn't think about her non-fucking-stop.

When the truth was, Jo was the only thing on my mind.

And this was hurting me far worse than it was destroying her.

Engaging more would only make things worse.

I turned my phone around, placing the screen against my desk, and I returned to my computer to finish the email I had been typing.

"We're going out," Ford said from the doorway of my office.

I shook my head. "I have an early flight in the morning. I need a good night's sleep."

He laughed. "I'm sorry, when did you turn into the biggest pussy? And since when do you need sleep? Go home. Get changed. I'll pick you up at eight, and don't even think about coming up with an excuse. I'm the one with a kid, and my ass is still managing to go out."

I dropped the folder I was holding. "If you're doing this to get my mind off Jo, I'm all right. You don't have to bother."

Dominick popped in, leaning against the doorframe. "What's happening? What did I miss?"

"We're going out," Ford told him, and then he looked at me. "Because I need a fucking drink."

"Why didn't you just say that in the first place?" I asked.

"Jesus fucking Christ," Ford groaned. "Dominick, either meet us at Jenner's or we'll see you at the bar."

I checked the time at the top of my monitor.

I had three hours.

Except I needed that drink now.

Ford left, and I looked at Dominick. "Any reason we should wait until eight to start drinking?"

He came into my office and took a seat in front of my desk. "Hell no."

"Perfect answer."

I walked to the wet bar in the back of the room—one of the first things I'd had built when I took over this space. Fresh out of law school, I'd told my parents that clients would be impressed by it. In all actuality, it was for circumstances like this.

"Cheers," I said, handing him a glass as I returned to my seat.

"Sounds like you're over this day?"

I nodded. "Not just this day. This whole fucking week."

"Have you spoken to her?"

"She's texted."

"And?"

I held the glass near my mouth. "And nothing. Unless she wakes up one morning and is no longer a Spade, she can't fix the situation, and neither can I."

"Do you think it's worth having a conversation with Walter?"

I laughed. Which was exactly what I had done the last time

he said something so fucking outlandish. "We've talked about this—and, no, I don't." I paused. "If you were in my shoes, would you?" I tried to think of a similar scenario, using one of his clients. "Would you request a meeting with Jerry Seinfeld to tell him you're fucking his daughter?"

"Is she even of legal age?"

"Jo's only twenty-two; she's not that far off."

He took a long drink. "Listen, if I couldn't live without her, then yes. If she was a one-night stand, no. I'd move on and forget about her."

"And if you lost Jerry as a client because of it?"

He smiled, but it was the kind of grin I hadn't been prepared for. "I'm going to tell you something you don't want to hear."

"All right."

"There is a whole world out there that doesn't involve work. A world that's more important than your clients and how much money they can make you."

I exhaled. "I know that."

"Do you?" His stare intensified. "I'm not so sure about that. From the way I understand it, you'd rather lose her than him."

"It's not like that."

"No?" He placed his arms on my desk. "Then, tell me what it's like, Jenner." He held up his hand as I tried to chime in. "I remember when things were at a standstill with Kendall," he said, referring to his girlfriend. "You and Ford practically had a goddamn intervention. If you remember—and it seems like you've forgotten—Kendall was my client's sister. Now, Daisy might have been a client I wanted to drop, but she was still a client at the time. I wasn't looking to settle down, and you and Ford whipped my ass." He adjusted his tie, his cuff links hitting the desktop when his arm landed. "That's what I'm doing right now, whipping your fucking ass because you're making a horrible mistake."

"And you know that ... how?"

"Because whenever you talk about her, you're happy. You smile. You're a different person. And after her trip to LA, you were the giddiest motherfucker in the world. You never act that way, and I honestly can't remember the last time I saw that side of you." He leaned back in his chair, taking his drink with him. "You've denied wanting a relationship with her, but no one believes that bullshit. She does matter, and you do fucking care."

"Well, shit."

I went back to the bar, grabbed the whiskey, and brought it to my desk. Since I'd finished my glass, I twisted off the cap and drank straight from the bottle.

"Someone's looking to get drunk."

I wiped my lips. "Not drunk. Wasted."

"You think that's going to help?"

I stared at my brother, honesty ripping at my chest. "It's certainly not going to help, but it's fucking necessary."

And that became the theme for the next three hours until Dominick and I stumbled out of my office. My driver was waiting outside to take us to the restaurant where I'd told Ford to meet us since there was no reason to go back to my place—we needed food and much more booze.

"You're both a fucking mess," Ford said as Dominick and I sat at his table.

Fifteen minutes late.

We were lucky we'd made it here at all.

"It's Jenner's fault," Dominick slurred. "He poured, and it continued to go downhill from there."

"Downhill?" I chugged the water in front of me and then

grabbed Ford's water glass and drank his too. "Uphill, brother. Way fucking uphill."

"What's he saying?" Dominick asked Ford.

Ford shook his head. "It's going to be a long night ..."

The server approached our table and said, "What can I get you to drink?"

"I'll have whiskey—"

"He'll have water," Ford said, interrupting me. He then pointed at Dominick and added, "He'll have water as well, and you can bring me a scotch. Make it a double."

"We just got denied by our baby brother," I told Dominick.

"Whose ass we had to fucking babysit when we were in Vegas," Dominick said.

Ford slipped off his jacket and placed it on the back of his seat. "Sometimes, we have to sit out a round. When we get to the club, you can resume the whiskey drinking."

"You're taking this"—Dominick pressed his thumbs against his own chest—"to the club?"

"I might need to rethink that idea," Ford admitted.

I nodded toward Dominick. "I'm not as fucked up as him."

"Yes, you are," they both said at the same time.

I laughed so fucking hard that I almost spilled Ford's water.

The server returned with Ford's drink and a basket of bread that I immediately reached for.

"This is delicious." I moaned, chewing the sourdough. "What club are we going to?"

"Why?" Ford asked. "Is someone eager to hook up?"

Mid-bite, I replied, "Fuck no."

"No?" He took a piece of bread and handed the basket to Dominick. "Why? Suddenly feeling ... taken?"

"*Ahhh.*" I tossed my napkin at him. "I see where this is going."

"Do you?"

"Fuck, don't you start with me too." I got up from my chair, holding the wooden frame, and said, "I'm going to the head. When I return, no more Jo talk. Understood?"

I flipped them off when they laughed and stumbled toward the back of the restaurant in search of the restroom. Once I got inside, I felt my phone vibrate in my pocket. I took it out, the screen showing a notification from Instagram that Jo had posted a new photo.

At some point, I'd set those up.

And I never stopped them.

Why the fuck did I do that to myself?

The alcohol flowing through my body caused me to slide my finger across my phone, pulling up the picture. She was standing near the water, a set of keys dangling from her hand, looking at the Miami skyline. The caption read: *Until next time, Miami.*

Damn it, she was fucking gorgeous. That body—that perfect, delicious, curvy body—was in a pair of cutoffs and a tank top, sneakers and a baseball hat.

She made casual look as sexy as naked.

"*Mmm*," I moaned as I stared at her, my dick getting hard, my hands clutching my phone, wishing it were her instead.

I knew her move date was coming up.

And I knew the next photo she posted would be in LA.

I didn't want to see it.

I didn't want to be tempted.

That girl was my weakness, and no matter what I did, I couldn't forget her.

But still, I needed more.

I pulled up her last message and read it again.

Jo: No, that's what you believe. I believe in us.

My thumbs were hitting the screen, and suddenly, I was pressing Send.

Me: If you believed in us, then why did you do this to US?
Jo: Would it have changed anything if I'd told you sooner? Wouldn't the outcome be the same? You'd still want nothing to do with me. I'd still be heartbroken over you.
Me: You should have told me before I touched you. Not after.
Jo: That's what you want to take back? How loud you made me scream? The way you ravished my body? Jenner, you could barely keep your hands off me. But if that's the part you wish you could do over, then good luck with that.

She was right.

I fucking hated that.

That despite how many women I'd slept with, none of them compared to her.

That even if I had known she was Walter's daughter, I didn't know if I'd have been able to stop myself. Because from the moment she'd sat next to me in the sportsbook, I had known I had to have her.

And the moment my lips touched hers, I knew I couldn't stop with just a kiss.

I'd needed to taste her.

I'd needed to touch her.

The same way I needed her right now.

Me: Why are you Walter's daughter?
Jo: Don't say it like that. Don't make it a bad thing. It doesn't have to be.
Me: Bullshit.
Jo: Stop being afraid that my father will fire you.

Me: I feel like a shady motherfucker who stabbed him in the back. He trusts me, Jo, and this would ruin that.
Me: Do you know what my other clients would say if they found out? Jesus, the whole fucking town would be locking up their daughters. I don't want my reputation to be hit that way.
Jo: Really? Because I'm pretty sure you've already slept your way through LA, and you weren't worried about your reputation then …
Me: You should have been a lawyer.
Jo: My smart mouth is one of the things you love about me.

Love.

Was that true?

Is that what this is?

What I felt?

What was fucking eating at me?

My thumbs stayed on the screen as I tried to come up with a reply.

But I had nothing.

No answer.

All I wanted was to tell her to get her ass to this restaurant right now.

But I shoved my phone back into my pocket instead.

TWENTY-TWO

JOANNA

"Jo," Gloria said as I walked into her bakery, "why do I get the feeling that this is good-bye?"

I moved over to the counter she was sitting behind, placing my hands on the glass. "I couldn't leave without popping in here one last time."

Her hands rested on top of mine. "I'm glad you did, honey." Her eyes held me in a way that told me she was seeing right through me. "I take it, things didn't go well with Jenner in Utah?"

I remembered rushing in here, knowing I'd had limited time before my girls arrived at our apartment, and I'd confessed the truth to Gloria. What I loved about her was that she hadn't judged me for lying to Jenner. She didn't seem disappointed with me either. She'd just listened and told me to be honest with him.

I shook my head. "He ended things."

She came over to my side of the counter, but she didn't hug me. She just stood close, fingering the long, chunky curl that rested across my shoulder.

"But he's not the reason I came in," I continued. "I wanted to thank you for everything and to get some pastries for the road. It's going to be a long drive to LA."

Her stare reached places far deeper than my chest. "California is going to be the start of something wonderful for you."

"I hope so."

She returned to the glass she had been sitting behind and reached inside once it was open. "He cares about you—you do know that, don't you?"

"I do."

"Jenner just needs time to work this through his brain. You caught him off guard—not what happened per se, I mean, you, in general. Love is an uncharted territory for him."

"Is there anything I can do?" I glanced down at my gel polish that my nerves had caused me to slowly pick off. "You know, to speed the process up?"

Monica had told me to be patient. My mother, who had dated sporadically since she and my father had divorced, had told me to be persistent.

"I've apologized," I told her even though I was sure she felt that. "I've offered solutions. I've told him I care about him. Nothing has changed. He still won't budge."

She pulled out a piece of fudge that was white and blue and set it on a plate. She cut it in half, handing me a bite, and took the other for herself. Even though I wasn't hungry, I didn't want to offend her, so I ate it.

Since Utah, Jenner had killed my taste buds, but I'd never had anything like this in my life. A mixture of creamy white chocolate with a subtle burst of blueberry.

"Gloria, thank you." I took another small nibble. "This is outstanding."

"It looks like you've lost a few pounds. We need to put some meat on those bones."

"Yes, well"—I sighed—"this has been hard."

Her hand moved to my shoulder. "I understand." Her fingers stroked the same spot, like she was seeing even deeper inside me. "You know, my son is the type of man who thrives on challenges and uses them as motivation. But, unlike Brett, Jenner doesn't allow them to come into fruition. He wants to crush them before they're born. When James entered Brett's life, that's what she was for him—motivation, a reason to change. Whereas Jenner tried to put out the flames before your fire even started. Except you're strong, Joanna. Stronger than he's ever experienced, and he knows he can't continue to fight—it's just not easy on his soul." She took out another slice, giving me the whole piece this time. "He lives by his word—it's his honor—and he feels that entering a relationship with you would go against what he's promised your father."

I moaned as I devoured the rest of the fudge. "How do I help him?"

"You can't."

"Then, what do I do?"

She reached inside the glass case and took out a piece of coconut fudge that she cut into quarters. "Do you see any chunks of coconut in there?"

I searched the small bits and shook my head.

"That's because I take the coarse pieces of coconut and puree them. No one wants to bite into a rough, stringy shred, but they love the flavor, so I change the structure." She reached into the case again and removed a half-moon cookie. "Most make theirs with a vanilla base. I find that boring. I use chocolate instead and add thicker icing, not the sugary fondant-like frosting most others use." She took a box from behind her and started filling it with fudge and blueberry cake, even several half-moon cookies. She tied the top and placed it in front of me. "Sometimes, they know what they want. Sometimes, you have to show them what they want. And sometimes, you have to come up with innovative ways to give them what they want." She wrapped her fingers around mine, squeezing. "Jenner hates coconut, but what do I give him every time he comes here?"

"And he loves it. He can't stop eating it and can't stop talking about it."

She smiled. "Exactly."

My heart clutched.

"Gloria ..." I took a long, deep breath. "I understand."

"Oh, darling, I knew you would."

She moved out from behind the counter and joined me, waiting for me to lift the box before she slipped her arm over the back of my shoulders. As she walked me to the door, she said, "The most intricate recipe I have is the blueberry cake. It looks so simple on the outside, but the inside is a beautiful, complex, layered web of flavors." When we stopped walking, she hauled me in for a hug, holding me in such a motherly way. "There's a reason why the cake is *our* favorite."

When we pulled back from each other, my gaze fixed on hers. "I can't thank you enough—for everything."

I went to reach into my bag to get my wallet, and she stopped me.

"Your money is no good here." Her fingers softly stroked my cheek. "Next time you're in town, please stop by. It would make me so happy to see you."

"I think you'll be in LA, visiting James and Brett, before I make my way back to Miami. During your next trip, how about I take you to lunch?"

"That would be lovely."

"Well, that was the easiest unpacking I've ever done in my life," Monica said, flopping down next to me on the couch that had just been delivered.

I slowly turned my face toward her. "But for some reason, I'm as exhausted as my credit card."

She laughed. "That bill isn't going to be pretty."

It wasn't, but we now had new living room furniture and a kitchen table, lamps, and bedroom sets—things we'd sold in Miami to start completely fresh. And with the steady salary I was earning, I would eventually be able to pay it off.

Not my father.

Me.

Just because I came from money didn't mean I took advantage of it.

"I know we're here—that drive took a century and was the longest thing ever—but I still can't believe we're *here*, here," I said.

A large window was across from me, showing a skyline that I hadn't studied in a long time. My dream was to always work for my father, but I hadn't thought he was going to hire me so soon. I got the impression he wanted me to have some experience first. But as I had driven him to the private airport after my graduation weekend, he'd offered me the job after some heavy begging. And even though I missed our friends in Florida, I was ready to start this next phase of my life.

"I can't either," she finally whispered. "I saw Manhattan. I saw thick, billowy clouds of steam coming up from the ground and chewy, hot bagels smothered in veggie cream cheese, and those incredible boho-chic boutiques in SoHo. I didn't see LA."

I leaned against her shoulder. "Are you disappointed?"

"No, babe, this is so much better."

I sighed, kicking my feet onto our new coffee table. "How

about I order us a boat of sushi and we open a bottle of wine and put on *Housewives* of any city?"

"I love you."

I giggled. "I thought you'd dig that plan."

"It's perfect."

And it was.

But what would be even better was if I heard from Jenner. He lived so close; I could be at his house in eight minutes if I hit every green light.

I wouldn't do that.

I wasn't going to call him either.

I was going to make him reach out to me.

"I feel like this is our last moment of freedom," Monica said. "Come Monday, you're all business, traveling to Utah soon and deep into the trenches of your new job. I have three interviews lined up for next week. We're working girls now, baby."

"We're so old."

She snorted. "Right?" She rested her fuzzy pink socks next to mine. "Speaking of old ... now that we're here, what's your plan? I mean, you haven't said his name in, like, a day." She put her hand on my forehead. "Are you feeling all right?"

"Very funny."

"Except I'm serious, Jo."

I reached for my phone and pulled up the shot that Monica had taken this afternoon when we first arrived. We were on our balcony, the sun shining directly on me, capturing my smile just perfectly.

I showed her the photo and said, "That's getting posted in the morning."

"And you're sure he checks your Instagram?"

I laughed. "Oh, I'm more than positive."

The timing of his texts told me he'd set up notifications.

Her brows rose, telling me she wasn't convinced. "So, your plan is to post a pic and just wait?"

"Sometimes, you have to show them what they want, Mon."

She was quiet for a few seconds, processing what I'd said, and finally replied, "Okay, okay, I can buy that." She leaned up on her elbows. "What comes next?"

"That's when I have to get a little creative and give him what he wants."

"Which is?"

I smiled. "Me."

TWENTY-THREE

JENNER

"The client is requesting that you fly to Miami tomorrow," my assistant said as I held the phone up to my ear, looking out the backseat window of my SUV.

Miami.

I felt movement in my chest as I took a breath, and I knew it wasn't just from the air that was filling it. "Tomorrow, Val?" I inquired. "Is it possible to accommodate that request?"

"Well, you're booked solid for the next ten days with barely even an opening for lunch. I suppose I could move things around, like I've done in the past, but it won't be pretty."

Miami didn't hold the same significance as it had the last several months.

That was because she wasn't there.

She was here.

And I still hadn't fucking seen her.

All I'd seen were pictures.

One of what I assumed to be the balcony outside her apartment, a high-rise I was quite familiar with—I'd helped my client build it.

Another one on the beach in Malibu.

A dinner at Nobu.

She was leaving breadcrumbs, and I was gobbling up every goddamn one.

"Fit them in when you can, but don't move anything around," I told her and hung up, keeping the phone in my hand to check the emails that had recently come in.

I felt the SUV come to a stop just as my driver said, "We're here, Mr. Dalton. I'll be parked along the side of the building until you're ready to leave."

I glanced out the opposite window, the twenty-story corporate office for Spade Hotels directly outside. "Thank you, Steven." He went to get out to open my door, and I added, "There's too much traffic today. I've got it."

I climbed out, holding my briefcase, and walked into the lobby. "Jenner Dalton here to see Walter Spade," I told the receptionist.

"Good to see you, Mr. Dalton," she replied. "You can head on up."

I went to the bank of elevators, waiting for one of the four to arrive. Once one did, I walked inside and hit the button for the top floor.

The door was almost closed when I heard, "Can you hold the elevator, please?"

I stuck my hand in the doorway, stopping it from shutting, and just as it began to slide open, my jaw practically fucking dropped as Jo stepped through the entrance.

"Thanks for holding it," she said, her breath hitching the moment our eyes connected and she realized it was me inside.

My dick instantly hardened. My hands were grasping air, so I didn't reach for her.

She halted a few steps in, almost teetering on her sky-high red heels. "Jenner ... hi." Her voice was almost like a gasp.

I shouldn't have been surprised. She worked here now; of course she would be in the building.

But I was.

Maybe it was seeing the business side of her that shocked me so much.

Dressed in a black suit that hugged those lean legs and curvy waist, a skintight red tank underneath her open jacket that showed the dip of those perfect tits. Nipples that were just turning hard, begging to be sucked and bitten.

Fuck, she looked hot.

"Jo ..." I replied.

She held a coffee in her hand and moved to the far wall. "This is a coincidence, I promise." She faced the front, giving me her profile. "I didn't know you were coming in today." She hit a different button than the one I'd pressed, a lower floor, where I assumed her office was located.

"I have a meeting with your father."

She finally glanced at me again, the sensation in my chest pounding even harder now. "I know you're not here to see me."

And then she looked away, leaving me with a fucking ache as the elevator began to rise.

The emergency button was only inches from my hand. Pulling it would stop the elevator from moving.

I was so fucking tempted.

To back her up against the wall and punish her with my tongue.

Ravage her.

To show her how much I missed her.

But I didn't.

I stared at the numbers as we climbed, each floor lighting up as we passed it. And seconds before we reached hers, I couldn't avoid her any longer. I took in that beautiful profile, feeling my breath leave my body as I exhaled, wishing that air was hitting her skin while my nose grazed across her.

I could almost taste her.

I could certainly smell her, that fall scent wrapping around me in this small space.

Part of me expected for her to be looking at me, for her eyes to be so fixed on mine, pleading, silently negotiating our future.

But they weren't.

She was focused on the door, and as the chime went off, signaling we'd arrived, she gazed at me over her shoulder, smiling. "Thanks for the ride, Jenner."

She stepped out and disappeared around the corner.

The minute the door closed, I adjusted my hard-on, the need to have her raging through me.

"Fuck." I pounded my fist against the wall. "Fuck, fuck, fuck."

I tried to get my shit together, hiding my throbbing cock as I arrived on the top floor, greeted by Walter's assistant the moment I stepped out.

"Good morning, Mr. Dalton. Mr. Spade is waiting for you in his office."

I nodded, turning down the hallway and walking to the very end, where Walter's massive office was located. I gave the door a quick knock, hearing him call my name before I let myself in.

He waved me over to one of the seats in front of his desk. "Jenner, it's good to see you."

"Likewise." I set my briefcase on the empty chair next to mine and took out Walter's file. "Are things going well?"

"Well enough. Could always be better." He stared at me as he lifted his coffee mug. "And you?"

I chuckled. "I couldn't have said it better."

His eyes narrowed. "I see that smile is gone. Does that mean the woman in your life is too?"

This was a conversation I needed to avoid.

But my top client was expecting an answer, and skating around one wasn't the best angle to take.

"You must be a mind reader," I replied.

"Enough bastards have sat in the same seat as you, and at this age, I can tell them all apart—the ones in love, the ones in lust, and the ones, like me, whose heart only belongs to themself."

"And I fall into the latter?"

"Not even close." He continued to stare. "What happened, Jenner?"

I took a deep breath, fingering the papers inside the folder. "Ah, you know, timing just wasn't in our favor."

"That's too bad."

I turned my attention to the top sheet in the stack. "Yeah ... well, some good things, unfortunately, have to end." My chest agreed, the fucking pounding inside becoming relentless. "I hope you've got some good news for me. You ready to negotiate on one of the pieces of land?"

As I looked up, he leaned back in his chair, crossing his fingers over his chest. "It wasn't an easy decision. The range in price varied so greatly between the three; each made a significant difference to my bottom line."

"We've been here many times before, Walter. We know it's an arduous process."

"It has been—there's no doubt about that. My accountant has worked overtime to spin these numbers in every possible way, coming up with my best option." He raised a finger in the air. "One second." Then, he lifted the phone from his desk, pressing several buttons before holding the receiver to his ear. "Joanna, are you free?" He paused. "Good. I'm meeting with

Jenner, and we're discussing the land in Utah. I'd like you to sit in on this meeting."

My back stiffened.

I had to see that gorgeous face again. That incredible body. The red tank and heels that I couldn't get out of my mind.

Fuck.

"She'll be right up," he said, setting the phone down. "She's been quickly learning the ropes around here, implementing several impressive strategies so far. And I've got to say"—he shook his head—"she's really doing a hell of a job."

Walter wasn't one to give compliments. He was more likely to complain about operations than comment on the positives. So, to hear this was impressive.

"She seems like an excellent fit for your team," I replied.

"Enthusiastic, hardworking, strong-willed. She's hungry, and she wants to make a difference around here." He opened his arms wide, almost glancing around the room. "And that's important because this is all going to be hers one day."

"Quite an undertaking."

He nodded. "She can handle it—she inherited that from me. As for her mother, she got Tricia's heart."

"What did I inherit?" Jo asked as she walked in.

The sound of her changed the way I breathed.

I moved my briefcase to the ground, giving her a place to sit, and looked over my shoulder, watching her come closer.

"I was just telling Jenner how Spade Hotels will be yours once I retire—unless you want me to sell it."

"You're not selling anything." She took a seat, her scent wafting over, enveloping me. "I fully intend to fill your shoes. My feet just aren't as big as yours, and I prefer heels." She smiled, her face slowly turning toward me. "Jenner, it's nice to see you again."

"And you, Joanna."

Goddamn it, she was sexy.

She certainly had been while she was in Miami, but the LA version of Jo had even more confidence, and it looked so fucking good on her.

"Joanna, why don't you tell Jenner what we decided?"

Was I surprised he'd discussed his plans with his daughter?

I wasn't sure.

I wasn't sure of anything at this moment.

Except how much I wanted to lift her off that chair and carry her to my SUV outside, sending my driver to lunch while I fucked her in the backseat.

"I'd love to." She turned her whole body toward me, the movement causing her jacket to open more, tits that were pure perfection taunting the hell out of me. "I'm not sure what my father mentioned prior to me coming in, but we had our accountant dissect all the options, weighing every possibility. I have concerns about each piece of land and the amount of credit we'll be tying up, but there's only one that truly fits the needs of our brand."

For the briefest of moments, she chewed the corner of her thick bottom lip, and I wanted to fucking groan.

"We'd like to make an offer on the mountainside parcel," Jo finished.

I shook myself out of the trance she'd put me in, remembering I was also in a meeting with her father, and replied, "That's the one I'd pick as well."

She moved her hair to one side, freeing up the other side of her neck, revealing the smoothness of her skin, the arch of her collarbone.

What the hell are you doing to me?

"My projections are high for this property," she added. "The additions I'd like to make to the design and amenities will be desirable for both summer and winter travelers, making this a destination that's unlike a majority of our other properties."

"And I agree," Walter said, dragging my attention away from Jo. "Now, it's time to work your magic, Jenner. I need you to get this land for a record-breaking low price."

I cleared my throat. "I'll do my best."

He leaned his chest against the edge of his desk, his hands folding in front of him. "You're scheduled to go to Utah in a few days to meet with the realtor?"

I nodded. "Yes."

"I'm going to fly the architect out there as well. I want you to discuss the details of the build-out with him, so he can start the rendering."

"No problem."

"And, Jenner?" Walter stalled, his gaze intensifying. "I'd like Joanna to go with you."

TWENTY-FOUR

JOANNA

As Jenner stared at my father, his chest rising and falling from all the deep breaths, his eyes didn't even blink.

I held the air in my lungs, waiting for Jenner's reply.

A trip to Utah was scheduled for later in the month, but my father hadn't mentioned that he wanted me to go on this one as well. I certainly wasn't disappointed by the news. I just wasn't going to let Jenner know that, nor how excited I was about the potential of joining him.

"All right," Jenner eventually responded. "Looks like we're going together ..."

I didn't trust myself to turn to him, so I kept my focus on my father and said, "Will you be coming along, Dad?"

He clicked his mouse, reading what I assumed was his calendar. "Not this trip, pumpkin."

Jenner and me.

Alone.

In the mountains.

I wanted to dance in my seat.

Instead, I said, "Walter," to reprimand him for his unprofessionalism—the term of endearment needed to stay away from the office.

He smiled. "Joanna, I mean." He glanced at Jenner. "One day, I'll get it right." When his eyes returned to me, he added, "I know we didn't discuss this trip, and it's coming as a surprise, but this project is your baby. You'll be in charge of all the marketing. I want you present for every step, including negotiations and meetings with the architect, working hand in hand with Jenner. I hope you'll be able to clear your schedule and go?"

Hand in hand.

Oh God.

I pulled my phone out of my pocket, pretending to check, knowing nothing would stop me from getting on that plane. "I'm going to have to shift some things around." I finally gazed at Jenner. "But I can make it happen."

He couldn't possibly look yummier than he did right now in his navy suit, the light-yellow, almost-gold tie hanging to his belt buckle. A crisp white button-down hid his etched abs, defined like piano keys running down his stomach. His pants hugged him in all the right places, concealing that delicious, long, thick cock.

I was sweating.

But I made sure Jenner didn't notice.

In fact, I kept my expression completely aloof as I stared at him and said, "How long will we be in Utah?"

He blinked.

Again.

"Three nights."

"And the two of you will be extremely busy," my father said. "There's a lot of work to be done."

"We can handle it," I assured him.

This time, I kept my eyes off Jenner, but I felt his.

They were roaming my body, heating my skin even more.

"My assistant will reserve the plane and book your hotel rooms," my father said. "Jenner, if you have a preference of where you'd like to stay, let her know."

"Will do," Jenner answered, lifting his briefcase from the floor and standing from the chair.

I slowly gazed up the length of him. He towered over me, making me feel so tiny.

"Let me know if you need anything in the meantime," he said to my father. And when he looked at me, all the air left my lungs, the hunger in his expression instantly making me wet. "I'll see you in a few days, Jo."

Oh fuck.

Thirty minutes into the flight, and Jenner hadn't said more than a few words to me. I'd already finished going through all my emails and every social media notification on my phone. No longer occupied, I was consumed by his presence.

What didn't help was that I could smell his cologne in the air.

God, it was enticing. Spicy, sensual—if sex and lust had a scent, it was him.

He sat on the other side of the jet. His laptop on a table in front of him, his fingers hitting the keys. The only time he ever took a break from typing was to pick up the coffee the flight attendant had delivered or to eat a piece of fruit from the plate she had given him.

All I wanted was his attention on me.

I shifted in my seat and reached into my purse, grabbing the box that I'd taken out of the freezer this morning. I carefully unwrapped the twine and opened the lid.

"In the mood for something sweet?" I asked, holding the box toward him.

He gradually looked up, his eyes holding mine for several seconds before they dipped to my hand. "Gloria's?"

I nodded. "I've gotten myself addicted, and fortunately, she ships."

He stayed quiet.

I'd expected that.

But he took the desserts from my hand and searched inside. "Coconut fudge?"

"I asked her to put together some treats. I wasn't specific." I shrugged. "She must have thought I would see you ... or something."

"Interesting." He took a piece out and handed the box back to me. "There're half-moon cookies in there too."

"Like I said, I wasn't specific."

I selected some blueberry white-chocolate fudge and took a bite. I was far from hungry. In fact, the thought of something sweet this early in the morning almost made my stomach hurt.

"I've missed this," he said, holding the chocolate in the air.

He was talking about the dessert.

Part of me believed he was also talking about us.

"One of the negatives to living here," I replied.

"The only negative."

I laughed, placing the box back in my bag. "I can definitely think of a few more."

He closed his laptop, his stare finding its way back to me. "Such as?"

I smiled, bringing the coffee up to my lips, keeping the cup there even though I wasn't drinking. When I set it back down, still holding his gaze, I responded, "Jenner, you're so cute sometimes." I grabbed my phone from the table and hit the screen, pulling up something—anything—that made me appear busy.

But even though my attention had moved on, his hadn't.

His eyes bore right through me.

And I felt their heat.

"The seller isn't looking to negotiate," the realtor said as we sat in her conference room.

Jenner was at the head of the table, the realtor and me on either side of him.

"Everything is negotiable," he countered.

"But when there aren't any comps in the area, we have nothing to use as leverage." She pressed her fingers together, forming a triangle with her hands. "Not a single piece of land like the mountainside parcel has been listed for sale or sold in the last six months."

"That's where you're wrong." He removed a piece of paper from his briefcase, placing it in front of her. He pointed at the center of the sheet, circling it with his finger. "This land right here isn't identical, but it's close."

The realtor grabbed the paper, examining it. "This didn't come up in my search."

Jenner exhaled, crossing his arms over his chest. "Because it hasn't hit the market yet. It's a pocket listing."

Her brows rose. "How do you know what they're going to offer?" Her eyes returned to the sheet. "And how did you get this?"

"I spoke to the seller."

"Wait ..." She entered something into the laptop that sat on the table next to her, returning to us several moments later. "You mean to tell me, you found this land, you spoke to the seller, and he gave you this information?"

Jenner chuckled.

And it was the most confident sound I'd ever heard in my life.

"Renee, let me explain something to you. When my client asks me to get him a record-breaking low price, I go to any lengths to achieve that." He nodded toward the paper in her hand. "Call him, talk to him. He's looking for a realtor; maybe you can score yourself the listing."

I was wet.

Again.

"I'd like you to bring that new comp to the seller's agent and tell him his client needs to come up with a better price." He stood from his chair, and I did the same. "The seller has twenty-four hours—and we will be countering, so don't come back to me with a best and final."

She nodded. "I'll go make the phone call."

We left the conference room and stepped into the SUV waiting for us outside.

"Wow," I said as I put on my seat belt, looking at him across the backseat. "Like ... wow."

He laughed.

"I had no idea you had that little tidbit of info—and I kinda want to strangle you for that—but, man, that small snack you dropped on her straight-up sucker-punched her in the gut."

"She's on our side, Jo, but she gets paid on the total sale. She wants the highest price, whether it's best for us or not. You have to remember that going into every deal."

The stunning mountains passing by his window couldn't even drag my attention away from him.

"Jenner, what you did back there, that was so smooth and flawless, in a way I've never witnessed before."

And sexy as hell.

But I was going to keep that part to myself.

"It comes with experience." He brushed his fingers over his

trimmed beard, reminding me of the way those whiskers had felt against my skin. "You'll learn the tricks, the longer you're in the business."

I continued to stare at him in awe. "How did you know about the property?"

"That's what your father hired me for. To go into a situation and know every angle because you never know when that angle will need to come into play."

"I have so much to learn." A heavy blush moved across my cheeks. "It's a good thing I've mastered the student role and I have an excellent teacher."

His jaw flexed, like he was grinding his teeth together, his stare so intense that it was vibrating through me. "The student role ..."

I took a deep breath. "Yeah, you know, just because I have my degree doesn't mean I want to stop learning." I dragged my teeth across my lip before I smiled. "And I'm going to be your student throughout this whole build-out."

His gaze thickened, his face telling me he was making the connection I wanted him to—the little nugget I was dropping in his mind from the day I'd shown up to his hotel, wearing a naughty schoolgirl costume.

Just as he opened his mouth to reply, his phone began to ring. He reached into his pocket and said, "It's the realtor. I'm going to put her on speakerphone." He hit the screen. "This is Jenner."

"Jenner, it's Renee. I just spoke to the agent, and they've budged a little."

"What's a little?"

"A dollar a square foot."

He laughed. "That's not a budge; that's a slap in the face. Tell them they need to do better. Much better." He was staring at the screen, but now, he looked at me. "If they want to close this deal, they need to be realistic. Our financing is rock solid. Our terms are more than reasonable. Remind the agent who we are and what we're coming to the table with."

"I'll see what I can do."

He ended the call and slipped his phone back into his pocket.

Could this man be any hotter?

Good God.

"What if they say no?" I asked him.

"They won't."

"How do you know that?"

A smile moved across his handsome mouth, a determination so strong that it was pulsing through me. "Because the land only appeals to a certain buyer, and organizations like Spade Hotels don't come around that often. The seller knows that. He also knows we're his only offer. So, he either plays fair or he goes back to waiting."

He was quiet for a moment, taking me in.

"Let me teach you your first lesson ..." He leaned in closer, his arm briefly grazing my shoulder, my chest melting from the contact. "If the seller's hungry and money is being waved in their face, they bite." His voice lowered. "They always fucking bite."

TWENTY-FIVE

JENNER

I stood at the front desk of the hotel and handed the clerk my credit card as I said, "Dalton and Spade. We should have two rooms reserved. You can use that card for both."

He typed something into his computer and said, "Yes, I see you're down for three nights." He glanced up, looking at Jo and me. "I'll use this card in case you incur any incidentals. Shall I make one key for each room or ..."

"One key is fine," Jo replied.

"Perfect." He stuck the plastic key cards into a coder. "I have two king-size rooms on the eighth floor." He placed the key cards into holders and handed one to Jo. "You'll be in 809." He then gave one to me and said, "And you'll be in 812."

Rooms right near each other.

So I could think about her only a few doors down, lying naked in her bed.

All night long.

The thought made me want to fucking growl.

He pointed behind us and added, "Walk through the lobby,

and the first set of elevators on your right will take you to your rooms."

Jo thanked him, and we rolled our suitcases to the elevator.

The moment the door slid open, I held out my arm and said, "After you."

As she moved ahead to the far wall, I got a hell of a view of her ass. Her skirt was skintight, hugging those fucking cheeks, and my cock ground against my pants as I craved to slip between them, rubbing my tip across that forbidden back hole.

When she turned, I made sure she didn't catch me staring and stayed near the front, pressing the appropriate button. Once we arrived at our floor, I let her get out first.

Her room came before mine, and as I passed, veering to the other side of the hallway, she held the card near the reader.

"Will you let me know if you hear from the realtor?"

I glanced over my shoulder, and her back was pressed against the door, like I was holding her against it.

I took a fucking breath.

"Yes."

"Is there anything else on the schedule for today?"

Several strands of long black hair were in her face, her lips glossy and parted, her eyes feral.

I couldn't think.

I couldn't even process.

I could only imagine, and the scene that was unfolding in my head involved her hands above her head and my mouth moving slowly down her body until I reached her cunt.

I swallowed, knowing I had to say something, and cleared my throat. "What are you asking, Jo?"

"I'm wondering if I should be doing something aside from going to my room ..." She swiped her tongue across her lip.

If I stayed in this hallway any longer, she was going to end up in my arms.

Joanna Spade was far too fucking dangerous.

I waved the card in front of the reader and opened my door. "I'll let you know if I hear from the realtor." I pushed my suitcase inside. "If I don't, you're free until tomorrow morning."

"That seems like an eternity."

I didn't want to go that long without seeing her.

Not after having her to myself all morning.

I'd gotten to smell her in the air and hold her voice close to my ears.

I'd gotten to look at her whenever I wanted.

"Enjoy it. Tomorrow is going to be much busier."

I went into my room and closed the door.

But I didn't move.

I stayed right where I was, thinking of her on the other side.

I needed to focus on work.

I needed to focus on the promise I'd made to myself the moment I found out who she was.

Walter Spade's daughter.

Off-fucking-limits.

But, goddamn it, the only thing I wanted was her.

I left my suitcase and went over to the minibar, removing several bottles of whiskey, dumping them into a glass that I held to my lips.

The liquor burned as it went down.

I wanted it to.

I wanted it to extinguish the thoughts in my head, the desire pulsing through me, the throbbing in my cock. I refilled the glass and took off my jacket, hanging it across the back of the chair and loosening my tie. As I was unbuttoning my shirt, I caught sight of the large bed behind me.

The headboard.

And all I could think about was tying her fucking wrists to each side, her legs spread wide over the mattress.

Jesus Christ.

I tried shaking her from my head, concentrating on work. The full inbox of emails that needed replies. The parcels of land I needed to study, the permits I needed to research, the numbers I needed to analyze.

But I couldn't focus on that.

I could only think of her.

And the raging hard-on in my pants.

I needed to come.

I glanced toward the door, my hands clenching as I looked at it, desperate to have her body in my grip.

And as I stared at the wood that separated us, I reached for my tie and pulled it off, and I unbuttoned the rest of my shirt. I untied my shoes and slipped off my pants and socks and walked into the bathroom.

As I reached the mirror's reflection, my cock was almost bursting through my boxer briefs.

I'd only have to round the corner to the hallway, walk out the door, and go across the hall. I'd only have to tap my fingers on her door, and she'd open it.

I'd only have to cup her face in my hands, and something told me she'd be mine.

Her pussy would soon be squeezing my dick.

Her screams filling my ears.

"Walter ..." I said out loud. "Walter Spade's fucking daughter."

I shook my head, slowly glancing at my eyes in the mirror.

"You can't do this, Jenner. You fucking can't."

My boxer briefs fell to the floor, and I went into the shower, turning the water on as hot as it would go. Once I felt the change in temperature, I stepped under the spray. I squirted some soap onto my hand and wrapped my palm around my dick. My other hand pressed against the back wall. As the water pounded against my chest, images of Jo came into my head. Her body was so fresh in my mind—I didn't have to search. She was there, always fucking there. And as my eyes wandered over the visions, I pumped harder.

Faster.

I twisted my wrist just like her mouth, as if it were sucking me right now. The soap slick and soft like her tongue.

Within a few strokes, I was there.

My hips reared forward.

My breath came out in hard, deep grunts.

"Fuck!"

My neck leaned back as I gripped the base, sliding my hand forward, milking the cum out of me. I hissed into the steam as each shot burst through my body. I didn't let up until I was empty, my hand finally dropping, my head moving under the water.

Before I closed my eyes, I watched my cum swirl around the drain.

This would do.

But it wasn't her.

"What can I get you to drink?" the bartender asked as I sat in one of the stools in front of the bar.

"Scotch, neat, and make it a double."

I'd done hours' worth of work, and now, I needed to be fed. Some of my favorite restaurants were in downtown Park City, a five-minute drive from here. But for some reason, I couldn't bring myself to leave the hotel.

She placed a menu in front of me and winked. "In case you're hungry too."

Blonde, perky tits, a smile that told me she was extremely

attracted to me.

Normally, I would bring her up to my room and fuck her. But since I'd been with Jo, I'd had no desire to be with anyone else.

I didn't know what the fuck was wrong with me.

She placed the scotch in front of me and said, "Any food?"

I handed her the menu, calling out the first item that was listed, "Red trout."

"Our chef's specialty." She typed my order into the computer. "So, are you here for work or pleasure?"

I wasn't interested in small talk.

I took out my phone, reading the notifications on the screen. "Work." I sighed. "Endless work."

"I'll let you get to it."

I was just typing out a reply when I got a whiff of a familiar scent.

A scent I knew better than anything.

I reached for my drink, my eyes closing as I swallowed. When I set the glass down, I didn't have to glance over my shoulder, but I did.

Fuck me.

Yoga pants that showed the gap between Jo's thighs, a tight tank top, sneakers, her hair braided, hanging over her shoulder with a baseball hat on her head.

There was something about seeing her in gym gear that made my dick fucking pound.

"I swear I didn't follow you. I just worked out, and I'm starving. The thought of going back to my room didn't sound like fun." She pointed to the other side of the bar. "Should I sit over there?"

"No." I reached over the top of the bar, grabbed the menu the bartender had taken from me, and set it beside me. "Here. Order."

She straddled the stool, scanning the large menu. "Did you get food?"

"I did." I cupped my hands around my drink, knowing I needed about five more of these, especially as I took a quick glance at her legs, the way they stayed wide across the leather seat. "I got the trout."

She pushed the menu aside. "Sounds good. I'm sold."

"Sold on what?" the bartender asked as she reappeared.

Jo crossed her arms over the bar, leaning forward, her tits pressing against the edge of the wood. "I'll take a cab and the red trout, please."

"Do you want to start a tab or—"

"Put her on my bill," I said.

The moment she was gone, finding the appropriate bottle of red, Jo said, "I hope you're billing my father for this. The incidentals for the room—because there will be some, as I had a couple drinks—and now this."

"I can afford to buy you dinner, Joanna."

Fire.

That was what I was playing with.

But, fuck, I couldn't help it.

"I don't doubt that for a second," she said. "But you don't need to—that's all I'm saying."

"Here you go," the bartender said, stopping me from replying as she placed Jo's drink in front of her. "So, have you guys been to Park City before? Need any suggestions on what to do in the area?"

"This is her second time," I replied, nodding toward Jo. "I've been coming here for a long time."

"And it's one of his favorite places to visit," Jo told the bartender. "I can see why he loves it here so much." She glanced out the massive windows behind the bar, showing a perfect view of the mountains. "It's an awesome spot to own a second home." Jo turned toward me, that gorgeous fucking grin spreading across her plump lips.

"Does that mean you're buying here?" the bartender asked.

"I checked out a house when I was here last. I'm going back to look at it tomorrow."

"You are?" Jo gasped. "You didn't tell me."

Why would I?

That was what I should say to her, but instead, I voiced, "I haven't really been in a position to tell you ... have I?"

She took a deep breath, nodding. "You're right."

"I hope things work out for you," the bartender said, leaving us alone again.

"I'm sorry," Jo whispered. "I realize I have no right to know what's happening in your life, but the disappointment that I didn't know just hit me really hard." She clasped my arm. "I'm so incredibly happy for you, Jenner."

Her touch caught me off guard.

It had been so long since her hands had been on me. I almost forgot how they made me feel.

How even the graze of her fingers could be so intense.

"There's no reason to be happy yet," I finally responded. "It's not mine."

She squeezed. "But it will be."

I wasn't sure if we were still talking about the house.

She released me, and the skin on my arm immediately turned cold.

"By the way," she added, "I'm taking full credit if you buy the house."

Her comment and smile made me chuckle. "Is that so?"

"*Mmhmm.*"

Cute and sexy—a combination that was so fucking lethal.

"Is it beautiful?"

I drained half my glass and said, "Would you like to see it?"

"Like you even have to ask."

I hit several buttons on my phone and tilted the screen in her direction.

"Oh my God, I'm dead over the view," she groaned. "Jenner, is that what you're going to wake up to every morning?"

The first shot was of the living room, and the second was of the master.

Even though I'd viewed the house the last time Jo and I had been here and I'd already learned who she was, when the realtor had taken me into that bedroom, I couldn't help but picture Jo in the bed.

The way the morning light would cast across her body as she woke up.

The way it would hit her tits as she rode me.

"Yes," I answered.

She swiped the screen, her finger gently hitting my hand each time. "That bathroom, wow. That's a tub I could soak in for days." She paused. "How many heads does that shower have?"

"Ten."

I'd stopped looking at the phone, now only gazing at her, watching her chew her lips, the temptation to pull them from her teeth so fucking strong.

When she stopped flipping through the shots, she looked up.

Inhaling loudly when she realized my eyes were already on her.

"I'm obsessed," she said, shifting in her seat, her legs crossing. "It's an amazing house. You did good, sir." Our hands brushed each other when she placed the phone in my palm. "Are you going to make an offer?"

"If I still feel the same way about it when I walk through the door."

"Ah, you will." She held on to the stem of her wine, twirling the glass. "When you love something, that feeling never dies."

"You don't think so?"

Her chin rested on her shoulder. "I know so."

Her eyes were still locked with mine when the bartender placed the dishes in front of us.

"Can I get you another round?"

"Yes," Jo and I answered at the same time.

Jo's stare gradually shifted toward her dinner, and she dipped her fork into the fish. "I'm glad I listened to you. This is excellent."

I took another sip of my scotch, the drink far more important than food in this moment.

But as I swallowed, she nodded toward my plate. "Aren't you going to have some?"

I tilted my head back, taking down the rest of my drink. After I licked the wetness off my mouth, I answered, "I'm just savoring it, Joanna."

The architect looked down at his notes and said, "I think I have everything I need." A camera hung from his neck, and he turned on the digital display, viewing the shots he'd taken. "I'm going to get the exact specs from the county, and we'll have another survey done. I know the rock and earth have been tested for weight and stability, but I'm going to have more in-depth tests done, so we don't run into any problems down the road. Do you have any questions for me?"

"I know your team will be putting together a physical 3D rendering. Is it possible to do a digital one first?" Jo asked.

He lowered his camera onto his chest. "I don't see why not."

"There are so many details involved with the aesthetics and facade of this hotel. I think going from drawing to digital would give us a real taste of what we're looking at," Jo said. "I would hate to make changes to the physical rendering if we don't have to."

He glanced down at his notes. "To be honest, it's an excellent suggestion. The structure of this hotel is unlike anything I've ever built for your father. I don't know if this is your influence or if he's feeling inspired by the mountains, but it's been a long time since I've been this excited to start a new project."

"This is all Joanna's creation," I told him.

I'd had a feeling she wasn't going to comment, so I did, making sure she received every bit of the credit.

For the last two hours, I'd listened to her conduct this meeting, describing the features she wanted to see when pulling up to the hotel. She even got as particular as the texture of the building, the shape of the windows, the slant and slope of the entrance. And what I'd learned was that she wasn't just a gorgeous face behind the brand; she was a powerhouse and as humble as she was beautiful.

I wasn't impressed.

I was blown the fuck away.

"I had a feeling," the architect said. He stuck out his hand in Jo's direction. "I look forward to working on this project with you. I'm positive my team will have questions—"

"I'm available twenty-four/seven," she replied before he could finish his thought. "Whatever you guys need, I'm here for it."

He nodded. "We appreciate that." He released her hand and moved to mine. "Jenner, it's always a pleasure."

"Likewise."

As he walked to his car, Jo and I made our way over to the SUV waiting for us in the lot. The driver opened the door to the backseat, and before Jo climbed in, she turned around, viewing the entire mountainside.

"Something tells me this hotel is going to do magical things for our company."

Now that it was their land, I agreed.

We had spent the entire day yesterday going back and forth with the seller, and after multiple rounds of negotiations, he finally caved and accepted our offer. Walter had been shocked at the price I had secured, ecstatic that it was fifteen percent lower than what they had asked.

"Jo, you're going to turn this into the most magnificent property. I'm excited to book the penthouse for a weekend."

She laughed, her gaze dropping to meet mine. "We would never let you book one of our rooms. You will always stay at our hotels for free. Besides, you'll soon have your own home, so you won't need to stay here."

"They haven't accepted my offer."

A warmth moved across her face as she said, "They will."

She took a final glance around and climbed into the backseat, her jacket riding up just high enough to give me the perfect view of her ass. The black pants were slick against her cheeks, showing the arch and curves and—

Fuck.

I looked away, the temptation far too strong, and I got in behind her. The driver shut the door, and before I even had on my seat belt, my phone was ringing from my pocket. My realtor's name lit up the screen.

I held the phone to my face and answered. "This is Jenner."

"Congratulations," she replied. "The house is yours."

I shook my head, chuckling. "I never thought they'd even consider that lowball offer."

"Their realtor told me they had two offers in the past that fell through because of financing. When they reviewed your proof of funds, I'm sure they realized you're a buyer they can't lose." The sound in the background told me she was on the road. "I'll take care of the inspection, and we'll start processing title insurance. I know you said you're flying out tomorrow. Do you want to do another walk-through before you leave?"

I checked my watch. "Could I do one in the next thirty minutes?"

"I'm headed to a showing right now, and I'll be tied up for most of the afternoon. I can text you the code, and you can let yourself in and lock up when you're done."

"That would be great. Thanks for your hard work on this," I said and hung up.

The moment I slid my phone into my pocket, Jo's hand was on me, her touch sending a jolt straight through my body.

"You got the house, didn't you?"

I exhaled, still trying to process the news. "I did."

"Yes!" Since she hadn't put on her seat belt, she slid toward the middle, throwing her arms around my neck. "Oh my God, Jenner, I'm so happy for you."

Her scent hit me first. Something I'd been smelling since this morning, but now that my face was near her neck, I could take a long, deep inhale of that fall pumpkin perfume. My arms wrapped around her back, her jacket thin enough that her bra strap was teasing my fingers, and so was the heat of her skin. Her hair tickled my cheeks as I got in closer, her body molding against mine.

Goddamn it, I missed this.

The feel of her.

The feeling inside me when she was in my arms.

"You're going to have so many amazing memories in that house," she whispered, squeezing my shoulders before she pulled away.

I didn't want to let her go.

I didn't want her to fall from my grasp.

But she was moving to the other side of the backseat, and it'd happened far too fast.

I didn't know what came over me, but as I looked at her gorgeous face, I said, "Do you want to go see it?"

She instantly nodded. "I would love to."

I gave the driver the address, and he headed for the road that took us up the steep mountain edge. When he parked in the driveway, Jo got out of the SUV first.

"The pictures didn't do it justice," she said, staring at the large two-story contemporary design.

The house was done in shades of slate and charcoal, and stone covered different parts of the exterior, adding to the unique construction.

"This house, Jenner"—she took a breath—"is so dreamy."

I walked with her to the front door, entering the code my realtor had texted me. Once I had it open, I let her go in first.

"Holy fuck," she gasped, her neck immediately tilting back as she took in the tall ceiling. "This is spectacular."

She moved through the large foyer and past the living room, stopping at the back of the house. This section was all glass, revealing a view similar to what the hotel would have, the scenery just of a different angle of the mountain range and the dips and valleys below.

I opened the door for her, and she walked out onto the patio.

"Jenner ..." She paused, almost like she was breathless. "This is a dream." She finally turned toward me, my stare already on her. "It's nice to see you smiling again. I mean, really smiling."

There was only one thing causing my grin, and it wasn't the house.

TWENTY-SIX

JOANNA

"So, you're on your way back," my father said from the speaker of Jenner's phone, where it was resting on the table between our seats.

"We're about to be, yes," I said. "The pilots are doing their final check, and we'll be taking off any minute."

"I know I've mentioned this already, but I couldn't be more pleased with the work you two have accomplished this week. I just read the email from our architect, and his initial thoughts from your meeting are quite impressive," my father said. "And, Jenner, I don't know how you scored us that price. I was expecting a seven or eight percent decrease, but fifteen? Unbelievable job."

"Joanna was an incredible help," Jenner said, his eyes only on me.

I was pleasantly surprised when he'd chosen to sit across from me rather than on the other side of the aisle, like on the way here. But that meant there were only two places to look—out the window or at him.

And no matter how hard I tried, his handsome face completely owned my vision.

"I might have steered the realtor's direction, but the meeting with the architect was all Joanna," Jenner continued. "She has quite a vision for this hotel."

"I see that," my father said. "The architect mentioned it's going to be my best property. Jenner, do you agree?"

"I do," he replied. "You know I'm rather biased when it comes to Utah; however, I don't think that's the sole reason. There's an elegance about this land, and the ideas that Joanna implemented are unlike anything this area has ever seen. Walter, your hotel is going to be a piece of art."

My father wasn't the type to praise one's efforts, only point out their weaknesses. I certainly wasn't expecting his compliments or Jenner's.

But something had changed during this trip.

The way he looked at me.

The way he treated me.

"I'll see you both in my office tomorrow morning for a recap," my father said.

"We'll be there," I replied.

"Have a safe flight," my father added before he hung up.

Jenner returned the phone to his pocket and watched me as the plane began to move toward the runway.

"Can I get you anything before takeoff, Miss Spade?" the flight attendant asked from the aisle.

I held my coffee in my hand, and some snacks were on the table behind me that I'd already dug into. "I'm all set. Thank you."

"And for you, Mr. Dalton?"

He gave a similar answer, and we were suddenly alone again.

"Thank you," I said softly, the plane picking up speed.

"You didn't have to say any of that to my father, but I appreciate it."

His hand rubbed over the side of his beard. "I was just speaking the truth."

I set my coffee in the holder and wrapped my arms around my stomach. "The night before we met with him, I had this dream about the hotel. I saw it clear as day, and I actually woke up and wrote it all down." I shrugged. "I didn't know if my thoughts would translate or if my ideas would even work, but I think it's worth trying."

"I'm not the only one who thinks it's going to work. I'm positive the architect does too." He pulled out his phone, tapping the screen a few times before he started to read from it. "*You weren't kidding, Jenner. She's a true visionary and certainly the most creative person on Walter's team. This design isn't just going to attract; it's going to win awards.*" He glanced up. "I've known him for a long time. We exchanged a few emails after our meeting."

"And now, I'm speechless."

"Don't underestimate yourself, Jo. You might be fresh out of college and a novice in this industry, but you were born to do this."

I couldn't help but notice how he fluctuated between my full name and nickname. I tried to decipher which he liked saying more and what occasion caused the difference.

But I couldn't.

I could only concentrate on his gaze.

"That means a lot to me," I whispered.

The plane lifted off the ground, and I looked out the window, watching us get closer to the clouds. "It's been fun, working with you on this project."

A heat filled my cheeks when our eyes connected. It

seemed his stare never left me—something he'd been doing more frequently the past couple days.

"You know, part of me thought you might strangle me during this trip. I'm glad you didn't." I winked. "We make a good team, Jenner."

We were just starting to level out in the air when he said, "I'm beginning to realize that too."

My chest ached from the look on his face, the intensity in his eyes.

I almost couldn't breathe.

"You know what else I've realized?"

I shook my head, not trusting myself to speak.

"How much I miss you."

TWENTY-SEVEN

JENNER

I couldn't fight this for a second longer.

Jo Spade needed to be mine.

I didn't know the ramifications of that decision, I didn't know what our future would look like, I didn't know how her father was going to react or how that would affect me—or us—but I had to be with her.

Because it was agonizing to be without her.

"You miss me?" she whispered.

"Those words aren't nearly strong enough." I gripped the armrests, so I wouldn't reach across the table and lift her from her seat. "I understand why you didn't tell me. I wish you had, I wish that weight weren't between us, but I get it." I studied her gorgeous face. "If you still want to be with me, then I need to find a way to talk to your father. I don't want to hide this from him." I took a deep breath. "I don't want to hide us." Our conversations were replaying in my head—each time she'd spoken about what she wanted and every time I'd told her it wouldn't work.

"I put myself through hell when I walked away from you.

Every single day has been a reminder of what I lost. From the meeting in your father's office right before we left and throughout this entire trip—it's all been fucking torture."

Emotion filled her eyes as I said, "I don't want to live without you, Jo."

"Jenner ... I ..." She swallowed and glanced out the window, her hand moving to her chest.

A sharp pain blasted through me as I tried to read her expression, fearing that I was too late, that she'd already moved on.

But she finally looked at me and whispered, "It's about damn time you came to your senses."

Her eyes confirmed what she'd said.

She wanted me.

"Get over here," I begged.

She quickly removed her seat belt and hurried over, sitting on my lap, throwing her arms around my shoulders.

I buried my face in her neck and squeezed her with all my strength, her body fitting so perfectly against mine. Holding the back of her head, I led her lips closer, moaning the second our mouths touched. I tasted her at first. Not gently. But with the desire that had been nagging through me for weeks, and when her lips parted, my tongue slipped through the opening, getting even more of her flavor.

"Fuck me," I hissed. "I've been thinking about these"—I tugged at her bottom lip and her top one—"since our last trip to Utah."

"I wish you hadn't waited so long to kiss me."

I held her face steady, scanning her eyes.

"I need to know that if things get hard or tough at any point, you're not going to dismiss me again." She clung to the back of my hand. "I need to know I'm really what you want, Jenner."

I pressed my forehead against hers. "Relationships are foreign to me. I don't know how to do this. I just know how I feel about you and what it feels like to not be with you." I gripped her cheeks even tighter. "That's something I'm never going through again."

"You make it sound like we're forever."

"We are." I leaned back, giving her my eyes, my emotions making my heart pound. "I let you go once, and it was a mistake. One that will never happen again." My thumbs traced the tops of her cheeks. "You're mine. Your heart, your body, your mind—all of it, all mine." There was one more thing bursting to come out, eating at my chest with fucking claws. "I love you, Jo."

I'd never said those words to another woman.

But I'd also never felt this way before.

I'd never wanted anyone as much as I wanted her.

"Jenner ..." Tears dripped from her eyelids, and I immediately wiped them. "I love you."

I kissed her again, this time much harder, and when I pulled back, I surrounded her bottom lip and bit down. "I need you. Right now." I adjusted her placement, positioning her pussy over my cock so she could feel how hard I was. "This is what you're doing to me."

"Here?" A bright red flush moved across her cheeks. "On Dad's plane?"

"In the bedroom in the back."

She took my lip into her mouth, the same way I'd just done to her, and when she released it, she said, "What are you waiting for?"

My fucking girl.

I lifted her off my lap and led her to the bedroom, closing the door behind us. It was a small space, just enough room for us to stand, with a double bed in the center and a narrow table on one side.

Once the door was locked, I slid my arms out of my suit jacket, loosened my tie, and worked on the buttons on my shirt.

She watched me from the bed, the hungriest grin on her mouth. "I've missed this view." Her stare slowly dropped all the way to my feet. "I'm just appreciating it for a second."

I could understand that.

In fact, I could give her more.

I finished the rest of the buttons and hung my shirt over the table before unlacing my shoes and stripping off my socks and pants, leaving just my boxer briefs.

"Those too," she said, nodding at my waist.

I dropped them down my legs and fisted my cock.

"Oh fuck, Jenner."

"Do you want this?"

She couldn't drag her eyes away from my dick, watching as I stroked myself. "Oh God, yes."

"Then, get naked."

Her shirt came flying off, and so did her bra, her pants lowering and her panties coming off with them. Within seconds, she was exactly how I wanted her.

Fucking bare.

My gaze took in her curves, the palm-sized tits that I loved to suck, her toned legs opening, fingers crawling down her body, rubbing my favorite spot.

"Jesus, Jo, you're fucking stunning."

She brushed her fingers across her clit.

"Does that feel good, baby?"

"Your tongue would feel better."

She wanted me to lick her cunt.

A request that couldn't be any sexier.

I knelt in the tiny space in front of the bed and pulled her ass across the mattress until her pussy reached my mouth. "I promise you"—I blew air across her, giving her just the very tip of my tongue, barely adding any pressure—"you will never forget this."

"Jenner ..." she moaned.

I breathed across her clit, just soft, normal bursts of air, gradually increasing the pressure. With each exhale, she quivered, rocking her hips, trying to get more of my tongue.

But I didn't give in.

I wanted to take my time.

I wanted to savor her pussy.

"You're torturing me," she cried, tugging my hair, trying to bring me closer.

I leaned back to kiss her lips, dropping as low as her entrance, rising to the peak of her clit. The view allowed me to see her whole pussy—every fold, every inch of skin, every part that needed to be licked.

"My fucking queen." I flattened my tongue and dragged it across her, her moans all I could hear. "Keep your legs spread," I warned, pushing them apart. "No matter what I do, I want them open. Do you hear me?"

She panted, "Yes."

She was perfect. Every goddamn part of her. But this part —*fuck me*—was exceptional.

I pressed my nose against her, inhaling her. A scent as addictive as the pumpkin perfume she wore. "You smell so fucking good."

Her skin was soft, smooth, like silk, my tongue lapping across her. And then there was the way she responded to me, how she shook when I flicked her horizontally, her body arching upward, her hips bucking.

Goose bumps rose over her flesh.

Wetness dripped.

I caught it with my tongue, spreading it across two fingers before they dived inside her. As I finger-fucked her, stretching her to get her ready for me, I circled, and I reached until I hit her G-spot.

"Oh my God!"

Her pussy was closing in around me.

She wanted the friction.

She wanted to fucking come.

"Jo, you're getting so tight."

I held her clit with my teeth, rolling my tongue across it.

Back and forth.

"Oh God," she breathed. "You're going to make me come."

I wanted to taste it.

I wanted to feel it.

I wanted to watch her fucking shudder as I licked her.

I pulled my finger out to my nail, and then arching it higher, I slid it back in, grazing that special spot.

Her hips shifted with each pass, her fingers bearing down on my head. "Jenner!"

As she screamed and wriggled, I saw the pleasure control her.

Own her.

Completely take over.

So, I switched up the pattern, moving my tongue vertically over the top, sucking her clit when the wetness became too much.

I was going to lick away every thought in her head.

Every worry.

Every tear she'd ever shed over us.

"Yes!" she shouted. "Fuck!"

I gave her the flat wideness of my tongue, the pointy tip, the length and width of my fingers, combining it all together at once. And I took my time because even though this was for her, it was very much for me.

Having her wetness coat my face and beard and run down my throat was as good as coming.

And she was about to. Sensing she was getting far too close, I slowed down.

Her hips lifted into the air, humping to my rhythm. Moaning, she tried to pull me closer, to speed me up, but I wouldn't budge.

I needed more of this.

I switched to my nose, rubbing it along her slit. I fucking hated that it had been so long since I'd been between her legs, soaking myself in her. I craved her pussy in ways I couldn't explain, in ways I didn't even understand.

And I was making up for lost time.

When the desire to taste her became stronger than just inhaling her, my tongue returned.

"Oh fuck, Jenner!"

Each word, each reaction made me lick harder.

Her hips began to sway again. Her arms reached above her, gripping the pillow like she was going to fall. Her knees bent, toes pressing into the mattress.

She was bracing herself.

And I didn't let up, giving her clit the most relentless caressing.

I twisted my fingers. I thrust.

I licked so fucking hard and quick that I could almost feel the rush happening inside her. Especially as she turned wetter, her pussy clenching my knuckles.

Her legs closed in, and she moaned. "I need your beard." She gasped from the roughness. "I need to feel it on my skin." Her lower back lifted, and her hands lowered, her nails stabbing my shoulders seconds before she began to shudder. "Jenner!" She sucked in a breath. "Oh my God!"

She pulsed around me, and I gave her one last push—a speed I hadn't used yet, knowing it would send her so far over the edge.

"*Fuuuck.*"

I watched her body shake, each wave coming with a new, louder moan. And as her orgasm erupted, her ass lifting after each tremor, the best feeling took over me.

There was nothing better than making your girl feel this good.

When she finally calmed, there should have been a satiated look in her eyes. But there wasn't. There was a feral one, and she was reaching for me, leading me up the mattress until our bodies were aligned.

"This mouth"—she ran her fingers over my lips—"is lethal."

"It's missed you." I held the back of her head. "Kiss me. I want you to taste yourself."

She briefly nibbled on her lip before our mouths slammed together, a pent-up breath releasing when our tongues touched.

Her hands were sliding around my body, tracing my chest and down my arms, across my abs until my cock was in her palm.

And so fucking slowly, she began to stroke it.

"I need you," she whispered.

Her legs wrapped around me, leading my tip toward her pussy.

And just as her wetness began to taunt me, I remembered something.

Something that made my fist want to pound the bed.

I pulled my lips away, squeezing her cheeks. "We can't, Jo." I swallowed, the thought so fucking painful. "I don't have a condom on me."

I hadn't brought one to Utah on purpose. I didn't want to be tempted.

In my mind, there was no way this was going to happen.

I wasn't going to let it.

Because no matter what I did, I couldn't change the fact that she was Walter's daughter.

But it had taken me this long to realize that I didn't need to change who her father was. I just needed to find a way to make it work.

"You told me you loved me," she said softly into my face. "Was that true?"

I pressed harder against the sides of her face, so she would feel these words as I said, "With every bit of my fucking being."

"Then, we don't need a condom."

My cock throbbed at the thought.

I never went without a condom.

But there had never been a woman like Jo in my life.

"You're on the pill?"

She nodded. "And I'm clean. I assume you are too."

I didn't hesitate.

I just reared my hips back and sank into her hot, tight, wet cunt, moaning, "Jo," so fucking loud into her mouth.

The rubber had always acted as a barrier, never allowing me to truly feel the heat of a woman.

But we were skin on skin, and she was fucking sopping.

And I was overwhelmed at this level of pleasure.

Her legs tightened around me, her arms circling my shoulders, and I got up on my knees and lifted her with me, pumping into her as I held her in the air. She began to move with me, meeting me, grinding over my dick.

"Fuck me," I roared. "You feel incredible."

I got us to the end of the bed and sat on the edge, my feet on the plane's floor as I straddled her over me. "Ride me." I ravished her mouth the moment it came near me. "Own my cum like it's yours."

"But it is mine, Jenner."

She teased my crown with her wetness, my fingers biting her in response, until she lowered all the way to my base.

"Goddamn it, Jo."

I tried to find air, to push away that climax that was already threatening, to just enjoy this moment.

But some things felt too fucking good, and her pussy was one.

My neck leaned back, my eyes aimed at the cabin ceiling, my balls tightened as she turned her hips, rocking her pussy forward and back, rising every other motion.

"Fuck!"

I held her waist, lost in those delicious curves, guiding her speed.

But she didn't need the help, nor could I control her.

This was what she wanted.

And she was fucking taking it.

As I looked at her again, her tits jumped from every bounce, her mouth opened from the pleasure. Her hair fell over her shoulders, hiding her nipples, and I leaned forward, taking one of those hard buds into my mouth.

Gnawing, sucking, licking like it was her clit.

I watched her face as she fucked me, a determination in her eyes.

There was no question in either of our minds—my cock was hers.

And she was claiming every inch of it.

Not letting up until I filled her.

"If you don't slow down," I warned, "you're going to make me come."

My fingers went to her clit, feeling the wetness that covered it, and I rubbed her.

She moaned, "You're going to do the same to me." Her teeth sank into my lip. "And it's going to happen fast."

I could see the sensation moving through her body.

I could sense it.

Because it was spreading into me.

My balls ached for a release, my body almost turning numb as she plunged over me.

"Jo." I couldn't hold off any longer. Not with the tightness that was taking over, not with the warmth that was swallowing me. "Fuck yes!"

Her speed increased, her hips swayed, and I swore I was going in even deeper.

"Oh, Jenner," she cried and then screamed as I added more friction to her clit. "Fuck!"

She was unraveling.

Shuddering.

Yelling out her orgasm.

And I was right behind her.

I arched my back, driving into her, repeating the same movement until the intensity blasted through me. I grabbed her with my other arm, each stroke milking me harder.

When she pressed her lips to mine, letting me taste her orgasm, it was my turn to lose it.

Her tightness narrowed around me, and each dip sucked more cum from my cock, my load soaking into her wetness.

"Jo ..."

I began to slow, and she took over, keeping up the motion until I made her stop.

My fingers left her clit, and I wrapped her in my other arm, pulling her against my chest.

When I finally caught my breath, I cupped her face, my eyes finding hers. "I'm so fucking in love with you."

Her long lashes blinked several times; her teeth found her lip.

But her smile was there.

It was always there.

"Jenner, my heart is yours."

TWENTY-EIGHT

JOANNA

The moment Jenner was within reach, I stood on the tips of my toes and wrapped my arms around his neck. As we hugged, I pressed my face to his chest, my cheek against his hard muscles. My eyes closed as my hands fisted his shirt. I inhaled as deep as I could to fill my lungs with him, his spicy cologne taking hold of me.

"Hi," I said softly, glancing up at his face.

"*Mmm.* I've missed you." He pressed his mouth to mine, giving me his tongue before he sucked my bottom lip into his mouth—his favorite of the two. "I thought about you all day." His hands lowered to my butt, squeezing my cheeks. "You know what didn't help?"

I grinned, already knowing the answer. "What's that?"

"That fucking picture you sent me."

My head tilted back as I laughed. "About that ... I'm sorry, I guess?"

While I'd been at lunch with two of my colleagues, I'd gone to the restroom, and before I dropped my thong all the way down, I'd snapped a photo and sent it to him.

"Do you know how hard it was not to drive to your office and fuck you on top of your desk?" He cupped my pussy over my dress. "Knowing I couldn't because I didn't want your father to get wind of me coming there." His mouth moved to my neck. "So, that wasn't very nice of you to tease me like that."

I squirmed as his tongue tickled my skin. "I thought you needed a sample of what you're going to get tonight."

His mouth went to my collarbone, kissing the sensitive spot near my throat. "You know how much I love your pussy, how much I crave it. You left me with a hard-on all goddamn day."

His exhales caused my nipples to pebble, my body to set on fire.

My legs begged to spread.

His hands moved to my face, holding my cheeks steady. "I spent hours at my desk, thinking about what I was going to do to your cunt tonight."

Tingles spread through me. "What are you waiting for?"

He took my earlobe into his mouth. "For my chef to leave."

My eyelids opened. "He's here? Now?"

I'd smelled something amazing when I walked into his house a few seconds ago. Since Jenner's office was off the entryway and he'd been sitting behind his desk, I hadn't made it into the kitchen to see that it was his chef and not takeout.

"He is," he said, "and dinner should be ready in five minutes."

"I'm starving."

He smiled, pressing his finger to the center of my lips. "You know that throb you're feeling between your legs right now? That's what I've been feeling since your little photo stunt." I went to respond, but he pushed down harder. "The second he's gone, my cock is going to slide in here"—he traced the slit of my mouth—"and then it's going in here." He dropped his hand to my pussy.

I moaned. "Where's your mouth going?"

"Baby, you know that I dream about licking your pussy." He grazed his nose across my cheek. "But if you need to hear me say it, then I can tell you, I haven't stopped thinking about how you're going to taste. How I want your wetness all over my lips and soaking in my beard."

I practically shuddered. "Jenner ..."

"I'm going to slip a finger into your ass and finger-fuck that tight, wet hole while I lick you, and when you come"—he moved his mouth to my ear—"I'm not going to stop. I'm going to do it again. And again."

I couldn't breathe.

"Are you wet?"

He reached under the bottom of my dress, touching the outside of my panties. The sensation of his fingers running along the satin sent an explosion through me. It only heightened when he moved the material to the side and touched my clit.

"Yes ... so fucking wet." He brought his fingers to his mouth, smelling me, licking me off him. "Now, it's time for dinner."

He led me out of his office, every step causing my body to ache even more for his touch. It felt like he had brought me to the edge of an orgasm, and suddenly, his tongue had stopped, leaving me there, hanging, shouting for more. And I was still internally yelling as we arrived in the kitchen, where his chef was plating our food.

"Good evening, Craig," I said, smiling at him.

My cheeks were flushed, like I'd just stepped out of Jenner's sauna, my breath labored.

I hoped Craig couldn't tell.

"Nice to see you, Jo." His gaze shifted to Jenner as he said,

"I've set you guys up on the patio. If you want to take a seat, I'll bring out an appetizer in just a second."

"Thank you," I replied.

Through the sliding door, Jenner brought me outside and onto his large pool deck. The view showed the gorgeous homes that were similar to his, sitting along the Hollywood Hills. And along the edge, before his property dropped, Craig had placed a table with candles and linens.

We took a seat across from each other, and Jenner lifted the bottle of cab that Craig had left for us and filled our glasses. The moment he was done pouring, I wrapped my fingers around the stem.

"Rough day?" he asked as I sipped.

"It wasn't until you made me drool in your office." I winked. "Not really. It was just a long day." I took another drink, holding the glass to my chest so the wine wouldn't be far. "We're putting together the marketing campaign for Utah, and the twenty-million-dollar renovation on our Napa hotel was just finished, so we're planning a whole reopening and kickoff for that property." I took a breath. "And working for my father is interesting—you know, when it comes to duties and expectations and all the things." I swallowed down a bit more wine. "There's just a lot going on."

"I know better than anyone what it's like to work with parents. I understand."

I nodded, knowing he got exactly what I was talking about. "And I miss Monica. She's been gone now for three weeks, and texting and FaceTime just aren't the same."

I couldn't be happier for my bestie. She'd scored a job with the most-sought-after stylist in LA—a connection she'd made through James, Brett's fiancée. But now, she was on the road more than she was home, traveling the world to style their clients.

"When does she get back?"

"Next week," I told him. "But only for three days, and then she leaves for Paris."

He grinned. "LA has been good for her."

"No, LA has been great for her."

I quieted as Craig approached with two small plates in his hands. "Homemade pork dumplings over a seaweed, cucumber, and kimchi salad." He placed them in front of us. "Enjoy."

Every time I ate over here, Craig's cooking continuously blew me away. He was better than any restaurant I'd been to in this city.

"Looks incredible, as always," I told him, my mouth watering.

"And it smells delicious," Jenner added.

He thanked us and went back inside the house.

"Wow." I moaned from behind my hand, chewing my first bite. "This is wildly good."

Jenner held his fork in the air, not touching his food yet. "Has LA been as good for you?"

"Eh, it's been all right." I shrugged. "I only scored the most delicious boyfriend in the world, who I'm completely obsessed with, and I have a job that's challenging in the most fulfilling ways." I chewed his favorite lip. "I'd say it's going great for me too."

His leg grazed mine under the table. "Minus the elephant in the room."

"Ugh. *Thaaat.*" I shoved a cucumber into my mouth. "Let's skip that convo and move on to something better, like what we're going to do tomorrow since we both have the day off."

Except, as he stared at me, finally chewing his first bite, the elephant wasn't gone.

It was very much standing between us.

And that was the impending conversation we needed to have with my father.

When we'd returned from Utah six weeks ago, Jenner had insisted we talk to him immediately. He didn't want there to be any secrets. He wanted us to be able to live freely without any weight bearing on us. His reasoning made sense. I just wasn't ready to go there. Before we tackled that massive task, I wanted Jenner to be positive that this was what he really wanted.

That *I* was what he wanted.

And every single day since we'd gotten back, he'd proven that to me.

He'd once told me that relationships were foreign to him, that he didn't know how to be in one.

But he was the most attentive, compassionate, loving man I had ever been with.

And he was right; it was time to tell Dad.

I just feared what that would look like and how Jenner would react to whatever transpired, so avoiding the situation was easier.

"I can't convince you to talk about your dad?" he asked.

I shook my head. "Not tonight."

"Then, let's talk about tomorrow."

I reached for my wine again. "Yes, tomorrow. What's on your mind?"

He finished the last piece of kimchi and said, "We can take our time waking up and go for a run at Runyon Canyon. Stop somewhere for brunch and come back to my place to get the massages I've scheduled for us. When those are done, I see a long nap before we get ready for dinner." He wiped his mouth with his napkin. "We have a reservation at Nobu."

I sighed, reaching across the table until my fingers landed on his. "I love you."

"Anything you want to add or change?"

"It all sounds dreamy."

Craig came back to our table, adding more wine to our glasses and removing our plates. "Are you ready for the main course, or do you want me to hold off for a bit?"

The sooner we finished this heavenly meal, the sooner Jenner's hands would be on my body.

"I'm ready," I told him.

Jenner agreed.

Once we were alone again, I said, "How about tonight? What's on the agenda?"

He glanced toward the Hills, where the sun was starting to set, an orange sky lighting up the space above our heads. "We're going to finish eating and have dessert." He turned back in my direction, smiling. "There's a shipment from Gloria waiting for us in my kitchen."

My eyes widened. "You didn't?"

He chuckled. "I fucking did." He leaned forward, getting closer. "It arrived this morning, and there's a shitload of blueberry cake and blueberry fudge in the box."

"Did I already tell you I love you? Because I need to tell you again."

"I love you too, baby." He moved his elbows to the table, getting even closer than before. "Once we're done, I'm going to strip off your clothes, and we're getting in the hot tub." He rolled his neck to each side. "I think we could both use it after a long week."

"You're talking porn to me right now."

He laughed again. "And then I'm carrying you into my shower, where I'll set you on the bench inside and spread your legs over the granite, and I'm going to get on my knees to eat your fucking pussy."

I took a breath, but I wasn't sure how.

I was positive there wasn't any air left in my body.

"If you don't stop," I warned, "I'm going to drag you into your bedroom right now and spoil this whole dinner."

He rubbed the back side of my hand, a sly expression crossing his face. "You liked tomorrow's plan. Is there anything you want to add to tonight? Anything you want to negotiate?"

My body was pulsing.

My pussy clenching.

"Let me guess, Jo ... you're fucking wet again."

TWENTY-NINE

JENNER

"Good morning, baby," I whispered, running my hand over the back of Jo's head, my fingers lost in her locks.

She tilted her face to glance up at me, eyes still heavy with sleep, hair wild from the way I had ravaged her last night.

Another Saturday, and I got this one all to myself.

"*Mmm,*" she yawned.

For the last two months that she'd been waking up in my bed, I'd learned that mornings were her least favorite time of day. She needed time to rise, time before she was ready for conversation. But seeing her face fresh without makeup, feeling her skin extra warm, having her completely naked in my arms—this was my favorite time of the day.

I couldn't get enough of her.

And I had no problem holding her just like this for the next several hours, but I was positive there was something she was craving, especially as the sun came in through my windows, casting its rays across her cheeks.

"Coffee?"

"*Mmm,*" she groaned again. "Please."

I kissed the top of her head. "Be right back."

I slid out from underneath her, grabbing my phone from the nightstand before I made my way into the kitchen. As I placed the first cup under the brewing machine, I scrolled through all the messages that had come in overnight. Aside from a multitude of emails, there was a group text that caught my attention.

Walter: I just received the digital rendering from our architect. I need the both of you in my office at 10 tomorrow morning.

The time on the microwave told me that was in two hours.

On a Saturday.

I sent a quick reply, telling him I would be there, and I made a second coffee, carrying them both into my bedroom, where Jo hadn't moved.

"Thank you," she grumbled, holding out her hand, gently sitting up to sip. Once she had a few swallows down her throat, she eyed me as I climbed into bed. "The most irresistible body and makes the best cup of coffee—my God, I'm lucky."

I laughed, pulling the blanket back over me, positioning her so she was close, carefully so she wouldn't spill. "Not to kill the mood, but you might want to check your phone." Her head tilted, and I added, "Your dad needs us to come in. The rendering is done."

She held her finger in the air, burying her face in the cup, downing what looked like half the coffee. "There, that's a little better. Now, say that again. Us? Going into the office? Today?"

I nodded. "In two hours."

"When he sees the design, this is either going to turn into the best day ever or he's going to wish he never hired me."

I brushed my fingers across her cheek. "It's not going to be the latter."

She shrugged. "But it could be."

I knew what would make this day better.

If I could walk into the office, holding Jo's hand. If I could sit next to her in the meeting with my fingers on her thigh. If I could look at her the same way I was right now without worrying that her father would know what was on my mind.

But I couldn't.

Because Walter still didn't know about us.

And every time I brought that up, Jo didn't want to talk about it.

"I wish I weren't able to read your thoughts." She grabbed a pillow and tucked it against her chest, resting her mug on top of it. "I'm sorry ..."

I set my coffee down and wrapped my arm around the back of her. "For what?"

"Everything. This. Us." She was staring at the top of her cup and slowly looked at me. "He needs you. Spade Hotels needs you. Every time I go into the office, I'm reminded of how integral you are to our brand and ..." Her voice faded out while she pressed her hand against her chest. "I'm worried I've ruined that. That's why I'm afraid to tell him, Jenner."

My fingers moved to her face, holding her so she wouldn't look away.

I didn't know if I believed this, but I still had to say, "It'll be all right."

I just wanted to take the worry from her. I didn't want it eating at her like it was doing to me.

She shook her head. "But it's not all right." She took a deep breath. "When I was in Vegas, I didn't think. I didn't understand. And now that I work there, now that I see your role, I do." Emotion started to fill her eyes. "If he fires you, it could be so detrimental—to him and to the future of our company."

I took the coffee out of her hand, setting it on my nightstand, and I pulled her into my arms, pressing my lips to the top of her head. "I'm only a lawyer, Jo. There are many others out there who are just like me, who can do what I do. I have an entire firm of them, and I can certainly suggest someone on my team who can help your father the same way I can—"

"No." She leaned back to look at me. "I know you're just trying to make me feel better, and I appreciate that, but there's not a single lawyer in this country who can do what you do. That's why you're the best, why Google says you're worth as much as you are—a number I can't even wrap my head around, let alone understand the meaning of."

She'd Googled me. She was so fucking adorable.

And even though this was a sensitive topic between us, I hated that she was hurting.

I brushed my thumb across her cheek, nearing those lips that I loved so much. "I can't predict what's going to happen or how he's going to react. All I know is, the sooner we tell him, the better we'll feel."

Her eyes changed, a look of fear entering them. "Are you sure about that?"

Jo, who had left my house fifteen minutes before me, was already in the conference room when I walked in. Despite our conversation this morning, we still wanted to play it safe. So, with Walter at the head and Jo at his right, I took a seat on his opposite side and folded my hands on top of the table.

"Thank you for coming in on a Saturday," Walter said, dressed as though this were a Monday morning press conference.

I'd done the same, wearing a black suit for the occasion, his retainer ensuring that I would be on and prepared, no matter the day or time.

"You asked for a digital mockup before the physical rendering," Walter said to Jo. "So, that's what the architect has prepared."

As excited as I was for this moment, I was also dreading it. The ideas Jo had given the architect were unique and sounded fantastic, but that didn't mean they would translate to a design that would actually work. I was worried like hell that I was going to hate it. That Walter was going to hate it. That I would give my opinion—something I would never lie about—and it wouldn't be in her favor.

That in front of her father, I'd have to go against the woman I loved.

And knowing how much Walter valued my opinion, it made me sick to think what that would do to her career.

Walter pointed a remote toward the wall of TVs, and they all turned on at the same time, showing the design of the building. He pressed another button, and the angle changed, revealing each side of the massive structure and the way it was embedded into the mountain. "The architect took Joanna's concept, and this is what his team came up with."

Jesus fucking Christ.

I was speechless.

The hotel was shaped like a tree trunk, protruding out the side of the rock, starting out wide at the bottom and gradually thinning as it grew the twenty-two stories, expanding again as it neared the top. The texture matched the look and feel of the mountains, the spiral grooves etched into the facade, like the rings inside a tree.

As the image continued to spin across the screens, I glanced at Walter and then at Jo, waiting for one of them to say something.

"Joanna, is this what you wanted him to build?"

I put my hands in my lap, so he wouldn't see me wringing my fingers.

She was slow to look at her father, staying reserved when she said, "Yes." She swallowed. "I know you had visions for it as well, and I tried to relay those to the architect. I realize this isn't what we discussed, but I've studied this town and our intended demographic, Dad. I've analyzed our competition. I truly believe in my heart that this is going to set us apart."

His face stayed stoic when he looked at me and added, "What do you think, Jenner?"

Jo had taken a gamble.

An expensive one.

One that had more than paid off.

I took a deep breath, slowly glancing over at Jo before I gave him my honesty. "There's nothing traditional about this build-out, nor does it match any of the buildings in your portfolio. But I don't think it should. What Joanna and the architect have created makes a statement. It makes the property desirable. People will want to stay there just to say they've been there. That right there is effortless marketing, and it doesn't get much better than that." My leg bounced under the table as I continued, "You know I've been all over the world, and not a single hotel I've been in is as beautiful as this one."

"I see," he replied.

He glanced back at his daughter, and I still couldn't get a read on him, his opinion and thoughts not making their way to his face.

"Joanna ..." he started and stopped.

My fucking stomach hurt for her.

I'd been in the same position as her many times in the past. I'd presented new ventures to my parents, waiting for their response, their aloof faces staring back at me in the boardroom.

I knew this was a moment she'd been anxious about.

I also knew this could be a huge breakthrough for her career—or not.

"I knew my inability to meet with the architect was going to result in a shift of control, that you were going to heavily influence this project." He shook his head. "I've been worried about what that would look like from a brand standpoint and how that could affect your future at this company. I certainly can't have my daughter having a vision so vastly different than my own. And then I see this and ..." His head dropped, and so did my goddamn stomach. "It's exactly what Spade Hotels needs." He gazed up at her, pride now filling his stare. "I couldn't be prouder. You really delivered on this one, pumpkin."

As I processed his words, relief passed through me.

Jo's face mirrored the same feeling, a warmth now growing across her lips.

She quickly looked at me, and I squeezed in, "Congratulations, Joanna."

Her grin grew, and she said, "Dad, you love it? Really?"

"It's stunning," he replied. "You've exceeded every expectation, and Lord knows, I set hundreds for this project." He smiled. "Never did I think you'd create something this special, but I should have known better—you've proven me wrong at every stage of your life. This moment, this achievement, this massive undertaking is certainly no different."

"To you," I said, holding my scotch in the air, a small table separating us at the restaurant.

Jo blushed, raising her champagne. "We're toasting to me?"

"And we will be for weeks to come. That design, Jo"—I

shook my head, clinking my glass against hers—"is fucking gorgeous."

"Thank you." She sipped from the flute. "I had a lot of faith in our architect, but I didn't think he'd capture my ideas practically word for word."

I set my drink down and reached across the table, covering her hand with mine. "You should have seen the way your father was looking at you. You're his whole world."

"The man about gave me a heart attack. I was positive he was going to tell me he hated it and then fire me."

"But he loved it."

"I'm honestly still in shock." She clung to the thin stem, staring at the bubbly. "You know, I always pictured myself working for him, but I never knew what that would really look like."

Our eyes finally locked.

"My parents divorced when I was ten. I lived with Mom mostly. Dad took me every other weekend, and most of those were spent flying to one of his hotels. A nanny would watch me while I played in the pool, so he could meet with the executive staff of the property." Her fingers tightened, and so did my grip. "I heard his phone calls, I listened to him talk to his employees whenever I was in his office, and I tried to picture myself on the other end of that conversation. It's one thing to be an alpha's daughter; it's a whole other thing to work for him."

"And impress him." I smiled. "But you have."

A gentleness came through her eyes. "I can't even tell you how overwhelming that feels."

"Baby, trust me, I know."

She placed her free hand over the back of mine, our fingers now stacked together, and she took several deep breaths, taking her time to say, "Today proved a lot to me, Jenner, and I know" —her voice softened—"it's time."

THIRTY

JENNER

When the waitress had taken our drink orders, I'd been tempted to ask for the entire bottle of scotch rather than just a tumbler with a few fingers poured neatly. But getting shit-faced at a dinner where I was about to tell my largest, most important client that I was dating his daughter didn't sound like the appropriate thing to do.

I needed to be aware.

Conscious.

I had to be on more than ever before.

So, I'd asked for a double instead, and I held the glass in my hand while the three of us sat in LA's finest steak house.

I'd taken Walter here before, so I knew how much he enjoyed the food. I'd hoped the dim lighting, which was far more forgiving than sunlight, and the dark wood accents would create a relaxing vibe for him.

Except he didn't appear relaxed at all.

In fact, for the last five minutes, he'd been on the phone, dealing with what sounded like an emergency at one of the properties.

Jo kept looking at me, gaining my attention each time her eyes widened, each time her head turned toward me. Without speaking, I knew she was wondering if we should postpone the talk to a later date.

But if we didn't do it now, we would continue to put it off.

I didn't want that.

I was ready to face this head-on, regardless of the outcome.

Walter's opinion wouldn't affect anything between Jo and me.

But what if he forbids us from being together?

What if he tells me to never get near his daughter again?

What if he fires her for this? Or forces her to resign?

What if he tells me he's going to ruin my reputation?

I couldn't think about that.

I couldn't think about the problems this could cause.

I could only think about the relief I would feel when I finally told him the news, and that was what I concentrated on during the silence and when the waitress approached our table again.

"Can I get you any appetizers?" she asked. "Or are you ready to order your main courses?"

Food was the perfect distraction.

"Can we get a couple Caesar salads to share?" I asked. "We'll also have the calamari and the beef carpaccio. I think that's enough for now."

"I'll get those started," she replied and left our table.

Jo had been holding her menu and placed it down in front of her. "I'm going to run to the ladies' room," she said, rising from her seat.

I tried to keep my eyes off her as she walked away from the table, but I couldn't.

Not when she had on that dress.

One that was red and short, only reaching the top of her

knees, hugging her ass the way I would if my hands were on her cheeks.

She was so incredibly sexy.

And she was mine.

"Just handle it, do you hear me?" Walter said.

The sound of his voice pulled my eyes away from Jo, and I instantly connected with his stare.

He hung up and shoved his phone in his pocket. "The fire alarms are going off at my hotel in Manhattan. No fire, but they can't seem to find the cause. Total fucking shitshow."

I reached for my drink, needing it much closer.

And before I was able to respond, he said, "What were we talking about before my phone rang?"

I tried to remember the conversation.

Utah?

Marketing?

The Napa renovation?

Jesus, Jenner.

My brain was so busy that I couldn't even remember five minutes ago.

"Ah," he said, "to be young and handsome again."

He had glanced away, and I was so lost in my thoughts that I had no idea what he was referring to.

"I'm sorry?"

"Every woman who walks by stares at you." He nodded in the direction where Jo had disappeared.

I held my breath as I looked that way.

The woman he was referencing was tall and blonde, her dress putting her tits on full display.

She held my eyes until she turned the corner.

"Is she on the conquered list?" He chuckled. "Or is she one you're about to follow into the restroom?"

Fuck.

I regretted the conversation we'd had over that dinner where he learned how much of a player I was.

But never had I imagined I'd be here.

"That's the old Jenner," I told him. "I'm a new man now."

"A new man," he mirrored. "Does that mean she's back in your life? Or there's someone new?"

The brief conversation we'd had was replaying in my head.

"She's back," I told him.

He took a piece of bread out of the basket and bit off the corner. "So, timing was on your side after all, then."

"Yeah ..." I eyed the bread, but I wasn't ready to put anything in my stomach. "Something like that."

"What did I miss?" Jo asked as she took her seat.

"Jenner was just telling me that he's off the market." Walter chuckled. "Take it from a perpetual bachelor who's seen it all; when a woman returns to your life, she doesn't leave again. That shit right there deserves to be celebrated." He raised his glass and clinked it against mine.

Jo looked at me, her expression telling me she wanted to make a fucking run for it.

My chest tightened. My hands felt unsteady as I lowered my glass and said, "Walter, there's something I need to talk to you about." I made eye contact with Jo again. "Something *we* need to talk to you about."

"I assumed that's why we're here." He moved his menu to the side, leaning his elbows on the table. "What's going on? Do you have more ideas for Utah? A change in the design? What?"

I'd spent all day trying to come up with the best way to discuss this with him. How to approach the conversation. What angle to take.

But as my mouth opened, I forgot every goddamn thing I'd planned.

My mind went blank.

I took a deep breath, holding in the air. "I'm in love with your daughter."

He looked at Jo and then back at me. "You're ... *what*?"

That certainly wasn't the way I'd wanted to initiate this talk, but, fuck, it suddenly felt like the right way. The words he needed to hear first before I backtracked to the beginning.

"Hold on ..." His eyes bounced from Jo to me, like we were getting cross-examined. "I need to make sure I heard you correctly." His cheeks were beginning to turn red. "You said"—he exhaled, his head shaking—"you're in love ... with my daughter?"

"Yes," I replied.

"What the fuck?" His face was now fully flushed, his voice getting louder.

"Let me explain myself—"

"Jenner, I would say you have a lot of explaining to do."

I quickly came up with a starting point and kept my voice low as I said, "I met Joanna when I was in Vegas for March Madness. I didn't know who she was. In fact, I didn't find out she was your daughter until months later, during our first trip to Utah."

His brows furrowed, and his fingers clenched, his knuckles sticking up like points. "I don't understand ..."

"Dad," Jo chimed in, "we're asking for your blessing." She reached across the space between us, her hand resting on top of my arm. "He's the man I want to be with."

He lifted his glass and took a long, heavy drink. When he returned his scotch to the table, he wiped his lips with the back of his hand, his mouth turning into a thin line. "Let me get this straight. You, the man I've trusted with every business venture for the last—I don't know—seven years, wants my blessing, so you can be with my daughter?"

My chest was so fucking tight that a finger tap would shatter it. "Yes."

His stare shifted to Jo's hand before he glared at me. "Looks like you already took what you wanted, Jenner, and it sounds like this has been going on for months."

"I didn't want to keep you in the dark, Walter. That wasn't—"

"But you did," he said, cutting me off. "Both of you did."

"You're right," I replied.

"And you've looked me in the face how many times since then?" His voice was staying the same pitch but getting grittier. "And never once did you mention that you were fucking my daughter—"

"Dad!"

"What, Joanna? Would you rather me sugarcoat the fact that you've climbed in bed with Hollywood's biggest playboy? Or maybe you're about to tell me that he's suddenly become celibate?" His eyes narrowed as he waited for a response. He didn't get one. "Do you understand the type of information Jenner is privy to? The responsibility he has to my company?" His fist pounded the table, the glasses rattling. "The millions of dollars I pay him every year?"

He was right.

Every word.

But there had to be a way to fix this.

As I attempted to budge in, he added, "And now, he's sleeping with my twenty-two-year-old daughter, who was in college at the time, and he's what, ten, twelve years older than you?"

Her chest rose and fell so fast. "Dad, I've never been happier in my life."

"At least one of us is." He waved the air, like he was

dismissing me. "Jesus Christ, Jenner, I expected more from you."

He was disappointed.

An emotion far worse than anger and disgust.

I poured the rest of the scotch down my throat, my heart fucking pounding. "Walter, I know I've crossed boundaries—"

"Boundaries," he hissed. "Had you brought that blonde with the big tits into the restroom and fucked her in a stall next to my daughter's, that would have been crossing boundaries. This"—he exhaled loudly—"this is a goddamn invasion."

I placed my hands under the table, squeezing them together. "I know I've put myself in a bad position with Spade Hotels. That's the last thing I want. Representing your brand is a job that's extremely important to me. But if you no longer want to work with me, I understand."

The sound that came out of his mouth was almost like a laugh. But one that told me he found none of this funny.

"It's important to you, huh? So important that you couldn't keep your hands off my daughter?" His head dropped, like he was collecting his breath, and there was a temper in his eyes when he finally looked up. "I once told you, when you find the right one, you hold on to her. You put a ring on her finger, and then you make her a mother. I just didn't tell you that the woman couldn't be Joanna—goddamn it, I didn't think I had to."

"Dad, it's not Jenner's fault—"

"Stay out of this, Joanna. This is between me and my lawyer right now."

There was no reason to convince him of the truth.

He wasn't going to listen.

So, I would take the blame instead.

The last thing I wanted was for him to be angry with Jo, for this to hurt her career.

For there to be any ramifications because of me.

"You're right, Walter. I wasn't thinking about your brand. I was thinking about the woman I'm in love with."

His stare intensified. "You have some fucking balls."

"If it comes down to Spade Hotels or Joanna, I'm not willing to lose her." I looked at my girl and added, "I will always choose her."

He licked across his lips, his knuckles white.

The silence like nails stabbing me.

"I don't know what to say to you right now, Jenner, but I will tell you one thing: there's no way in hell I'm about to share this meal with you."

His napkin stayed on his lap.

His ass planted on the seat.

He wasn't moving.

That meant only one thing.

He wanted me to leave.

I got up from my chair and stood across from him.

I wasn't going to make Joanna choose.

I would never put that kind of pressure on her.

This was her father.

Her employer.

So, I reached into my pocket and took out my credit card and dropped it on the table. "Call me when you're ready to talk," I said to him.

I didn't wait for a reply, for the look in his eyes to worsen.

I just left the restaurant and got into my car and drove the fuck away.

THIRTY-ONE

JOANNA

The second Jenner walked away from the table, I gasped, "Dad—"

But he cut me off, holding his finger in the air, his face grim and stiff. "I need a goddamn minute, Joanna."

Air huffed out of my lungs. My feet were desperate to sprint toward Jenner. The nerves, running rampant in my body, caused me to fidget.

What did I expect?

For my father to smile and accept the news?

For him to wrap his arm around Jenner and invite him into the family?

I didn't know.

I couldn't anticipate. I'd had no expectations.

But as I watched my boyfriend leave the restaurant, my father practically fuming in his seat, this wasn't what I'd wanted at all.

I finally turned toward my father again, watching him lean back in his chair, his arms crossed over his chest.

"You caught me off guard, young lady. You know I don't

like it when that happens, especially when it involves my daughter."

Regardless, I couldn't let Jenner take the blame for something that was my fault.

I couldn't let another second pass without my father knowing the truth.

"Dad, before you start, I need to confess something."

I paused as he lifted his empty glass into the air, calling over a waitress to get a refill.

I requested another glass of wine as well, and the moment she left our table, I said, "When Jenner told you he didn't know who I was, he wasn't lying. Every bit of that was the truth." I gripped the sides of my seat, my fingers so slick against the leather. "I didn't tell him, and he had absolutely no idea I was your daughter until we were in Utah, months later, when I finally came clean."

His expression didn't change. "What are you telling me, Joanna?"

"This whole thing is my fault. Not his."

He was silent, blinking hard as he stared at me. "I still don't understand."

My fingers reached lower to the bottom of the seat, clenching the width of it, holding on. "We started talking in the sportsbook of your casino. He told me his name and that he was a lawyer in LA, and I put it together. I knew who he was, Dad, and I didn't care. I didn't stop it."

"Were you ever planning on telling him?" He shook his head. "What the hell did you think was going to happen?"

I shrugged, the movement so honest. "I have no idea. But I didn't think we would be here, months later, spending every free moment together." My voice softened when I said, "I love him, Dad."

He ran his hands through the little hair he had left. "Jesus

Christ."

"He wanted to tell you," I said almost frantically. "We talked about it daily, and he urged me to set this up, so we could have this conversation with you. But I was the one avoiding it, the one who didn't want to discuss it, who waited until now to tell you the truth."

He eyed me. "Jenner took responsibility for this, Joanna."

"Because my boyfriend would never throw me under the bus."

My mouth closed as the waitress returned, our drinks in her hand. Several runners were behind her, delivering the appetizers Jenner had ordered.

Two salads.

Calamari.

Beef carpaccio.

Food I was most definitely not going to touch, my stomach revolting at the mere sight of it.

Time ticked by once we were alone.

Our forks stayed on the table.

Our hands didn't even move.

"Does he treat you well?"

I filled my lungs, my chest quivering from the air.

Tears sprouted without any effort. They were just there, burning.

"Better than I can even describe." I glanced toward the front of the restaurant, hoping Jenner was standing by the entrance. But he wasn't. I could feel in my gut that he was long gone. "When I told you I've never been happier, I meant it."

He watched his hand flatten on the table, fingers spread, and then his gaze gradually lifted to me. "I don't know what you want from me."

"I want you to be okay with our relationship." My arms circled around my stomach. "I want you to trust Jenner. That man is so ridiculously loyal to you; it's not funny. I want you to accept that this isn't his fault; it's mine." I leaned on the table, needing to get closer to him. "And you know what? I wouldn't change what I did, and I've said the same thing to Jenner. Because if I had told him who I was and that I was your daughter, he never would have given me the time of day." I swallowed, trying to breathe, trying to imagine what life would be like without him. "And I never would have known what it feels like to be loved by him."

His jaw flexed as he ground his teeth together. "I'm not happy."

"That's fine, Dad. You don't have to be happy. You can be angry and upset. You can be disappointed. I deserve all those things. But don't take this out on him. Jenner doesn't deserve that."

Just as my voice faded, our waitress returned to our table and said, "Are you ready to order your meals?" She noticed our untouched plates. "Or do you need a little more time?"

Without looking at me, my father replied, "I don't think we'll be eating. In fact, why don't you box up all this food"—he nodded toward me—"so she can take it home?"

He reached into his pocket and removed his wallet and handed her his credit card. She took it and disappeared.

At the same time, we both glanced at Jenner's card, sitting on the tablecloth between us. As I was about to pick it up, he did instead, slipping it into his wallet.

"I need some time, Joanna." He drank the rest of his scotch. "I need to process this ..."

"That's fine," I told him. "I get it."

More silence began to beat away until the waitress returned with my father's receipt and the boxes to pack up the appetizers. Once she emptied the plates, she put the containers into a bag and set it next to me on the table.

My father stood, and as I gripped the handle of the bag and my clutch, I followed him out of the restaurant.

Jenner and I had driven separately, my car staring back at me in the parking lot.

Maybe, deep down, both of us had known this was going to happen.

My father's driver pulled up, and Dad stalled in front of the backseat, his fingers gripping the door handle. "I'll see you at work tomorrow."

I walked closer and leaned in, giving him a kiss on the cheek. "Yes, you will, Dad. Good night."

The second I got into my car, I pulled out my phone, hoping to see a text from Jenner.

There was a screen full of notifications, not a single one from him.

I started the engine, and as I drove out of the lot, I called him.

He didn't answer.

I tried again, my call going to voice mail.

I wanted to go to his house, but there was a chance he wasn't home.

He could have gone to Dominick's to drink his face off.

Or to Ford's house.

He could even be sitting at a bar, wondering what the hell he'd gotten himself into.

But I knew that if he wasn't answering my calls, he needed space, so instead of driving to his house, I went to my apartment, and I was so relieved to see Monica on the couch when I walked in.

"I didn't expect you tonight—" Her voice cut off when our eyes connected. "Oh fuck, babe. What happened?"

I left my heels by the door, not trusting myself to walk in them, and I hurried over to the fridge, grabbing a bottle of wine that I brought to the couch. I tugged out the cork that was halfway in and guzzled straight from the bottle.

"It's like that?" she asked.

She knew what tonight was.

We'd been texting about it for days. She'd even given me a pep talk before I left for dinner.

"*Mmhmm*." I wiped my mouth. "It went horribly bad." I handed her the wine, watching her drink straight from the bottle. "Like Jenner left the restaurant, and Dad is beyond pissed. He will barely even talk to me. Jenner isn't answering my calls."

Her eyes went wide. "Okay." She gave me back the bottle, encouraging me to lift it to my mouth, and while I chugged more down, she said, "It's okay. We'll figure this out. Somehow. Yes, somehow, we'll make this better."

"We will?" I tested her. "How?"

My best friend usually had the answer to everything.

But this time, I just didn't know.

As I was waiting for her to respond, still holding my phone in my hand, it vibrated.

A new text appeared on the screen.

Jenner: I'm at Dominick's, getting shit-faced, but I need to know that you're all right. And I need you to know I love you.

"See," Monica said as I showed her his message. "Like I said, everything is going to be just fine."

"Fine?" I mocked. "*Fine* is the worst word in the world. No one wants to be fine."

"*Fiiine*, then it's going to be great." She pointed at my phone. "Reply to your man and then come here." She held out her arms. "I think we could both really use a hug."

THIRTY-TWO

JENNER

"Fuck," Ford said as he stared at me from the other side of my desk. "That's some serious shit."

Dominick and I had just finished filling him in on everything that had gone down at the restaurant last night and then the drinking that had transpired at Dominick's house after.

I'd been buried in meetings all day, and this was the first opportunity I'd had to catch up with my little brother.

As we sat in my office, Dominick poured us drinks. My hangover from last night was just barely lifting, and the scotch wasn't going down as easily as I wanted.

"What has Jo said about all this?" Ford asked.

"We haven't talked that much," I admitted. "I called her when I got home from Dominick's. I was a drunken fucking mess. I barely remember what she said. And our conversation this morning was brief—both of us were running late to work and heading into meetings." I pushed the glass toward my computer, getting it farther away from me. "This is the first time I've been free all day."

"I wonder what it was like for her, facing her father at work today," Dominick said.

"Me too," I replied. "Hell, she had to face him when I left the restaurant. I'm curious what he said to her and what she said to him."

"So, now what?" Ford asked. "Do you carry on like the conversation with Walter never happened? Do you put things on pause with Jo—"

"Fuck no. There's no pause," I said, cutting him off. "Jo Spade is mine. I came clean. I did the right thing. If he doesn't want to work with me anymore, that's on him. But it's not going to affect my relationship with his daughter."

"Says the dude who was never going to fall in love," Ford joked.

I flipped him off at the same time my phone vibrated, and I lifted it out of my pocket, staring at the screen.

"Jesus ..." I groaned. "Speak of the goddamn devil."

Walter: Let's talk. Meet me in the bar of my hotel.

"Walter?" Dominick asked. "What did he say?"

I glanced up from my phone. "He wants to meet up at his hotel."

Dominick came back with, "Don't burn the place down, please. It's my favorite spot in LA."

I looked at my brother. "Is it?"

"That's where I met Kendall."

"Oh shit, that's right," I replied. The grand opening was the night he had met his girl on the rooftop. "Don't worry; nothing is going up in flames this evening."

My thumbs hit the screen, typing out a reply.

Me: I'll be there in 15 minutes.

As I stood from my chair, grabbing my jacket from the back of it, Ford said, "What the fuck are you going to say to him?"

I slipped my arms through the holes, adjusting the front on my chest. "Don't know."

"That you're going to date his daughter whether he likes it or not?" Dominick challenged.

I chuckled. "Sure, I'll use those exact words, and we'll see how well that goes over."

"I'm glad it's you and not me," Ford said. "I have enough drama in my life between having a four-year-old and needing a full-time nanny."

"And then there's baby mama," Dominick added.

"We don't talk about baby mama," Ford snapped back.

"Listen," I said to them, "while you two bitch this out—or whatever you're doing—I'm going to go."

When I reached my doorway, I heard, "Good luck," and I kept walking down the hallway and into the garage, where my driver was waiting for me.

"Spade Hotel," I told him, and I looked at the screen of my phone, tapping the necessary buttons to call Jo.

After three rings, her voice mail picked up, and I started my message. "It's me," I said. "I'm on my way to meet your father. He wants to talk. I'll call you when I get out." A beat passed, and I added, "I love you."

My office wasn't far from the hotel, which had made it convenient when Walter was in the thick of construction, the short commute allowing me to get there fast and promptly.

Something my client had appreciated at the time.

Now, there wasn't a fucking thing about me that Walter liked.

In the few minutes it took us to arrive, I replied to a couple emails and watched the hotel come into view. Once Steven pulled up to the lobby, the bellhop opened my door.

"Welcome," the bellhop said. "Will you be staying with us this evening?"

"No, just visiting," I told him.

I walked inside, veering toward the right, where the bar took up a large section of the lobby. Walter had had a heavy influence on the design of the bar, all of it done in dark wood and drab colors—an old-school feel in a modern space.

I saw him the moment I rounded the corner, sitting at the bar, his hands wrapped around a tumbler.

I held my breath as I closed the distance between us, standing behind the chair next to his. "Can I take a seat?"

He nodded.

The bartender immediately approached and said, "What can I get you to drink?"

I pointed at Walter's glass. "I'll have whatever he's having."

A quick peek around the room told me we were far from being alone. He'd chosen a public spot, where eyes were everywhere, ears were open. The last thing his PR team would want was to hear that Walter had given his lawyer a verbal lashing in front of hotel guests.

This was going to be civil.

I just didn't know which way he was swaying.

Once the bartender placed a scotch in front of me, Walter took a drink of his and then said, "I spoke to Joanna after you left the restaurant last night."

"I assumed."

He kept his eyes straight, not looking at me. "She told me the story of how you two met. You didn't know who she was; therefore, you didn't stop it from happening." He gradually moved his stare, locking with mine. "But once she told you the truth, what happened, Jenner?"

I didn't know if this was a test or if he truly didn't know the answer.

"I ended things." I wiped the corners of my mouth. "I told her it couldn't work, that I wouldn't do that to you." I sighed. "That was one of the hardest things I've ever done, Walter."

"But you found your way back to her." His voice was flat.

I had no idea where this was going.

"Yes." I attempted to lift the scotch to my lips but didn't. "Our second trip to Utah is when that happened."

"That's quite a gap in between." His eyes narrowed. "I'm trying to understand this, Jenner. To wrap my fucking head around it."

"I love her." I looked at the bottles that lined the center of the bar, my heart remembering that feeling when I'd walked away and the feeling when I couldn't fight her any longer. "And every day she wasn't in my life, I wanted her to be. It was miserable." I turned toward him. "I wouldn't have rekindled things if I wasn't serious about her. I wouldn't have taken the chance, not with the relationship I have with you. You need to know that—that I went into this, knowing I would more than likely lose you as a client and I was all right with that as long as I got her."

He exhaled. "Jenner, you've been with me a long time. We've worked on billion-dollar projects together. Last night, I was willing to give that up."

"And today?"

He drained his scotch and called the bartender over for another. "Today, for the first time in a long time, I saw my daughter's smile not as bright as it usually is. I saw her mope through meetings and eat lunch at her desk instead of going out with her colleagues. That's not her. That's the result of this." His finger traced the air between us. "Prior to today, I'd never seen her happier. Hell, I thought it was her job that was giving her that smile." He paused. "Now, I know it was you."

I was silent for a few moments before I said, "I won't hurt

her." I halted and then added, "You need to know that Jo's safe with me."

That was a promise I'd never intended on making, one I'd never even contemplated before.

But I could say those words to Walter and mean them.

"You bet your ass you won't hurt her." He gripped his cup like it was a gun. "I'll hang you by the fucking balls if you do."

I took a breath. "Walter, you can trust me. I know that's easy to say from this end, and given what you just learned, you're doubting that, but my personal life has absolutely nothing to do with the decisions I make for your company and the way I represent your brand."

"One of the things my daughter emphasized was your loyalty to me." He circled the glass over the wooden bar top. "I've calmed down a lot since last night. I'm not saying I'm going to shred our contract. I'm also not saying I'm going to invite you to my poker game next week." He licked the scotch off his lips as he emptied another glass. "It's going to take me some time to accept the new role you have in my family."

A role I wasn't ever stepping down from.

But I kept that point to myself.

"My ex-wife would tell you I'm inconvincible, stubborn as an old mule. And maybe so, but I need you, Jenner—something I don't want to admit. But like I've said in the past, I've gone through enough lawyers to know I have a good one. And since I can't replace you, the best thing for me, my company, and my daughter is to find a way to accept this."

Any man with an ego like Walter's would have had a hard time, admitting that. I knew this conversation wasn't easy for him, but he also knew I respected him, and I wouldn't be sitting here if Jo were just another girl I wanted to fuck in a restroom stall.

"I won't do you wrong," I told him. "You have my word."

I shot back my whole drink and chased it with some water that the bartender had poured for us at some point.

As I was setting the glass down, Walter said, "I think you forgot this." He placed my credit card in front of me. "I should have used it for the dinner that none of us ate."

I chuckled, sticking the card in my pocket. "That's why I left it."

"Don't worry; I'll be deducting the amount from your bill this month."

"I expect nothing less." Knowing we'd reached the end of this little talk, I got up from my seat and held my hand out to him. "Hopefully, our next dinner will end a little differently."

"Let's hope."

He shook my hand, and once he released me, I patted his shoulder and walked out of the bar and through the lobby, climbing into my SUV that was parked outside.

"Where to, Jenner?" Steven asked.

"One second," I told him and checked the screen of my phone.

Jo: Oh boy. Call me when you leave him. I'm at the office, catching up on work. I'll be here for a while.

THIRTY-THREE

JOANNA

I couldn't stop checking the time, waiting for a call or text from Jenner. Almost an hour had passed since he'd left that voice mail, telling me he was meeting with my father, and I could only imagine what was going down between them.

My father hadn't spoken a word about last night's dinner during any of the times I'd seen him today.

That didn't surprise me.

He wasn't the most open communicator. I had a feeling he wouldn't discuss it again unless I was the one who brought it up.

Still, there were so many unsolved thoughts.

Where this left the three of us.

What Jenner and I were going to do if my father wanted to murder my boyfriend every time he saw him.

If Jenner was going to represent our company.

Instead of constantly dwelling on my life today, I'd been trying to busy myself with work, burying my mind in marketing.

Each attempt had been extremely unsuccessful.

But I had so many projects that needed attention, so I decided to stay at the office long after everyone left. To get in the zone, I played some music and made myself some tea, trying to really focus on the social media campaign we were about to launch.

It took almost nothing to distract me, jumping the second a text came through, disappointment filling me when it wasn't Jenner's name on the screen.

Monica: So? Any news?
Me: Nope. Crickets. Where are you?
Monica: About to board the jet to Vegas, where I'll be for exactly three hours to help a client get ready for her concert, and then we're flying to New York.
Me: Your life is so fabulous; I can't stand it.
Monica: Text me the second something happens. I feel like I'm waiting on pins and needles.
Me: Have a safe flight. Miss you already.
Monica: XO.

I was just setting my phone down when there was a knock at my door.

I didn't know who it could be. I was positive everyone in the department had already gone home for the night.

"Come in," I said.

Flutters shot through my body when the door swung open, and Jenner's deliciously handsome face came into view. He closed it behind him, and I heard the sound of the lock.

"What are you doing here?" I asked, standing from my desk, rushing to the front of it, where he met me, my arms instantly going around his neck.

He cupped my cheeks, holding me steady. "I've missed you."

The feeling was so mutual that I could weep. "You have no idea how much. I know we talked last night and this morning, but today has been hell without you."

A devilish grin grew across his beautiful mouth. "I drank so much at Dominick's. I don't remember a thing I said to you."

"You just kept apologizing that this happened." My body aligned with his as I held his back, gripping his suit jacket, so plush and firm in my hands. "And you told me how much you love me—several times."

"At least you know I'm an honest drunk."

I took a deep breath. "How did it go with Dad?"

Without saying a word, he leaned down and kissed me. I breathed him in, tasting the flavor that was so unique to Jenner, swallowing the reassurance I felt from his mouth. That feeling only increased when his hands dropped to my waist and he hauled me even closer to him.

I was breathless by the time he pulled away.

"I've been thinking about your lips all day."

My heart pounded as I said, "Does this mean you're trying to avoid my question?"

He took my hand and led me to my desk, lifting me onto the wooden edge before he took a seat in my chair in front of me. He quickly glanced around the room that I'd spent the last several weeks decorating, his eyes eventually returning to me. "You've got a nice office."

It wasn't large by any means with just enough space for a love seat and a couple of plants, a floor lamp and wall art. I'd expected a cubicle, so it had been quite the pleasant surprise.

He licked across his bottom lip as he added, "I'm getting a feel for it. I intend to spend a lot more time in here."

My face turned as I tried to process what he meant. "More time?"

"Now that I can visit you here."

And then it clicked.

I grasped his hand, holding it between mine. "So, Dad's not going to kill you?"

He laughed. "I might not be playing poker with him and his buddies next week, but I'll still be alive." He kissed the tops of my fingers. "He's warming up to the idea of us. It's going to take him a little while."

I exhaled a huge sigh of relief. "Next time you have news of this magnitude, can you lead with it? My heart can't take the buildup. I've been dying inside."

"But it was so fun, watching you squirm."

I gently kicked his knee. "I had a meeting in his office this afternoon with his PR team. I felt his eyes on me the whole time, and when it was over, he asked me if I was all right. I'd barely talked. He knew how bothered I was by this."

He ran his fingers across my chin. "He just wants you happy."

My heart throbbed as I stared at him. "This moment, Jenner—right now, right here, with you—this is my happiness."

"Come here, baby."

I pushed myself off the desk and moved to his lap. My legs stretched across his, and the rest of me snuggled into his chest. "You know we go back to Utah next week, right?"

"I'd like to extend the trip, so we can vacation for a few days before we return to LA." He turned my face, so I looked at him. "Can you take the time off from work?"

"*Hmm.*" I bit my lip. "I don't know ..."

He tugged on my mouth to release my teeth. "Don't tease me, Jo ..."

His eyes told me his warning was because I'd gnawed on his favorite lip, but I still answered him and said, "I think I can swing it."

"Good, because I can't move into the house without you."

My back straightened, my eyes widening. "You're closing?"

"In three days." He kept his thumb on my lip, tracing across it. "I was going to surprise you when we got to Utah, but I think we've had enough surprises this week."

I buried my face in his warmth, squeezing my arms around him. "After relocating to LA, I feel like I'm an expert mover. I've got this."

"We won't be doing any heavy lifting. I just need your input on furniture and decorations. You know, shit my decorator is going to put together for us."

I leaned back to take in his eyes. "Us?"

"Did you really think you weren't going to be heavily involved? You're going to be staying there as much as me. That house is for us."

"Jenner ..." I scanned his eyes, my heart beating so fast that I swore he could hear it.

"I told you forever, Jo. I meant it."

I couldn't wait.

I had to taste him again.

I slammed our mouths together, and his tongue found its way between my lips. His hands moved to my hips, our bodies grinding, that need immediately thrumming.

"Oh God," I finally breathed.

He felt far too good.

His kiss.

His grip.

His presence alone.

I was wrapped up in all of it, and I didn't want him to let me go.

He glanced around the room again and asked, "Are there any cameras in here?"

I smiled, knowing exactly where this was going. "Nope."

"Then, what's stopping us from getting naked?"

"Absolutely nothing."

I tore at his tie, pulling the knot until it was loose enough to slip off his head. I then went to work on the buttons of his shirt, popping each one through the hole until he could get his arms out, the jacket coming off as well. I stood from his lap, so he could remove his pants and I could reach behind my back to lower the zipper of my dress.

Except the moment my fingers hit the tiny piece of metal, he growled, "Leave it on." His eyes dipped to my feet. "Those too." He pointed at the desk while he unbuckled his belt. "And I want your ass up there, sitting."

I lifted myself onto the edge, where I'd been just a few minutes before, and watched him strip, leaving his suit pants and shoes and socks where they landed on my floor. He eventually stood in front of me, completely naked.

"Damn ..." I took my time, my eyes traveling the length of him, my body lighting on fire from the sight, my pussy tingling as he pumped his cock. "For the record, I don't know if I'll ever stop saying that when I see you naked."

His arms surrounded both sides of me, making me feel so tiny on this desk. "For the record, I'll never stop worshipping your body." He kissed down my cheek, stopping at my jaw. "It's so fucking perfect, Jo."

I tried to find my breath as I said, "It's yours," and I moaned as his mouth lowered.

His knees hit the floor, and he lifted my feet until my heels were resting on the desk, his face moving under the bottom of my dress.

The feel of his beard on my thighs and the instant lapping of his tongue made me scream, "*Ahhh!*"

He didn't tease.

He didn't drag this out.

He just went for it, lick after lick across my clit, swiping his tongue to each side, two of his fingers finding their way inside me.

He ate me like he needed me as much as I needed him.

"Goddamn it," he hissed. "You taste so fucking good."

I closed my legs to brush my skin across his whiskers, holding the edge of the desk because his tongue, his fingers, his power were making it hard not to fall.

Every inhale, I sucked in more air that was full of his scent.

Every exhale, I trembled from the way he was making me feel.

"Jenner!"

His tongue was brutal, not showing even the least bit of mercy as it flicked over me, going as low as my entrance, hitting each side before solely focusing on the top of my clit.

And in that spot, the strength in which he licked, the orgasm threatened to come.

My arms straightened, and my head fell back, the ends of my hair making a noise as they scratched across the desktop.

And that sound was constant because my body couldn't stop swaying into him.

Because he never let up.

His fingers, slick with my wetness, moved in and out of me, making me cry, "Oh God," and with each plunge, I got louder. "Fuck!"

The bottom of my dress was now so high that he was able to glance up at me, this hungry, almost-animalistic look in his eyes. "Come on my face."

I tried to fight it.

I tried to at least hold off for a few more seconds.

But I couldn't.

A burst of sensations exploded through me, and I shouted out in pleasure. Shudders were taking over my body, and I moaned, "Jenner," after each wave.

My legs wobbled as I tried to keep my feet steady, but his licking was relentless, his fingering so consistent that balance was the last thing I had at this moment.

And I loved every fucking second.

When the orgasm finally began to die down, he lifted his face, his lips instantly finding mine. He meshed us together, my mouth coated in my own wetness, and before I could even take a breath, his cock thrust inside me.

"Oh my God," I gasped.

Everything tingled.

Every part of me so incredibly sensitive.

His forehead pressed to mine, and he growled, "You're so goddamn tight." He kissed me again. "And wet."

He held my waist, using my hips to pull me toward him, stroking his long, thick dick inside me. When he was fully plunged, he twisted his hips, causing me to buck, my back arching in response. He then reared back to his tip, and my body immediately missed him, begging him to enter me again.

"Faster," I urged, digging my nails into his shoulders.

His beard scraped across my cheek, his teeth nipping the same spots he'd just roughed up with his whiskers.

That kind of pain was something I now craved.

A feeling so unique to Jenner.

One I knew I could no longer live without.

"God, you feel so fucking good," he moaned.

My legs circled around him, locking us together. "Harder."

And that was what he gave me—deep, consuming jabs that had my entire body vibrating over this desk.

But within a few pumps, he was lifting me, moving me to the wall, holding me against it.

This new position, the way he placed me over him, his tip grinding across my G-spot, I was reminded of how quickly he could bring me to that place.

"You're tightening up on me ..."

My arms crossed around his neck; my mouth hovered above his. "Because you're going to make me come."

"Is that what you want?" He sucked on my lip, releasing it to say, "To come on my fucking cock?" His rhythm picked up, giving me more speed and so much more power.

"*Yesss!*"

"Then, we're going to come together."

He reached down and rubbed my clit, driving into me at the same time that I was bouncing over him. I could feel my pussy squeezing around him, holding him inside me.

As though he could read what I needed, his movements became sharper, more intense, while our lips intertwined, my hands grasping for him.

To hold on.

To prepare.

Because the rise was back.

And as he rubbed my clit and hammered that beautiful cock into me, the feeling came on stronger.

"Jenner!" I clung to him. "Yes!"

He was dominating me, each punch of his dick pounding me against the wall, his breathing sounding like growls as he worked up his orgasm.

"You're fucking milking me."

And that was when he came—I felt it the second he shot his first stream.

"Jo," he roared across my face. "*Fuuuck.*"

We were releasing at the same time, our bodies shuddering together, synced in a way where it could only be love.

I held on, wrapped in him, losing myself completely until there was only stillness between us.

"My God," I panted.

That was when he carried me over to the small couch and

took a seat. He kept me straddled over his lap, his cock still inside me.

He didn't even pull out when he said, "Kiss me."

My breath hadn't yet returned, but I pressed my lips to his, tasting the lust on his tongue, the desire in every bit of air that he exhaled.

His hands softly, slowly roamed my body.

"I can't get enough of you," I finally whispered.

"You don't have to, Jo. I'm not going anywhere."

My heart throbbed from his words, from the expression on his face, from the way his eyes were looking at me.

"Ever?"

A smile moved across those ridiculously sexy lips. "No, baby. Not ever."

EPILOGUE

WALTER

The long red ribbon was stretched across the entrance of the hotel, several feet behind me as I stood at the makeshift podium. My team had worked endlessly on the grand opening. Every time we unveiled a new hotel, it took more planning. More money. But Utah's budget really took the crown.

The media was in attendance. Celebrities. My family. Friends. Many familiar eyes looking at me from the crowd.

But there was a set just to the side of me that meant the most. She was holding a pair of scissors that were almost the length of her body. A smile on her face that made this father so damn proud.

"I want to thank my daughter," I said into the microphone. "I don't want to embarrass her, but many of you don't know that Joanna graduated from the University of Miami a little over eighteen months ago and came to work for me. As any father would, I tossed her to the wolves." I winked at the crowd. "I made her learn the ropes. I put her up to the test and this"—I opened my arms wide, glancing up at the vast thirty-foot overhang above our heads—"is her creation." I took a breath as I scanned the faces looking back at me. "Most parents can't say that their little girl designed the best hotel in their portfolio." I gazed at my pumpkin. "But I can. I'm so proud of you, Joanna."

Thank you, she mouthed to me.

"I'm honored to introduce you to our newest addition." I moved back, turning my body toward Joanna as she held the scissors to the red ribbon, waiting for me to give her the signal to cut it. "Park City Mountainside."

I eyed my daughter, and as each side of the ribbon fell, an applause erupted from the crowd.

Everyone rose from their seats, entering the hotel, and Joanna and Jenner made their way over to me.

"Congratulations," Jenner said, clasping my hand, reaching forward to wrap his arm around my shoulders—the kind of hug the younger generation gave nowadays.

"And to you too," I said, patting his back. "You know you deserve just as much recognition. You worked your ass off on this one."

He released my hand, his arm dropping as he said, "You should have heard some of the rumblings in the crowd. They were blown away by the exterior alone, and they hadn't even been inside yet."

"If they think this property is magnificent, wait until they see what you and Joanna are spearheading next."

Jenner's arm slipped around my daughter's shoulders. "Baby, are you ready to do this all over again in South Beach?"

"You mean, head back to one of my favorite cities in the world and eat Gloria's desserts every day?" She grinned at me. "I'm more than ready."

"Speaking of Gloria," I said, gazing at the faces that walked by, looking for hers, "have you seen her?"

"She's here," Jenner replied, turning around, waving his

hand in the air, and I assumed he'd spotted her. "She's on her way over."

Gloria approached with her son, Brett—a close friend of Jenner's, who I'd now met several times—along with his fiancée, James, a woman who needed no introduction. Neither did Monica, my daughter's best friend, who was a permanent staple in our family.

Monica threw her arms around me. "What a wicked place," she said, hugging me like a second daughter. "I love it here, like, so, so much."

"You know there's a room for you anytime you want to come," I told her. "That's true for any of my hotels."

She smiled. "And when you're ready to up your style, you know I'm your girl."

I laughed. "I'll keep that in mind."

"Hell of a hotel," Brett said, shaking my hand. "James and I are thrilled to be staying here this weekend."

"Yes," James agreed. "It's absolutely beautiful, Walter. Thank you for inviting us."

"I appreciate you coming," I told them, and then I looked at Gloria, tapping my stomach that seemed to have a heavier bulge than yesterday. "I sampled some of your desserts this afternoon when my team was prepping for tonight's gala. Don't tell my pastry chef that I said this, but yours are the best I've ever had."

Gloria blushed and replied, "You're too kind."

"Had my daughter not brought your desserts over for Thanksgiving, I wouldn't have ever found you, and this never would have happened." I pointed at the entrance behind me, where past the lobby and into the lower belly of the hotel was Gloria's newest bake shop.

My guests were going to be able to snack on her treats anytime they wanted.

"Half of LA now knows about her," my daughter said, smiling at her friend. "And we wouldn't have it any other way."

While they hugged, Ford and his daughter came over along with Dominick and his girlfriend, Kendall, as well.

"This place is gorgeous," Ford said, picking up his little girl in his arms.

I remembered when mine had been that size. When her tiny hands would hold on to me so tightly. When her pigtails would tickle my face.

When I could protect her from everything.

"You should be proud of your brother," I said to him. "He worked his tail off on this hotel."

Ford clapped Jenner's shoulder and said, "You're always making us proud, buddy."

"I hope you'll be joining us for the gala tonight?" I asked Dominick and Kendall.

"We wouldn't miss it," Dominick replied.

As I was looking at Dominick, I felt a tap on my arm, and I glanced toward the source.

Little Everly still had her finger on me, and she whispered, "Daddy says he's taking me skiing tomorrow. But he says I can only go if I'm a big girl and I don't cry at your party."

"Is that so?" I asked her, chuckling. "What happens if your daddy cries at my party? Did you make that part of your bargain?"

"Daddy!" Everly yelled. "What if you cry—"

Ford started tickling his baby, distracting her from finishing the rest of her question. Her head fell back, her mouth opened, and the cutest, loudest giggles came out of her.

I leaned into my daughter's ear and said, "When are you going to give me one of those?"

She looked at me. "A grandchild? Dad, we're not even

engaged yet. Besides, you keep me so busy; I don't have time for anything, let alone a child."

I did keep her busy, but that was because I needed her.

She was far more talented than her old man with an eye for design and a personality that kept her marketing team engaged and motivated.

Of course, I hadn't believed that at first.

In fact, Utah was a role I never intended to give her.

I didn't think she had the skills. Right out of college, she didn't have a lick of experience, and she was far too green.

But after finding out that the two of them had gotten together—a bit of news that had shocked the hell out of me—how else was I going to see if Jenner was the right man for her?

I laughed to myself as I watched the two of them, lost in conversation, arms wrapped around each other.

They thought they had fooled me.

They thought they had kept their relationship a secret.

But what they didn't realize was that I knew everything that went on in my hotels.

Especially if my daughter was staying in one.

And the Vegas property made it even easier because there were cameras on every inch of the interior.

Jenner Dalton was a dirty fucking dog.

He wasn't the type of guy you let your daughter date, and my initial instinct had been to put a stop to it.

But deep down, I knew if Jenner mended his ways, if he gave up being such a playboy and was in it for the long haul, then he would be perfect for Joanna.

I just had to make sure he wasn't going to break my pumpkin's heart.

Their first trip to Utah might have broken them up, but I was positive the second would glue them back together, and that was why I insisted she go with him.

Neither of them would ever know it was my doing.

I preferred to keep it that way.

So, I waited to see how long it was going to take him to tell me the truth. Every time we met, every time we spoke on the phone, I listened to him struggle with the secret. And when he finally shared the news, I wasn't easy on him. I certainly wasn't going to let him think he was the alpha in this family.

That role only belonged to me.

But what I did do was test him.

I wanted to see what meant more to him.

Spade Hotels or my daughter.

He made the right choice.

And even though I had given him a hard time, even though I'd borne down and buried him in pressure, he'd become a part of my circle the moment I saw the smile on my daughter's face.

The same one she wore now.

Happiness looked good on the both of them.

I looked away from Joanna just in time to see Dominick come closer and stop at my side.

He gripped the top of my shoulder, like we were shaking hands again, and said, "Walter, we'll see you inside."

Kendall and Ford and Everly followed him.

Joanna then checked the time on her watch, our eyes connecting as she said, "Dad, I have to go get ready for the gala." She kissed me on the cheek.

"Don't be late," I warned even though I knew she'd be early.

Jenner shook my hand again, his head nodding, his fingers squeezing my shoulder before he linked fingers with Joanna.

I turned and watched them walk through the entrance.

Even though they had a home in the area, they were spending the weekend at the hotel, participating in the festivities her team had planned.

Little did she know, when they boarded the plane Monday morning, they weren't headed for LA, like she thought.

Jenner was taking her to Bali.

And the ring he was going to propose with was currently locked in the hotel's private safe.

She would always be my baby girl.

She would always be a Spade.

But soon, she would also be a Dalton.

Interested in reading the other books in the Dalton Family Series

...

The Lawyer

The Single Dad

The Intern

Or check out Signed, which stars Brett Young

ACKNOWLEDGMENTS

Nina Grinstead, every time I reach this section, a million thoughts come into my head on what this journey has looked like for us. All the late-night and early-morning talks. The texts. The plans. The dreams. Each book has looked so different, but nothing about us has changed. We're in this together until the very end—and I'm talking about walkers, not words. *Love you* doesn't even come close to cutting it. Team B forever.

Jovana Shirley, whenever I send you my final manuscript, I exhale the biggest sigh of relief. Not because it's done—although that too—but because it's in your hands. You have this unbelievable ability to always know what I'm *trying* to say and this incredible vision and talent that can polish my books into something I'm so proud of. YOU make me shine. Like I say every time, I wouldn't want to do this with anyone but you. Love you so hard.

Hang Le, my unicorn, you are just incredible in every way.

Judy Zweifel, as always, thank you for being so wonderful to work with and for taking such good care of my words. <3

Chanpreet Singh, thanks for always holding me together and for helping me in every way. Adore you, lady. XO.

Kaitie Reister, I love you, girl. Thanks for being you.

Nikki Terrill, my soul sister. Every tear, vent, dinner, virtual hug, life chaos, workout, you've been there through it all. I could never do this without you, and I would never want to. Love you hard.

Sarah Symonds, you understand my words more than anyone, and I have a blast, being on this journey with you, my friend. Thank you for always being there, for all your love and support. I wouldn't want to do this without you. Ever.

Ratula Roy, this was a special one for us, a rainbow behind the clouds, and you helped me capture that beauty. You always have my back, my heart, and my love. Forever, baby. Love you.

Kimmi Street, my sister from another mister. There's no way to describe us; there's just something special when it comes to our unbreakable bond. Nothing and no one will ever change that. I love you more than love.

Extra-special love goes to Valentine PR, Kelley Beckham, Kayti McGee, Chris Fletcher, Tracey Waggaman, Sally Ilan, Elizabeth Kelley, Jennifer Porpora, Pat Mann, and my group of Sarasota girls, whom I love more than anything. I'm so grateful for all of you.

Mom and Dad, thanks for your unwavering belief in me and your constant encouragement. It means more than you'll ever know.

Brian, my words could never dent the love I feel for you. Trust me when I say, I love you more.

My Midnighters, you are such a supportive, loving, motivating group. Thanks for being such an inspiration, for holding my hand when I need it, and for always begging for more words. I love you all.

To all the bloggers who read, review, share, post, tweet, Instagram—Thank you, thank you, thank you will never be enough. You do so much for our writing community, and we're so appreciative.

To my readers—I cherish each and every one of you. I'm so grateful for all the love you show my books, for taking the time to reach out to me, and for your passion and enthusiasm. I love, love, love you.

MARNI'S MIDNIGHTERS

Getting to know my readers is one of my favorite parts about being an author. In Marni's Midnighters, my private Facebook group, I post covers before they're revealed to the public and excerpts of the projects I'm currently working on, and team members qualify for exclusive giveaways.

To join Marni's Midnighters, click HERE.

ABOUT THE AUTHOR

USA Today best-selling author Marni Mann knew she was going to be a writer since middle school. While other girls her age were daydreaming about teenage pop stars, Marni was fantasizing about penning her first novel. She crafts sexy, titillating stories that weave together her love of darkness, mystery, passion, and human emotions. A New Englander at heart, she now lives in Sarasota, Florida, with her husband and their yellow Lab. When she's not nose deep in her laptop, working on her next novel, she's scouring for chocolate, sipping wine, traveling, or devouring fabulous books.

Want to get in touch? Visit Marni at ...

www.marnismann.com

MarniMannBooks@gmail.com

ALSO BY MARNI MANN

STAND-ALONE NOVELS

Even If It Hurts (Contemporary Romance)

Before You (Contemporary Romance)

The Assistant (Psychological Thriller)

THE DALTON FAMILY SERIES—EROTIC ROMANCE

The Lawyer

The Billionaire

The Single Dad

The Intern

THE AGENCY SERIES—EROTIC ROMANCE

Signed

Endorsed

Contracted

Negotiated

THE BEARDED SAVAGES SERIES—EROTIC ROMANCE

The Unblocked Collection

Wild Aces

MOMENTS IN BOSTON SERIES—CONTEMPORARY ROMANCE

When Ashes Fall

When We Met

When Darkness Ends

THE PRISONED SERIES—DARK EROTIC THRILLER

Prisoned

Animal

Monster

THE SHADOWS DUET—EROTIC ROMANCE

Seductive Shadows

Seductive Secrecy

THE BAR HARBOR DUET—NEW ADULT

Pulled Beneath

Pulled Within

THE MEMOIR SERIES—DARK MAINSTREAM FICTION

Memoirs Aren't Fairytales

Scars from a Memoir

NOVELS COWRITTEN WITH GIA RILEY

Lover (Erotic Romance)

Drowning (Contemporary Romance)

THE SINGLE DAD

DALTON FAMILY SERIES: BOOK THREE

The Single Dad is coming June 28, 2022, Ford's sexy, steamy, single dad romance ...

If you would like to pre-order The Single Dad, *click* HERE.

SNEAK PEEK OF UNBLOCKED

FRANKIE

His mouth caressed the skin across my navel as my back arched off the bed. My nails dug into the mattress; a long, drawn-out moan escaped from my lips. His kisses quickly turned to licks. The tip of his tongue changed to a point during the upstroke, traveling as high as my nipples, and went flat during the downstroke where he paused at my folds. My legs spread, waiting for that pointed wetness to flap against my clit.

Nothing but air swished over me. His breath. Exhales that triggered the throbbing to pulse even faster.

"Please," I begged. "Please make me come."

A tease. That's what this was.

I couldn't remember a time when I had craved a man's tongue this deeply. I hadn't begged him with just my words, but with my hands, too, drawing his face even closer. I combed his soft locks as I drove the back of my head into the bed, anticipating the feeling that would shoot through me when he eventually gave me the pressure I needed.

His breathing continued, his mouth hovering over my sex while his hands moved to my nipples. He squeezed with a fierce intensity. My stomach shuddered from the ripple of pleasure.

"Please," I repeated. "I need your tongue."

"If I give you my tongue..." His voice startled me. Up until that point, I hadn't heard him speak. I hadn't seen his face, either, now that I thought about it. "You'll be moaning too loud to answer your phone."

My back straightened, and I glanced between my spread legs and bent knees. The night's darkness casted a shadow over half his face hiding everything but his parted lips and wide tongue. Both dove forward and traced the inside of my folds, flicking across the middle and sucking slowly.

"Screw my phone," I grunted.

Lick, suck...breathe. Lick, suck...breathe.

My hips bowed to his pattern, his rhythm. The wetness he created mixed with my own arousal and it began to drip down my thighs and onto the sheet. The pressure he was using wasn't strong enough to give me an orgasm. He was gentle—too gentle. That was all I'd ever had...I needed more now.

"Harder," I said. As soon as the word left my mouth, he stopped touching me. I wanted him back and even closer. I reached for his hair, but there was nothing. The tongue that teased me so delicately was gone, and the fingers that had squeezed my nipples. Darkness filled the space where he had been.

"What the..." My voice trailed off when I heard the ringing.

You'll be moaning too loud to answer your phone.

The ringtone was a siren, a sound that wouldn't blend into background noise, and one I had specifically chosen for my father so I would never miss his calls.

Where the hell had this man disappeared to? How could his tongue and fingers simply vanish in seconds?

I sat up and pushed my back against the headboard, a movement that made me gasp. My eyelids popped open.

My eyes...hadn't been open before?

I scanned the room for evidence of this mysterious man who had pleased me in the middle of the night. From what I could see, nothing looked out of place and there weren't any clothes on the floor. My blanket and sheet were still on the bed, and I was wearing my pajamas. I turned toward my nightstand and felt the wetness...a small spot on the bottom of my cotton shorts and a dampness between my thighs. I knew if I smelled my fingers, my scent would be all over them...

And it was.

He was just a dream.

I lifted my phone and cleared my throat. "Isn't it a little early to be calling?"

"Business doesn't sleep, therefore neither do I. You know this about me, probably better than anyone else." I said nothing. "Technically, it's quarter to five."

"This had better be an emergency, then."

"Call it what you'd like. Be at the office in an hour, Frankie."

"Wait..." I needed caffeine and a scalding shower—and for the wetness that still clung to my sex to be completely dry—before my brain would really start to work. He would hang up before I had time for any of that, so I forced myself to recount yesterday's hot items. Everything had been settled prior to me leaving the office from what I recalled. Why else would he call? It was too early to open escrow on any of our accounts as none of the lenders were open yet, and funds only processed during banking hours. Emails could wait. It had to be a meeting with one of our international clients. Their trips to the States tended to be so short, they didn't bother getting acclimated to our time zone so this wasn't uncommon. I was just surprised by the short notice. "Who's the appointment with? Giovanni? Hamad?"

"On your way in, why don't you grab me a bagel with the veggie cream cheese I like. And a latte, extra hot, with that foam stuff on top and real sugar, none of that artificial crap. Oh, and Frankie, don't be late."

He disconnected the call before I had a chance to repeat my question or say good-bye. That didn't matter. He knew I'd be there within the next forty-five minutes with his bagel and coffee exactly the way he had requested it. That was how he had raised me to act, and that was one of the reasons he would soon be handing me his company.

"Take a look at those papers," my father said, pointing to the folder at the end of his desk. His peppered hair was longer than usual, swept back and sprayed, almost like a headband that framed his crown—a suggestion from his most recent fling, I suspected.

I set his bagel and coffee in front of him and sat in one of the chairs. I opened the folder to find Block Development printed at the top of the first sheet, the words encircled with long, sleek, winding branches that added warmth to the contemporary logo. Derek Block was known for using wood and naturalistic aspects in all his architectural designs. His overstated earthy elements were what set his work apart. Under the logo was a press release that highlighted his most recent venture: an apartment conversion in the Back Bay where he was renovating one hundred and eighty-one units. The development, listed as Timber Towers, was an exclusive, state-of-the-art green building with an array of amenities that included underground parking. This was his first project in Boston; his prior build-outs had been in intimate beach towns throughout New England. Thanks to the connections I had at the building division office, I'd been notified over a year ago that Block had filed permit applications and that the city had awarded them. I only lived a few blocks from the site, and I'd been watching its progress.

"So?" my father said, wiping a glob of cream cheese from the corner of his lip.

"My research shows he employs a full-time agent and handles all sales in-house," I answered. "It's a dead-end."

"Your research is correct, except for this building."

The papers dropped from my hand, and a smile spread over my face. "He's shopping for an agent?"

"Not just any agent, my dear. He wants the best agent in Boston...and she just so happens to be my daughter."

I felt my cheeks turn red. My father was a hard and often ruthless businessman, and his compliments were rare. When they came, I cherished them.

"I certainly can't be the only candidate. There must be others vying for the job?"

"Correct again." He sifted through several sheets until he found the one he was looking for and rattled off the names of my competitors. I wasn't surprised by the agents Block had chosen to interview; they were all competent—one with more experience than me, another who was known for sleeping with her clients. None had Jordan International, a forty-year-old agency backing them, or the mentorship and knowledge of my father, Garrett Jordan, the man who'd built the company from the ground up—or the connections we had secured over the years, or our database of buyers. Our reputation in this city was flawless, all of which Block undoubtedly knew.

"When's the meeting?"

"At seven."

My steel and yellow gold Rolex showed I had a little time to prepare. The watch was five years old; I'd bought it right out of college after closing my first large sale. My father always said that in order to successfully sell luxury real estate, you had to experience fine luxury for yourself. Our agency didn't represent knock-offs, and our clients weren't looking to buy them, either.

"I'm going to go prep," I said.

He nodded silently, his eyes moving to his computer screen. "Frankie," he said as I reached the door to his office.

I turned around, gripping the framed arch. "Yes, Dad?"

"Land this one."

I nodded back, mirroring him.

Flipping on the lights in my office, I sat behind my desk and booted up my computer. Several emails had come in from my assistant, Brea, providing even more information on Block Development. While I read through the first article, she called my cell.

"I'll be there in ten minutes," she said. I could hear traffic in the background. I pictured her walking to the subway. "Did you get the emails I sent?"

"I'm reading it all right now."

"All I could find was info on Mr. Block's company, but nothing on him personally."

"I'm sure what you found will be perfect." The clock on the wall chimed. It was now six o'clock. "It's too early for you to be on your way here."

"I want to dig around a little more and see if I can get you some key talking points."

She was the most dedicated assistant I'd ever had. I didn't doubt this was a reason she was coming in, but I knew it wasn't the only one.

"Brea..."

"Don't worry. I'm fine."

I moved over to the window, looking down at Faneuil Hall and Government Center. The city was so gentle at this hour. "Are you?"

"I'm having a hard time sleeping, that's all." There was honking in the background. "You don't sound so rested, either."

"It's early. That's all."

"No...it's more. Let me guess: the dreams are back?"

I turned and rested my back against the window to let the icy glass cool me off. Just the mention of those dreams had me sweating. "I can't believe I told you about those."

"Girl, you've got just as much dirt on me." It now sounded like she was running—and probably in heels. "So they've returned just as powerful as before, I take it?"

"They've most definitely returned." Despite it being a dream and a man who never showed his face, his tongue had felt so real. Too real. I pushed off the window and walked back over to my desk. "If we start going down this road, I won't get any studying done."

She laughed. "See ya in a minute."

I smiled as I hung up and skimmed through the article that filled my screen. I was really so lucky to have her.

If you would like to keep reading, click HERE to purchase Unblocked.

Printed in Great Britain
by Amazon

87885288R00202